DREAMLAND
—OTHER STORIES—

First published in Great Britain in 2021 by
Black Shuck Books
Kent, UK

Versions of these stories previously appeared as follows:
'The Night Parade' in *Wonderland* (Titan Books, 2019)
'Mari Lwyd' online at sinisterhorrorcompany.com (2020)

Set in Caslon by WHITEspace
www.white-space.uk

Cover design and interior layout © WHITEspace, 2021

978-1-913038-68-7

Dreamland:
Other Stories

Edited by
Sophie Essex

BLACK
SHUCK
BOOKS

NECTAR

It was nice, having a fruit bat for a lover. Or at least, it wasn't not nice. He brought her fruit. Figs, mangos, dates, bananas. She was sure that those fruits didn't grow here. He didn't pick them from a farm or grow them himself. He must steal them from the supermarket. Or perhaps he bought them. She didn't know that much about him. They barely spoke outside the bedroom. And even in the bedroom, their mouths were too full.

Every morning she came down to the table laid: cloth as white as a snowstorm, tiny china, red poppies in a faceted glass. Fruit was cut bite-size and displayed on a three-storey cake stand. He hung upside-down from the chandelier and watched her as she ate it. He tied a starched white napkin around his black velvet throat but he didn't eat anything. Or not that she could see, anyway.

She told herself she did not miss her former lover, the vampire bat, whose dietary habits she understood some people found distasteful, but that she found preferable to her insectivorous bat lover and her fish-eating bat lover. She liked his conical muzzle and the naked pad of his nose. She liked his minuscule back teeth. She liked his peculiar loping gait. His nose could locate areas where the blood flowed close to the skin. His ears could detect the regular breathing sounds of sleeping animals. She told herself she didn't miss waking to the nip of his tiny teeth. But sometimes when he came to her, there was already someone else's blood on those teeth. She told herself that really was a dealbreaker.

K
I
R
S
T
Y

L
O
G
A
N

She had read that other creatures could use the same infrared radiation to locate blood hotspots under the skin. Boas, pythons and pit vipers. She thought about taking a boa, python or pit viper for a lover. But it all seemed a bit phallic. A bit crude. She should content herself with her fruit bat lover. He was a good bat. He was punctual. He was neat. He remembered birthdays. He would never leave her.

She stuck a small silver fork into a cube of mango, wishing it would bleed.

GRIMMER HOUSE

⇌DAY 1⇌

Grimmer House groans an angry crack and whines from the rush of October wind whipping its old boards. The two-story gothic revival trimmed in clapboard was once a structure to be revered, rising alone out of a small field that then became a street and eventually a cul-de-sac. Look at its gable-front mouth stretched in a wide, guttural hiss, with a peak so sharp it could halve a thoughtless bird. The long and dirty windows like too many cartoon eyes. Layers of cracking paint, the color a sterner shade of brown, just shy of black, with a slim green trim, though there's no record of when the painting took place. You would have to scrape the walls until your nails were bloodied with flakes to unearth the original color. Only the house knows that it was once pure white.

Built just off-center of Central, Indiana, Grimmer House now hunches over modern homes that look nothing like its own kind: a squat ranch and a practically plastic two-story home painted yellow as innocence. Houses bearing no long-dead namesake, no ghostly chill, and certainly no stone fireplace with a lion's head roaring at the center. No hand-carved staircase sloping up and out of sight in the dark, no drip or scratch of faucet and wood floor. Repairs are undeniably in the nature of Grimmer House, but the flaws only mirror its grandeur. The house can't be blamed for its marrings.

9

Of course it is collapsing in on itself.

Jeanette Mason stands in the center of the entryway, staring up at the remains of the stained-glass windows that have shattered so many times there's hardly any color left. The high windows along the staircase are mostly filled with the clear but still marbled replacement glass, and through the clear she can see the world. Grimmer House has known her heart-shaped face for the last ten years of her life. And yet somehow for her it is like she has always existed here, even before she was alive. The wood carvings in the ceiling poke down at her like stalactites while the grandfather clock near the front door resounds its hourly Westminster Quarters chime. Watch closely to see her body shudder with the clicks of the clock.

Maggie Mason sits in the living room with her eyes trained on the brightly-colored characters flashing across the screen. Now and then she will stand and follow along with the action – running the room while pretending to fly or slashing her arms like an animal with claws. Of these characters she watches daily, her favorite is the one called Supernova because she is the most powerful of all. Supernova knows what people say in their minds, not with their mouths.

At barely six years old, Maggie is too young to think her home is strange. She loves the nighttime humming, the loose shutters that slam against her bedroom windows like clapping hands, how her father lifts her to stick a fist into the mouth of the stone lion in the fireplace. Already she is accustomed to echo and eerie silence. She thinks her house is special, that it can hear her and is alive.

Jean is still staring into the rainbow glass when the metal knocker cracks through her head.

"Someone's at the door!" Maggie shouts from the living room and gallops to answer. She uses all her strength and both hands to pull the doorknob until the wood relents and allows the guest to enter.

A woman with frosted hair emerges from the shadow under the archway. "Why, hello there, Maggie May. Do you remember me?"

Maggie shrugs. "No."

"I'm Linda Cunningham! From the library!"

"Can I read your mind?"

Linda leans back and laughs to mask her surprise. "That's a bit forward."

"Maggie," Jean interjects. "I don't think Mrs. Cunningham wants her mind read."

Maggie stares for a moment before bolting back to the living room.

Linda looks up and smiles awfully. "Needs to work on those manners, I think. When are you planning to repaint your front porch? All that peeling is ghastly."

Jean rolls her eyes. "Please. Don't be dramatic."

Linda laughs like someone said something funny, links arms with Jean and leads her in a promenade. "I hope you don't mind me coming over early. It's just such a nice evening that I thought I'd take a sunset walk. Barely even need my coat."

Jean is never in the mood for weather-related conversation. She disconnects from Linda's arm and walks ahead. "Your costume's hanging in the kitchen. Come on."

"Your booth was missed at the Corn Roast this year," Linda says, transitioning to a tone that is decidedly envious. "Everybody kept asking, '*Where's Jean's pumpkin seeds? Where's Jean's pumpkin seeds?*'"

"Things have been a bit," Jean hesitates for her least favorite word, "*crazy* lately. And Maggie's in kindergarten now..." She trails off, hopes this will do.

"You could always join November book club? Get out of this house from time to time." Again, that laugh like an alarm, like some invisible figure whispered a dirty joke or flirtation directly into her ear. "I'm sure Logan wouldn't mind."

"No, Logan wouldn't mind…" Jean pauses, unable to remember her lines. "Your costume's in the kitchen."

As Jean leads her through the dining room, Linda pauses to place her hand over the lion's angry mouth as though she might suffocate it.

"I don't know why you don't throw a Halloween party. I see you already have the cobwebs—"

Get her out, something in Jean demands.

"Your costume is hanging on the pantry door… See if it's Cleopatra-enough for you."

Finally arriving in the black-and-white kitchen, Linda lifts the thin plastic over the costume.

"Oh, Jeannie, you've outdone yourself. Looks like you went a little lower with that neckline than we discussed. You're so *bad*."

"Mm," Jean nods. "So, if you're happy with it."

"Well, I'll have to try it on at home of course, but I'm confident. Here's the hundred, as promised, and a little extra for that porch?"

Jean pockets the cash and makes the grimace she usually saves for her husband. She wishes she could tell Linda to screw her charity, but even the impulse exhausts her.

Linda runs her palm along the kitchen counter. Her nails are an agitated red. "You know you'll need to do some fixing up if you're planning to sell."

The statement is a strategic stab into Jean's stomach. "Planning to… sell?"

"Danny mentioned that since Logan opened up that new location in Valpo, you might be thinking of an upgrade? Something nice and modern? Can't say I blame you. Though I'm sure you're more than used to it by now."

"Yes," Jean thrusts her hands in her pockets and straightens. "We are used to it."

"Bye-bye, Maggie May!" Linda calls on her way back through the living room, but the girl doesn't register the remark. "Prettiest red hair. Runs in the family, hmm? You shouldn't let her sit so close to the television. She'll wind up with glasses and cataracts."

Jean quickens her pace to the front door.

But Linda idles in the entryway, turning about the room, judging and marveling at once. Her glance flicks through the minimally furnished space – the oak-paneled walls, the bronze full-length mirror, the three-tiered chandelier, and finally, the grand staircase curving toward a darkening hallway.

"Can I walk up the stairs?" Linda inquires, her hope apparent.

"Why?"

"It's just, this house is so historic, so… it's…" She seems to stumble over her rehearsed language. "You know, I knew the family that lived here before you."

"Did you."

"I'm sure you've heard the stories. Anyway, there are just so few of these historic houses left. You never have anyone over to appreciate it, so I thought I'd take advantage a little while I'm here."

This is my house, get out, you can't have it, Jean wants to say, but frowns instead. "Suit yourself."

For once Linda does not speak and instead moves to the first step of the staircase, resting her hand on the bannister. The steps wince under her weight, and small splinters rise below her palm as she unsettles the wood. The house is irascible as a cat brushed in the wrong direction, but Linda is stunned by the glamour. An elegant curve upward and higher still, as though she is a queen above it all; that she might speak and her people would hear her, praise her, paint her with the clear and colored glass as her shimmering background…

But it is a gray day so there is no shimmer, and when she reaches the top, she remembers there is also no queen. All the dark doors on the landing are closed. Disappointed that she can't peer inside to catch a glimpse at Jeanette Mason's secrets, she turns to make her way back down, but first touches the stained-glass window – the blue, then the red – when her skin brushes against some bubble or crack and opens just a sliver, enough to send a stream of blood winding down her wrist.

"Damnit!" Linda snatches her hand away from the window. "Damnit, Jeannie, your house bit me!"

"What?" Jean calls, distracted, from the entryway.

Linda rushes down the stairs without touching the bannister. "I'm bleeding."

"How did that happen?"

"Cut it on the glass somehow, I don't know. I'm going home. Thank you for the dress."

Linda frowns in Maggie's direction, looks once more to scan the stairs, and then departs from Grimmer House with the intention of telling everyone she knows about how strange Jeanette Mason has become, how her daughter is a brat, and how that ugly old house is in desperate need of a new coat of paint.

When Logan Mason comes home from work, he's wet with kitchen sweat and goes straight for a shower. Maggie stands at the foot of the twenty-six-step staircase and watches him spiral out of view. He does not wave from the landing like she wishes he would, but she loves him still, helplessly so.

Dinner is served, a lasagna without ricotta, and together the family eats at the dining room table. Thick red curtains are drawn over the windows. The table is long, every seat set with placemats and cloth napkins. There is wine for Jean and beer for Logan and the silverware is real. The iron chandelier hangs heavy above their heads.

Maggie eats a special meatless portion of the

lasagna by picking it up with her fingers and placing the noodles flat on her tongue. She knows how to use a fork but doesn't feel like it, and she rarely does anything she doesn't feel like doing. The only thing she's not allowed to do is go into the basement. She can watch TV all day if she wants, or swing on the tire swing in the backyard, or play dress-up and do rain-dances in the attic.

"Daddy, I want to be Supernova for Halloween."

Logan drinks from a can and looks at Jean. "What's a Supernova?"

"A cartoon character."

"You've been reading comic books?"

"It's a show she watches during the day," Jean clarifies. "Do you realize that if this chandelier fell from the ceiling it would kill us all?"

There is a silence. There is never much but silence. Maggie laughs at nothing while Logan sticks his fork into the center of a sauce-laden square and cuts.

Logan chews happily. Food is one of his only true joys in life, and the sound of his teeth and tongue on meat and noodle is more soothing than a prayer. He's never been one for God, but if food isn't a blessing, he doesn't know what is. Jean is a fine cook, always has been. Maybe that's why he still loves her. But really it's this house. Grimmer House was their wedding gift to each other. Only a month married when they bought the house along with all its remains at auction. Having grown up only blocks away on Pettibone Street, Logan developed a kind of unrequited affection for the place. He envisioned a future in which the house would mold to his needs and his family would praise him for his single-minded focus and drive toward stability. He learned too late that the beauty wasn't worth the price tag. A grand house did not mean a grand life. There were constant repairs, so much time and energy involved in maintaining such a beast. Biting into the soft Italian sausage, he wonders if the only thing he truly loves is food.

Jean's voice breaks through his meditative state. "Did you tell Danny Cunningham that we were selling the house?"

Her tone is cool, but Logan knows that means she's silently steaming inside.

"I just mentioned that we could afford it now, is all."

"So, you were bragging?"

He takes a long, slow bite of lasagna to give himself a moment. *Twist it somehow*, he thinks, crushing the warmth against his gums. "We discussed this."

Jean feels a distinct tug on her hair and bristles. "I know we discussed it."

Logan can feel his wife pulling at the power again. Something has her more prickly than usual, but there's no route to discovering the reason.

"Lasagna's great," he says.

"Of course it is."

Jean smiles at Maggie and Maggie smiles back, like they're in on some secret together and Maggie just can't remember what it is.

At night the house moans openly. The wind touches every board and every breath between metal and glass. Frozen fingers reach, stretching, through the thin bedroom windows, down so many stairs to the main floor, past Logan sleeping in the living room, clawing to get at the throat of the house, the kitchen where a heavy door leads to the basement. This is the room where no one goes anymore and not even the cold can reach.

Logan stretches on the couch, rubbing himself as he wakes. He'd been dreaming again of the woman with red hair and full moon eyes. *Return to the dream*, his mind begs, and he almost drifts again when his briefly-opened eyes catch a shadow. The shadow rests in front of the bay window that frames the front yard and the open field beyond. It does not shift when he sits up to reach for it. He realizes the shadow is not a shadow but his daughter standing and staring out the window with her eyes mostly closed and her mouth slack with drool.

He kneels and shakes her until she wakes with a fierce blinking of her tiny lashes.

"Dad?" Her voice flutters. Looking again out the window, she hugs his arm like she's hiding from something. "There was a storm."

After he carries Maggie back to her bedroom, Logan sinks into the couch and looks out the window. He can't shake the sensation that she's still there, that she left her shadow, and when he sleeps he dreams of his daughter standing before him and staring, just staring.

⟿DAY 2⟾

At dawn, Grimmer House stretches and yawns itself awake. Miniature glass orbs on the lampshades tremble, the grey stones in the fireplace readjust, and sleeping birds rush away from the roof to find a more agreeable resting place. Though the curtains are drawn, and the bright orange sun still buried, Jean wakes as she always does. Her four-poster bed firms when she turns, sick of her weight. Rising, her first act is to make the bed as it wants to be made. She dresses in the same clothes as yesterday and carefully closes the door behind her.

On the first step of the staircase she trips, tips forward, gut dropping with her body, then regains balance on the next step. So many times she has almost fallen and broken her neck.

At the little table in the black-and-white kitchen, bright as a sitcom, Logan drinks coffee with cream and assesses his wife's figure: the lift of her hips in her jeans, belted tight at the waist, her sharp shoulders.

He mutters something so quickly that she can barely hear him over the coffee pot's choke.

"What?" she asks, busying herself with the dishes from last night. She doesn't sit with him in the morning anymore and never dreams of cooking breakfast. She tries to stay active when he's home to avoid conversation.

"Maggie was sleepwalking last night."

She turns from whatever task and faces him. "Sleepwalking?"

"Yeah, she made it all the way downstairs. Said there was some sort of storm."

"Too much television," Jean says with a shrug and turns back to the sink.

Once her family is gone, she begins her ritual of sitting at the kitchen table and lighting a cigarette. There is only a short slip of time, so she must use these hours, precious ten, then eleven, then twelve strikes of the clock, wisely, in the silence. A cold air snakes down from the chimney and into the kitchen, passing through Jean's body, and makes its way to the back of the room. She hesitates only a moment before taking her cigarette and unlocking the basement door with the key above the mantel. The cold goes first and then Jean closes the door behind her. See how she drifts down the staircase until the red of her cigarette hovers alone in the dark.

Jean locks the basement door behind her, places the key back in its spot on the ledge, and calls for Maggie to meet her in the kitchen for lunch. She can feel herself going off and on sometimes, more frequently these days. Then and then not. Time seems to be jumping, or she is jumping through time, drawn ever-faster toward some unstoppable shadow in her mind, some doom… She slices the sharp cheddar into small squares and places them on crackers, arranging them in a neat circle on a plate. A small cluster of grapes fits soft in the center. The appearance of perfection is almost too easy to master.

"Mommy, can I be Supernova for Halloween?"

Jean is now standing next to the fireplace, the grandfather clock chiming the half hour, and she can't remember moving from the kitchen to the dining room. The lion winks at her.

"You can be anything you want, honey," she calls back.

Then she is next to her daughter and her hair is the loveliest red. She runs her fingers through, and it feels wet like rain.

Logan comes home to his daughter asleep on the living room couch with the weather channel blaring. He turns down the volume with the remote and looks into the dining room for his wife.

"Jean?" he calls, walking up the staircase, missing the bit of blood on the window. Her room is empty, bed pristine, and so is the bathroom and Maggie's room. He calls again, though it seems useless, and goes downstairs to check the kitchen.

In the living room, he wakes Maggie by brushing his hand on her hair. "Maggie, where's your mom?"

She grumbles and turns over. "In the basement."

"What?"

There's a small sound from behind and he spins to see Jean standing near the fireplace. "I didn't hear you come in."

"Where were you?"

"I was in the basement."

"Why?"

"Just cleaning up. Is leftover lasagna okay for dinner?"

Flustered, Logan is able to manage a nod before she turns and walks away.

Jean warms their portions in the microwave but does not join them at the table. She cannot remember the last time she ate a whole meal. During dinner, Logan focuses on chewing, pleased with the leftovers, and answers Maggie's questions about the difference between a severe thunderstorm watch and a severe thunderstorm warning.

For once the loudest sound comes from Grimmer House's human occupants, as Logan's snore fills the first floor. The sound is so intensified by echo that he wakes himself.

With one eye pressed into the cushion, he sees a smoky darkness sway in front of him. He is freezing, and his chest tightens as though gripped by a strong hand. No moonlight reaches the room to allow him some clarity. *It's the house,* he thinks from nowhere, an epiphany: the house is working against him, trying to frighten him with this ghost. When he sits straight, the shadow is clearly his daughter again. This time her torso is tilting. She is about to fall when he leans forward and catches her in his arms.

"She's coming!" Maggie shouts, eyes still shut.

Logan is stunned by his daughter rolling in his arms like a person possessed. She's only having a nightmare, but it feels more like a dream he needs to wake from. *It's the house*, again and more certain.

He shakes her awake and she clings to him. "She's coming! I saw her!"

"Saw who?" Logan asks.

Maggie's voice is so tight it's curled in a ball. "The storm."

He lifts her from the couch and cradles her in his arms all the way up the stairs. When Maggie asks him to stay in bed with her, he can't refuse. Instead of sleeping, he stays alert and listens for a sound from Grimmer House, for a sign that the house means his family harm.

In the next room, Jean sits up in bed. She hears a voice so small it could be coming from a mouse in the wall, a voice saying *forgive me, forgive me, forgive*.

~DAY 3~

When the house wakes, Jean knows there is not much time.

She can hear Logan and Maggie in the kitchen already, up early together. Her body sinks further into the bed with the hope it will swallow her. To be as heavy and as permanent as this four-poster bed, screwed into the wall. The whispering comes back again, though this time it is so rushed and close in her ear that she cannot interpret its language. What does the house want her to know? Flattening her face to the mattress, listening for a pulse, she holds her breath and tries and tries and tries to hear whatever instructions Grimmer House has for her. But the sound of dishes clanking in the kitchen overpowers. *Stop it*! she almost shrieks, but instead starts to cry and eventually falls back to sleep.

There is darkness first, and then a scratching sound, like the rodents she hears skittering in the walls at night. Her eyes are open and there is still darkness. That scratching, so much like the mice in the corners, and how she dreamt of swallowing them, gray fur in the back of her throat. She can feel the fur now. She sits up, reaches for the light she knows must be there, and it's true: she has woken in the basement. Two old twin beds sit parallel to each other; the cement wall is covered with drooping photographs and lipstick-kissed posters of movie stars. In the corner, a disoriented field mouse scratches away. The dense air reeks of day-old cigarette smoke. Never mind how she got there, what time is it? On cue, the grandfather clock chimes her name from above: *Jean-ette, Jean-ette... Jean-ette, Jean-ette... Jean-ette, Jean-ette... Jean-ette... Jean-ette...* and then eleven long, deep beats straight to the heart.

"Forgive me," she whispers, and turns off the light. "Forgive me. Forgive me."

Jean has been staring into the darkness for so long that she is slow to hear the crying reverberating softly through the walls. She shakes her head and follows the sound to the second floor, where Maggie is perched at the top of the landing, legs dangling between the balusters. Her arms are wrapped around her stomach as she cries.

"Why are you crying?" Jean asks.

"There's a Halloween party at school tomorrow. I don't have a costume."

Jean sighs. Another failure. "I'll make you a costume."

"No, you won't," Maggie pouts. "You never do anything you say you will."

This makes Jean want to cry again but instead she smiles. "Supernova, right?"

Maggie nods and wipes her eyes. Jean sees her becoming so slender that she slips straight through and smashes on the floor like an egg.

Jean cuts up the dining room curtains to form the red body of the costume, lets Maggie draw the exploding star emblem for the chest. By the time Logan comes home, Maggie is racing around the house in her costume, pretending to fight off villains by stretching her arms outward and pressing tiny fingers to her temple. Jean watches from the living room couch, overexerted, but for the moment satisfied with her accomplishment. She has seen too many of her efforts crumble before her, so this success rings through. The chiming of the clock is more soothing now. She has done something right.

"Supernova?" Logan asks.

Jean is smiling somewhat. "Supernova."

"She looks great."

He is genuine and somewhere inside her, a crack appears.

"Now you'll have to take her trick-or-treating next week," Jean says.

He pauses, almost says, *maybe we could…* But that door is closed, has been for years, half the time they've owned this house, and why try the handle again all on account of a costume and a somewhat smile? Logan nods and turns to the staircase.

With his back turned, he cannot see Jean's face fall, the success of the costume suddenly lost, how fragile happiness can be, and when the half-hour resounds, she wants to cry again for the minutes, the hours, the years.

Maggie vrooms into the dining room for dinner and runs to Jean, assuming it's playtime; her costume is still on, and more than anything in this world she wants to read her mother's mind. She stretches her eyes and stares into Jean's face. Jean stares back and sees her sister's wide eyes, that longing look.

Maggie says, "You're scared of something."

"Sit down and eat your lasagna."

"*Again?*" Maggie asks.

"Have you been having trouble sleeping?"

Logan looks up from his leftovers – somewhat toughened now from age, but still enjoyable – and sees his daughter shaking her head.

"Did you wake up downstairs the other night?" This time it sounds like a threat.

Maggie is a little afraid of her mother sometimes. She looks down and says, "No."

"Maybe now's not the best time to be talking about this." Logan nods toward Maggie, wary of what she might remember.

"Are you sure she was sleepwalking?"

"Yes, Jean, I'm sure. It's not a big deal," he says for Maggie, then lowers his voice. He knows what he's about to suggest will trigger a reaction, but he says it anyway. "Maybe we should return to our conversation about a psychologist?"

"How dare you?" Jean gasps, sudden betrayal flowing through her. She turns to Maggie and says, "There is nothing wrong with you. Don't let him tell you that there's something wrong with you."

He starts to feel it again, the house inside him somehow, making him deepen his voice, compelling him to grab his wife and throw her into the mouth of the fireplace. "Well, hold on a minute. I'm not saying there's something wrong! She's experienced a tough loss, we all have, that's all."

"No one in this house is crazy. How dare you suggest that, that, that…" Again Jean is starting to lose track of time, of language, of space. She imagines tongues of fire flickering from her pupils. "There's *nothing* wrong with Clarice. Nothing! She's fine!"

"My name is Maggie," Maggie mutters.

"Clarice isn't crazy," Jean continues, speaking straight to the chandelier. "I'm not crazy."

Logan slams his palm on the table so the dishes shudder. "Every time!"

Maggie looks back and forth between them and starts to cry. When they yell like this she always cries.

Jean presses her palms to her ears. The house is so loud with its walls crumbling and fringe rustling and glass clinking. Even the iron above their heads whines to be released. She grabs Maggie and shakes her. "Listen to me: if this chandelier fell from the ceiling it would kill us all!"

Maggie cries harder and runs to hide in the fireplace with her head between her knees. She doesn't know why there is so much yelling. If she had Supernova's powers, she could make it stop.

Her fear is too much for Logan. He stands, walks around the table, and slaps his wife across the face. "Stop it!" He yells louder than he ever has. He can feel the sound inside him. "Stop acting like we can't hear you!"

"You *can't* hear me!" Jean screams with a surge so strong it could be a lion's roar. When her voice cracks, she covers the warm side of her face with her hand.

Logan knows then that his wife has completely unhinged, the same way her late sister unhinged. That's the only word he can think of to describe the behavior: *unhinged, unhinged, unhinged.* To separate from sanity. Once again, he questions if his wife could hurt herself, if she could hurt Maggie, or him. He grips the table and clears his throat. "You need to get your shit together, Jeanette. Are you hearing me?"

She stares into his eyes above her and says only, "Yes."

Jean dismisses herself from the table without looking at her family. She considers how much Maggie already knows or will remember – hopefully nothing. *Keep none of me,* she thinks. It would be better to forget. She moves slowly up the staircase and rests her hand on the railing the whole time. But the stairs are dizzying, the angles off-kilter, and it seems to her that she is not walking beside but instead crawling up the wall.

The rain lightly tickling the windows is enough to wake her. Jean can feel what the house feels more and more. Maybe she has been alive for too many years now, already so many lives lived, all the lives of this house in her bones.

A door down the hall opens and closes. Then a soft knock.

"Come in."

Logan closes the door behind him. The room smells foul. He hasn't slept here in over a year.

"Yes?" Jean asks into her pillow. "Did you need something?"

Logan exhales. "I need to apologize for my behavior at the dinner table. I never should have laid hands on you and I'm deeply sorry for that."

Jean tightens in her ball on the bed.

"I won't ask you to forgive me, but I will ask you to consider Maggie in all this. I'm worried about her. I'm worried about you." He starts to walk the room to give himself something to do, a place to look at other than the curve of Jean's spine. "I know that you're grieving. And I am too. But I don't let it torture me like you do."

"I'm not crazy," Jean whispers. "Clarice isn't crazy."

Logan shakes his head. "I'm not here to fight with you about your sister. That's your business."

Nearly every night Logan dreams of his wife's red-headed sister, her circle eyes, her loud mouth. She moved in with them, here, before Maggie was born. Clarice claimed she saw things no one saw, heard things no one heard. She waged wars with the world, with her mind, with substances. She snuck strange men and women into the house in the shadow of early morning; she stole money and jewelry and silverware; spun webs of disconnected, incoherent lies; manipulated and broke her sister's heart, broke Logan's heart, until the night almost a year ago when he found her crumpled at the foot of the stairs like he might find a dead mouse or a trampled spider. It was dark and she was dressed all in black, so at first he couldn't see her broken neck.

Thinking about that night, his eyes start to tear and it feels uncomfortable, a faucet he needs to fix, but the leak is stronger than his will to hold it in. He sits on the bed and rubs Jean's shoulder under the blanket. "I loved her too, you know. And I felt sorry for her because of the way she was. But you did everything you could to help her."

Jean bites the bone in her middle finger.

"It's time for you to forgive yourself. But if you keep acting like this, Maggie never will."

She wishes she could tell him that she no longer has control over her capacity to forgive, but she can't seem to find the words. Instead she rolls back over and says, "That's enough. Please go."

He exhales, lifts his hand from her back, and leaves the room. Then his weight on the stairs and the inevitable collapse on the couch. In the next room, Maggie shifts in her bed. Scattered raindrops are swallowed by the chimney, collecting on the vines that grow there. In the living room, a fresh layer of dust settles on the old piano. Mice scratch away in the basement. Every sound, Jean can hear it all, as though the house has opened its ears to her. She stands and crosses from her room to Maggie's in the dark.

"It's me," Jean whispers, walking toward the bed. "I'm sorry I yelled earlier. I didn't mean to scare you."

Something in the softness of Jean's voice makes Maggie feel less fearful now.

"It's okay," Maggie says. She hesitates, then adds, "I miss Aunt Cee. I think about her a lot."

Jean smiles a little. "I miss her too, and think about her all the time."

"Is that why you've been in the basement so much? Because that was Aunt Cee's room?"

Jean sits on the bed and touches Maggie's hair. The hair she always wished was hers. The hair her mother gave to her sister, the hair her sister gave to her daughter. She feels more than ever the distance between who she wanted to be and who she became.

"You don't need to worry about that," Jean says. "The most important thing is that you feel safe here."

Maggie's eyebrows wrinkle. "I am safe here."

"This house is yours and no one can take it from you. Do you understand? Say it for me, okay?"

"This house is mine."

"Yes, good girl. Once more."

"This house is mine." Maggie feels powerful, suddenly, like Supernova.

"Exactly." Jean smiles with all her teeth. She has given Maggie something at last. "Now go to sleep, Supernova, and sweet dreams. No more scaring your father, okay?"

Maggie nods and rolls over. It's only after Jean closes the door that Maggie realizes her mother had read her mind.

There is a woman with red hair and a storm again. The storm a part of the woman, or the woman a part of the storm. Maggie tries to close her eyes and ends up opening them, blinking several times in the darkness. Now she is awake and in the living room, staring out at the last empty lot in the cul-de-sac. A silver slit of lightning cracks through the black sky. She gasps. Three streetlights in the circle flicker on and off and on. All the electricity in the house and on the street dies with a single shudder. It feels cold like there's a wind inside her. Pressure building in her ears. She squints into the nighttime outside her house and sees something else, and darker still, a darker darkness shooting down from the sky like a thick root or a crooked finger. Her body seems to lift in the air, hover for a second at the sight of the storm touching down, until there is a thundering and she lets out a scream.

Logan jolts at the sound. But even louder is the roar of a helicopter in his head. He stands, stumbles to the window. Maggie is transfixed. A mass of cloud has taken shape across the lawn and, like his daughter, Logan stands in awe of the tornado. The ground shreds as the storm crosses the empty plot. Wind hits the house hard and a single gust shatters the weakest windows in an instant, covering the room with glass. Maggie screams again and somewhere in Logan's head a voice whispers, *hurry*.

With Maggie in his arms, Logan runs for the kitchen, fumbling with the key above the basement door. Rushing down the stairs in the darkness, he throws Maggie on the closest chair. She immediately starts to cry, though he can hardly hear her over the wind. Now the tornado is banging at their door.

"Mommy!" Maggie cries out. "Where's Mommy?"

"She's coming," Logan tells her. "She'll be right here." He hopes this is not a lie.

"Get her," she begs. "Please go get her!"

Logan groans and carries her to the back corner of the room. For his daughter's sake, he makes a focused effort to speak in a voice both calm and stern. "Sit here and don't move a muscle. No matter what happens. Promise."

He waits for her nod in the dark before taking the stairs two at a time. The door slams against the kitchen wall at his touch. The wind is here and blackness surrounds, seeping through the broken windows, swirling behind his eardrums, so much wind that he cannot tell where the storm is, or if they are already inside. "Jean!" he bellows as loud as he can through the living room, and again while running up the quaking stairs to her bedroom, empty.

"Damnit!" he yells. "Jean!"

There is dirt in his mouth when he calls her name. Down the stairs and the front door splinters open: darkness there, too. He pauses in the dining room and looks around for the last time. Wind hurls silverware and broken crystal and filthy water at him, slitting and soaking his skin, as though forcing him toward the kitchen to safety, to where his daughter needs him.

If Jean is still here, she is a ghost, vanished. The tornado is consuming their one-hundred-year-old house and Logan tells himself there's nothing else he can do to save her.

Even with the wind funneling down the chimney, Jean can hear her husband shouting her name. She is crouched, unseen, below the throat of the hearth like another log on the fire. When his legs finally move away from her sight, she smiles. Her hair is glittered with glass and the pressure in her ears builds so that the roar becomes a scream. This storm has come to swallow her and the house together.

A vortex shakes her and lifts her from the floor. Her body knocks twice against the stones. She cannot hear Maggie in the basement crying *Mommy, Mommy, Mommy.* A howl twists in the air as the tornado strikes through the center of the room, and Jean can see the black cloud's broken hands reaching out. See how she reaches out, too, for the storm.

The fireplace spasms before it collapses, taking part of the ceiling down with it. The swallowing, fragmented darkness consumes the kitchen too, ripping the basement door clean as a flick, and down below Maggie is thrashing in the arms of her father. *Take it,* Logan thinks, stunned to serenity, *take it all.* Overhead the iron chandelier spirals until its neck cracks at last and crashes to the floor.

Half of the house is reduced to broken browns and crushed grays by the time Central, Indiana's first tornado slips back into the sky. Furniture flattened, walls collapsed, lost doors and everything wet with rain. Grimmer House appears defeated, ravaged, yet somehow pulsing still. The grand staircase remains, as does the whole second floor. The wood carvings in the entryway ceiling poke down at the remains while the grandfather clock buried near the staircase manages its hourly Westminster Quarters chime.

The people in town would never know more than what the local papers could report. That the tornado was an F2 and ultimately caused minimal damage. How the Historical Society evaluated the structure, and confirmed plans to begin the restoration of Grimmer House the following spring. The body of Jeanette Mason had been found crushed by the fireplace stones. Now she can be found next to her sister in Maplewood Cemetery.

What the papers couldn't write, only Maggie Mason will remember. That the storm was a future she somehow summoned. How the wind went through the windows like water filling a cup, tangling the curtains and spewing rainbow glass upon the floor, until wind was all there was, all there could be, her human form made wind. How disaster ate them. And then she tore the house in half.

OF THE WAYS

The year has grown old and tired – it drops its treasures from fumbling branches; from stiff, crooked twigs that snatch at the air as their leaves fall, too slow to save them. Gold, copper and bronze is piled, dragon-hoard deep, around the pillars of the trees.

You have chosen this path, so why does a frost brittle the edges of your heart?

She wades through dry leaves, the seashore hiss breaks against her ankles, and she is able to dictate the rhythm of this ocean, but the hills she glimpses beyond the wood are building in swells of grassland, rutted earth, and sallow crops, to meet the horizon in a line of dark hedges like the crest of an oncoming tidal wave. There is no reason to stop walking though, no one to turn back for. Not any more. She has travelled the length of spring, summer and autumn, roaming far from the weighted blanket of home.

Its comfort became smothering, you had to throw it off to breathe.

The air of the outdoors is sharp, scraping the sorrow from her throat, scouring tears away, cutting bonds and promises. The movement was enough at first, away was all she desired. Then a craving for direction crept up from the oldest part of her awareness, and at that moment she realised she was lost: missing down stinking alleyways, forgotten in blaring roads, disappearing beneath layers of brick and concrete.

I will lead the way – holding the treasure of memory in the casket of my skull.

P
J
R
I
C
H
A
R
D
S

For the hooves, the soft pads, the scrabbling claws, for the soles of tanned hide, the studs of boots, the stab of staffs, the rumble of wheels, for the fleet and the lame.

She walks the tracks now, learning to delve the strata till her feet touch the land; clenching her toes to feel for the seams and faults that crease the ground, the mineral veins and percolated water, twining in its depths.

The Ways are paved with skulls and bones, great curved tusks, broad antlers, dagger horns, long teeth for tearing, blunt ridges for the meditation of cud, chisels to strip bark, tiny flecks of enamel for rendering seeds to a sweet dust.

She caresses their shapes beneath her feet as she walks. The bare trees and their brittle fallen leaves thin out, and the cloudy daylight glows timelessly from every direction.

Her eyes hawk the horizon, watching for the next hilltop beacon, or the slate walls of oncoming storms, or the signs left on the sky by arrowheads of migrating birds as the wind carries them south.

I lead without looking back, trusting they will follow.

And they do follow, those who feel her presence. They notice when she passes by, pulled by the season-tides; the venture that calls to fledgling minds or laments within nostalgic, faltering hearts. She reminds them to move on, to keep in step with the rhythm of the land.

Because if they don't, the line will be broken. The spine of the land will snap.

She doesn't know how many are behind her, or how few.

It doesn't matter as long as the ghosts that roam the rolling, sea-drowned plains are remembered – there are seasons of fate as well as life. As stragglers or hoards, every step is a consecration.

She has fled from where hope bled to death on the tarmac – metal twisted into silver filigree, glass smashed to diamonds, indicators broken into rubies and topaz, glittering in strobing sapphire blue. The endless days when grief fixed her with its unblinking stare, and rooted her to the instant when the world split, when she was severed from the path she had planned.

Some steps must be taken on trust – in the dark, as the ground crumbles. As you fall.

All that was good and precious sealed off from the soft earth; its green maps to freedom despised in scraps fouling gutters and damp corners, or driven off with blades and poison. Her Way forgotten.

There were ages when winter never died and the blizzards filled my footprints, and the Ways were almost lost beneath all the cold white death – then black death, battlefield blood, the heaviness of stones piled into walls, cruel iron enclosing wild land…

Still I walk.

She knows where the sun is, even as it shivers behind the clouds; turns her face towards it, closes her eyes, and, for a moment, sees the unbroken web of shadows it has cast from every tall stone raised by the ancient wanderers – markers of the Ways.

Keep moving.

She pushes onwards until the balance of twilight steadies her pace, and thirst and hunger drag her from the fields towards scattered streetlights and dollhouse vignettes framed by windows. There is always something to scavenge from the edges of the mundane world: windfall apples, food and water left out for the birds (she never takes it all), a tithe of eggs, vegetables and honey from farm-gate boxes (she pays with poems), and most rarely, if she is recognised (with a double-take and a smile of wonder), there will be an open door leading to a hearth and a hot meal shared without questions.

I cannot stay.

She slips away before dawn, leaving her thanks in the form of maps drawn in the condensation she breathes over windowpanes, to be revealed when winter chills the glass.

I leave a part of myself behind with every cycle of the sun. Yet I do not diminish.

Along roads, to lanes, to paths, to tracks, back to the Ways. She trails her fingers through the crystals of frost on the tips of hedgerows, the warmth in her hand melting and setting the ice into fresh patterns; tiny arrows pointing in the direction she travels.

The sun shatters like golden glass over the land, the blue of early morning washes her clean. Pledges and promises hang like mist in the damp air with her sighed breath.

My crown grows again.

Her long strides roll the miles and memories far behind, and a smile smooths the lines on her face. She lifts her gaze from the ploughed earth and salutes the squabbling rooks and gulls that are turning the clods for worms – they hush and bow (she nods). She waves up to the wind-tumbling crows, and they weave into a black ribbon that swirls high above her, paying out like a kite-string and bursting into a raucous chorus (she understands a word or two: *Far! Go far!*).

Its branches press against my scalp. Striving towards the midwinter light.

Pale light.

Blue light.

The pain of recollection is a ripping of metal through flesh, a shattering of skulls. The rooks and gulls erupt in screaming columns around her *fly! fly! fly!* and she is choking on their feathers, beaten to the ground by their wings, head down, hands grasping at the broken soil, voice rising with theirs.

The points pierce.

Her fingers touch bone. There is silence.

She holds tight to the hands offered up by the earth, clasps them in both of hers and leans back allowing them to take the burden of her body – then a pair of antlers heave from the ground: short, neat, pleasingly asymmetrical. Shaking, she smooths the soil from the tines, wipes them clean on her coat, holds them against her hammering heart.

The defiant heat of movement melts the frost, keeps the heartbeat striking against death.

The antlers warm in her hands.

Reveals a Way back to life.

She lifts them to examine how perfectly their ridged branches taper to slim, ivory tips – and as she does so, the low winter sun breaks through the clouds and turns them to dazzling gold. Instinctively, she shades her eyes with the antlers and they touch her forehead, stroke back through her hair and settle, their weight nothing more than the breath of the breeze. The gentle caress of a forgotten hand.

And when she lets go, they do not fall.

NOT JUST MUSEUMS

It was the second time in as many days that Marie had overheard a child's question and wondered where it came from.

The first time, she'd been returning to her hotel, disoriented by the unfamiliar night-time street, the exaggerated, slanting light, the voices that came close and vanished, and, revealed by railings, the unexpected spaces that seemed blacker than the sky. When she'd turned the last corner, her path was blocked by a woman with two tiny dogs, and she'd slowed then to make way for a man and small boy walking near the kerb. As these two passed, the child had said: "Will they shoot those doggies too, Dad? Will they?" After a second, Marie turned, itching to learn what the answer would be, but it was too late, already, to hear anything.

And now, Marie watched as a little girl with pink cheeks and wet blue eyes – a bland poppet lacking only a Victorian hoop and stick – gazed up at her mother and said: "Mummy, why do they keep men in there?"

Her mother made a little movement of surprise. "No, darling," she said, and her eyes strayed briefly to Marie. "Of *course* they don't keep men in there. We've been here before, haven't we? They're red deer. You remember? Look, see, over there? Can you see their antlers?"

The child stared up in open disbelief. "I'm cold," she said. She dug one rubber heel into the grass and stuck out her lower lip, and then, obeying a sudden inner call, she ran off to the head of the woodland path, leaving her mother no choice but to follow.

Why, thought Marie, would the child say that? Had she ever seen a prison yard? Or was it something she'd seen on television, something that made her think that horrors lie in wait at the end of suburban streets, and in the wooded corners of public parks? In fact, the wire fence that she'd seen as a prison's bars, though tall, was flimsily made, the horizontals slack and widely spaced; an obstacle to deer, not enterprising humans. And it was only there, at the viewing point, that this poor barrier could be seen; elsewhere, dense thickets of low-level trees grew up and through the border, apart from where, at the furthest edge, they met a high wall and a row of lean-to sheds. The herd of deer was over there. They stood beneath a tree whose fractured trunk and branches had turned, in death, lustreless and white.

Marie shoved her hands into her pockets. The air was damp, cold, as still as the low sky, made of the same stuff. If she stared up, from that nothingness, grey masses seemed to bloom, like a blank wall that comes to life if examined long enough. Perhaps she'd go back. It took ten minutes to walk through the park, and then, after that, another ten to the hotel. Night came on so fast.

Not far inside the fence, crows crowded the rim of a feeding trough, and their beaks beat a tattoo, like hail, as they pecked at the stuff within. Their gleaming eyes looked as if they were remembering, as one by one they all looked up and began to cast themselves away into the air. They flew in a wide circle to the crown of the tree that held the centre of the field, sending shivers as they landed, through the thin threads of its few leaves.

The herd was immobile, over there, under the dead white tree. The russet of their hides burned through the gloom. One of them, a hind, advanced, and perhaps it was the confusion of the forms behind that made it seem as though its legs were disproportionately thick. It fell forward onto its knees, and to Marie it looked as though its skin slid too freely, sagging around its breast. She moved closer to the fence. You could hardly distinguish one from another. Only the outline of the kneeling deer was clear, where its narrow head and extended neck inclined towards the grass. A beast at the centre of the herd moved out, but immediately its definition faded, so that it seemed only slightly darker, only slightly fuller, than the air. Perhaps one of the collective had reared up; perhaps it was a leg she saw, although, for a moment it appeared as though an arm reached out, as though a brown hand shot forth from a sleeve of wrinkled hide, high above the others.

Why were they so close together? Why were they huddled so near that each flank touched another's? She took a step back; without realising, she'd been resting her face against the wire, and now she felt cold water on her skin and smelt its slight metallic odour. How dark the wooded area had become. How dark the 'nature trail' path behind her. The crows wheeled up and glided to the top of another bare black silhouette, and as they landed they shrugged and pulled in their wings, and turned their heads towards her.

The receptionist smiled warmly at Marie as she handed over her room key. "Not just museums today then?" she said. "You made time for some shopping too? Well, why not? We all deserve a treat don't we? Especially on holiday."

Marie glanced down at the pink carrier bag. It looked, she supposed, quite flashy, and not at all as if it came from the pile behind the counter in the charity shop near the park. The plastic bulged at the seams, and its contents, brown and pliant, were visible through the top.

"Yes, that's right," she said with a laugh and an agreeable smile that she only dared drop when the lift doors had closed behind her. She held the bag against her chest as she rode up to the fourth floor.

"A bargain," the elderly man behind the counter had said. His voice trembled in time with his hands as he packed, as though he were moved by powerful emotion. "It only went in the window today. I said it wouldn't be there long. A real bargain, that is. A real bargain you've got there."

She didn't try the coat on then, but now, in her room, in front of the mirror over the desk and its scattered pile of information leaflets, she slipped her arms into its sleeves. It was made from the skin of a sheep and it doubled her bulk and hid her shape, or rather, made it something else's. She pushed her fingertips into the creamy fleece lining, and traced them along the rugged seams which age and usage had creased and darkened. Here and there a crackling had crept into the skin, but, still, she thought she could detect the oily scent of lanolin.

She lay down on the bed and lit the side lamp, looking obliquely through the window, to where the rain was glittering down.

She should have left the coat in the cloakroom. But then again, although it was too hot to wear inside, when she'd taken it off and carried it, a chill had run straight through her spine. It was impossible, it seemed, to get her temperature just right.

The ivory statuette was naked but for a loin cloth, inlaid with a streak of red. The same bloody inlay had been applied to the hands, to the knees, to the minutely detailed beard, to the ecstatic, heavenward eyes.

She moved on. A bronze rococo ewer with a bare-breasted woman for a handle, and growing from its base and belly and spout, fish with lions' manes, and curled half-human creatures hauling the ropes of ripe, wind-billowed sails. Next to it, a daybed, the utility of its frame buried by carved extravagances, by peonies, and doves, and snakes, and leaves embellished with gold. Nearby, a woodpecker, worked in porcelain, crushing a black beetle in its beak. These might be grave goods, thought Marie, and I might be caught inside a tomb.

The open entrance to the room had appeared closer than it actually was; it felt as if she were walking on the spot as she approached. When she reached the wide lobby, she found it half-empty, lit only by the frosted light that filtered down through glass. At the far end, away from the main doors, soundless figures drifted.

Was she hot, or cold? Was this the start of a fever? Her wet breath settled on her face and she was uncomfortably aware of the damp prickle of the fleece against her neck. The pockets of the coat grew deeper as she pushed her fists down into them. She felt the stitches start to break.

Perhaps just the one museum today. She'd go back to the hotel, take a nap. And then, in the evening, a boat trip on the river, maybe a walk over Tower Bridge. She only had two nights left before the train back to the coast. The streets of her little town were deserted now, sleeping out the winter. The old timbers of the pier were black with rain, and only the drunks stayed faithful to the benches that looked out to sea. She thought of her desk, her paperweight, her mug, the Association office and "It's always the quiet ones, isn't it?" and "We're only having a laugh, Marie" and "Sometimes I think I don't know you at all." One long day was there, waiting for its end.

She'd walk up through the park, before she went back to the hotel, up to the deer enclosure.

The herd was centred in the field, below the tree, whose trunk, she saw now, bore enormous thick-scaled growths, as though the vitality within had surged up and out to meet the other world, and, finding nothing for it there, turned back upon its host.

Some of the animals stood, but others lay, cramped together as before, so close that their bodies made a low mound that might, if not for a stirring here and there, have been built from that reddish clay that, after rain, can turn a ploughed field bloody. Necks and heads emerged from the mound, and their ears, in the failing light, were the skeletons of leaves.

There was no one else there. Only her. A slow drizzle pattered into her hair and settled on the resistant surface of the coat. She reached out and wound her fingers through the cold wire of the fence.

The stag rose and took a step and the movement shuddered down its thick neck and rippled across the barrel of its body, settling to stillness. Its jaws were working, and its heavy throat shook. Did it have some disease? Its knees looked too large; four domed discs which caused the skin to stand away from the bone, bunching strangely above and tenting tautly below on the way to the sharp-toed feet. The creature's black, indifferent eyes turned and gazed beyond Marie, and it shook its head as if its wide-branched antlers, its shattered crown, were a humiliation.

They were all rising now, as if commanded, but their bodies were ambiguous, overlaying one another so they became one larger composition. Was it two separate animals she saw at the side of the group, or one?

A fox, plumped against the cold, slipped into the enclosure and trotted out towards the herd, conscious of itself and them, a stealthy interloper, tensed for confrontation; the crows hopped away from it, mocking.

What was that? Marie turned an ear towards the fence as though it were a wall. Was there, after all, someone – men – in there? A low voice, a higher answer? It might only be the creaking of a tree, something falling, a bird.

They were moving forward towards the fence in slow increments, rotating their positions. She thought of Roman soldiers, advancing behind their shields. One elongated head, comprised of many, appeared and turned, displaying row on row of upright ears. The group flowed with supple lassitude across the ground, where fallen leaves, wet from the rain, reflected the sky like mirrors. A pale corona hung about them. White breath smudged their mouths.

The stag broke away from the mass, huge against a slender tree. It bowed its head towards the grass, and there, Marie could see a darker line that ran across its shoulders and along its spine, like a rough-sewn closure in its skin.

She stepped back, composing herself, sensing *company*. She turned. There was nobody there, but the air was thick with presence, with the felt exchange of energy that runs through a surging crowd. The pressure bore down, electric, alive, as she walked slowly and deliberately to the head of the woodland path. Was this what a panic attack was like? A shift, similar to falling without warning over a sheer drop, like crashing to the bottom of a pit. A blackening of the mind, a bone-deep doubt.

She wasn't used to the city: that was all. That was it. The feeling was fading already. As she pulled up the collar of the coat, she thought: tomorrow, I mustn't do too much.

~<>~

Towards the end of the next afternoon, Marie stood before an oil painting in a busy room. Hounds, backs viciously arched, ribs raised, teeth bared against red tongues, foregrounded a nocturnal forest that opened, in the distance, to the sheer face of a cliff. The white neck, the regal head, of the dogs' doomed quarry showed between the shadowed trees. She'd been standing there too long, perhaps; someone was whispering behind her. She moved towards the right. There, within the scene's black centre; a cradle of glowing light, an executioner's hand, the nightmare swoop of steel, a flaming artery, a curtain, held aside.

The day was beginning to fade when she found her way outside the gallery. Taken by the crowd, she walked through the door of a resting bus whose number she now knew, and climbed to the upper deck, relieved, in a way, that this was her last night. The city was not how she'd remembered it. This time, beneath its vivid lights, its human variety, its artefacts, she saw the wide grey horizons of her home, and heard the swell of its winter tides, and smelt its bitter iodine. Sometimes a mist rolled in, back there, and took the walls away, and the sun laid a white path, impossible to follow.

Every seat of the bus was taken by the time it reached London Bridge, but at the south side of the river the passengers began to leave, until soon she was the only one left there on the upper deck. Someone in the street, looking up, might have seen her and recalled the time they'd waited in a white corridor and despaired at ever hearing the sound of their own name. When she recognised the columns of a Georgian portico, she rang the bell for the bus to stop.

Although it was near dusk, the park gates were still open. She hurried, a little breathless, up the long slope of the central walk and, at the top, passed through the gate that led to the wooded nature trail and the fence of the deer enclosure. The herd was in the distance, by the far wall, by the lean-to sheds, a distance that released them from the confines of their forms and made their movements seem as soft as falling ash. They rotated in one mass, subtly exchanging position, yielding to each other. Their darker parts were charred wood, the rounds of their bellies were rust. Like leaves caught in clear water, they seemed suspended above the stuff that might circle them ashore.

Vacancies between their necks captured the light, weaving simulacra within them, the lineaments of wings, of feathers, of rigid manikins, and eyes, conjured from a spell of nothing, that peered in strange pearliness before they blinked away. A head turned, flattened by that same deceiving light, creating, within its cusps and flexures, the cryptic mirage of a human face.

It was just an impulse, she knew, and one that might get her into trouble, but, with a quick glance around, she understood that, suddenly giddily inspired, it was one she would indulge. The wires sagged and swung beneath her feet, but the coat shielded her from injury as she pulled herself over the top and down to the other side.

As she approached, the herd jolted forward, as though the movement of time had accelerated, or had cut out for a black second, to adjust itself to her. The size of them was a surprise; they were embanked monuments, ridged and hollowed, made from ruddy earth, and reverently, like a supplicant, she made herself small before them. They waited, rooted, organically sure of her, and when she was close enough to touch them, they moved apart, dividing their one self, with stately slowness, with ceremonial dressage, to form an elaborate autumnal arc, opening the glowing foyer to the temple's fiery heart.

"Is it you?" a low voice said. They'd closed around her, nuzzling her, containing her. Human feet and hands extended from their sides, from the ends of their tight-tendoned limbs. Her coat-skin tightened as her stomach dropped and rounded, but its collar loosened at her neck as she fell, in gratitude, back sloped, legs tensed, to the safety of all fours.

The dawn broke a sickly pink. Marie followed the deer's slow high steps as they moved towards the centre of the field, her heels raised and her fingers held stiff and straight upon the grass. There was a woman coming for them. Hell – let her do what she has to, Marie thought: I'll do anything, *anything*, now.

She heard the woman more than saw her. Now, she had to turn her head to the side, because her eyes had grown so far apart. The woman was wearing something that flowed, sinuous and heavy, across her stony skin.

A sharp blow on her rump sent her running. Her hands slapped down on the sodden earth, and her feet scrabbled madly to keep up. Another blow; it was cushioned by her thick pelt, but lacking understanding, any clear thoughts at all, stunned and stupid, she changed tack, springing off towards the first opening she saw, leaping towards refuge. What was this? *Of course*. She was being driven away from the herd. Too late, her bare feet touched straw and a door slammed shut behind her. In the dark, weight shifted, near to her. A sliver of white light appeared, and within the wavering touch of it, a face.

"Welcome," the woman said. "We've not had one of you for a while."

And then Marie saw the others; their ragged, fingernail-raked coats, their whiskered, ancient, chewing faces, the half-blind blankness of their eyes. She breathed in the hanging scent of their manure.

"Can I stay?" Marie said.

Black silence broke over her. But in her heart she understood that the answer must be "Yes."

FILL THE THICKENED LUNG WITH BREATH

The window. Dusk. Ilse watches the cabs come and go below. Rain slicks the street with the shine of a freshly groomed dog, flashes of chrome yellow bright enough to sting her eyes in the gloom. She blinks, the after images ghosts against her lids. Memories of adventures long gone swiftly crumble like candyfloss to sharp sugar in her mouth, then depart, nothing but a gritty trail on her tongue. The doorman runs in and out of the rain, Charon steering his charges across the Styx, his grey coat spattered with drops, Dalmatian fresh, barking directions, slamming doors.

It has been raining for days; it never seems to stop. Every gloomy morning Ilse half expects to wake up floating, the furniture bobbing around her, her bed a dinghy. The ring of a navigational buoy would not be out of place. The light is never good but lately it seems as though the city is in a near constant winter fog. Soft grey despondency seeps in through the window, staining everything with its indifference.

The curtain in Ilse's hand runs like sand against her skin as she pulls it further to one side, time slipping through her fingers, unstoppable. It heaps on the floor unhindered, a tiny island in the sea of the blue shag pile. She is waiting for someone, or thinks she is. Maybe the girl in the coat is just a memory. Her lungs are thick with them, after all, choking her when she wakes, all at sea. Another girl in another town in another time. Maybe.

Every passenger who jumps into a cab takes a little more of the city's colour with them. The yellow pulses greedily as the cars swallow each one up, practically slobbering as they devour the life force of their occupants, the chewed up bones and ground down sinew revving their engines as the vehicles screech away into the fog and the night beyond.

Ilse shudders but still watches. She is good at waiting.

As dusk descends her patience is rewarded, just as she knew it would be. The bright red slash of coat sharp against the steadily draining tones of the city is able competition for the hungry cabs, pulling one's eyes helplessly in the girl's direction. Every evening she strolls along the street, unhurried, unconcerned colour against the coming of the night, with no need of the voracious taxicabs. Until now the simple fact of her has been comfort enough, but this evening Ilse wants more. She discovers she has an appetite too, ignored for too long, and is suddenly hungry to see her face, to hear her voice, to know where she is going, where she has been, everything and anything. Enough of this fog and the constant waiting. Her feet and hands twitch at the wildly simple idea of throwing the door open, running down the winding stairs, ever down, until she runs out of nondescript carpet, hits the lobby, and makes a break for the outside. A smile touches her mouth as she lives it in her mind, every step, every breath, the sudden lightness of her thoughts lifting her lips, throwing muscles into places they have not been for far too long.

She almost moves. Almost. Her muscles flex and her blood runs a little faster in her too tight veins. Habit, however, is a tireless mistress, and she remains fixed to the spot, to her place in the world. Removed. Afar. Ilse thinks of the other girl as her beacon, wants her to be what snaps her out of the inertia and fear that hold her in this room, her red coat a talisman. Yet now it feels more like an omen and the portent weighs her down anew, anchoring her even more firmly in place, unyielding to temptation, to freedom.

How she came to be here, watching and waiting, is a mystery to Ilse now. She remembers a summer's day, the sun high in the sky, Charon wishing for a summer shower as he helped her with her bags. The heavy-sweet tang of heat across her skin, the slow trickle of it between her legs, pearling down the small of her back, beneath her breasts, peppering her upper lip. She can almost taste it now, standing in the cold grey room, the only colour the sea blue ocean of shag.

Ilse sighs and…

At first there is just a smudge, something catching at the corner of her eye – a hair perhaps, a lash – but soon it is tumbling, spiralling, gathering strength as it rushes from the four grey corners of the room. Her earlier hopefulness disappears, swallowed by the familiar foreboding. She wants to close her eyes, to turn away, but she knows the storm will only come with her. There is no hiding unless she can change. It only comes when she rests in a single form for too long, and she does not want to see, does not want the hurly or the burly, wire sharp against her nerves.

How she longs to be on the sidewalk with the girl in the red coat.

Ilse falls to her knees and wills herself to change. It used to be so easy. Everything was. Now she croons to herself softly, singing the song of her mother's people, of the Ones Who Knew, and slowly she begins to change. Wind rushes in her ears and, although the windows are closed and locked, she can feel a sharp salt breeze licking at her skin. Her hands sink into the carpet, too pale skin seeping into the blue and the blue seeping into too pale skin. She feels herself spreading, welcomes the release of it, feels the same warmth of that long ago summer's day between her legs. Flushed. The change is always the same, a better lover than her human ones, and, as she watches her skin rippling slowly, sinuously outwards, away from her but still of her, entwining with the fibres, becoming them, she gives herself up to its sweet cherry pleasure.

The wall is close and her body sings to it, welcomes it, meets it, and soon enough she is also brick and paper, paint and render. Convergent boundaries have her reaching further, throwing up mountains, straining for change, burgeoning, yearning, into the curtains, sandy-beach fabric and pebbled stitching at the edge of the azure carpet-sea. Her body cannot meld with the glass, there is too much of the outside in it, but she is happy to surround it, happy to edge up into the ceiling and spread herself across it, her lithosphere drum tight and snug. She gives herself over to the metamorphosis, every atom heavy with earthly ecstasy, salt thirsty and burning, burning, but safe in the knowledge her human concerns yet thrive – she will still be able to keep watch on the ferryman and the girl in the red coat.

The grey has receded, its incursion a failure.

So, for now, she sleeps.

Waking, Ilse scrabbles for the side of her dinghy, the sharp slap of water on the deck enough to panic her. Using the edge to pull herself up, she takes stock of her situation and cannot help but gasp as she realizes how far out at sea she is; she must have been drifting for days. There is no sound but the water and her thumping heart. Her gasp becomes a thousand breaths long, her head swimming with what must be true. Weakness woven wickedly in her marrow has her fighting to stay sitting. She may have been asleep for time unaccountable, but she is bone-weary, dog-tired. Frustration leaks like oil from her pores, and she tips her head back and howls at the moon above her, baying over and over until she falls back in the dinghy and lays stock still, except for the harried rise and fall of her chest. She stares up at the sky, at the stars patchworking the heavens and pointing her in directions she cannot know.

She is not certain how long she stays there, but eventually she becomes aware that the moon has begun to sink and the light in the east – she assumes it is east for surely that is where the sun always rises, Mr Hemingway – has begun to gather, bleaching the constellations one by one from the sky. What can she do? She has no oars and the dinghy has no motor. She is floating ever onwards with no idea where she has been, where she is, or where she is heading. Or perhaps she is in the same place she has always been and here she will stay, the same old dinghy, the same old waves.

As the sun rises, the warmth touches Ilse's skin and the familiar heat finally rouses her into sitting again. Homer's wine dark sea surrounds her, but it is the blue of an old sherry bottle her great-great aunt would sneak her nips from when she was too young to know what it was except forbidden. It laps at the dinghy, soothing her senses as she listens, her limbs heavy as she whispers sweet nothings back.

Yet, the greyness is gathering once more, she can feel it, far off for now but always there, always waiting, and she wants nothing more than to slip into the water's waiting embrace, to lose herself in its lover's arms, to reach for oblivion, every sinew straining for release. It is too much temptation and, almost before she knows she is going to do it, Ilse has swung herself over the side of the little red dinghy and is plunging down, down, down, vast feathers of bubbles streaking above her to mark her progress. Her hair dances and leaps in the wash, graceful pirouettes and gymnastic arabesques, folding and floating as she sinks, the salt water brisk against her skin, sharpening her senses, keeping her awake lest she give herself over to the somniferous lament of the deep. Her lover wraps themself around her, claims her, drops and molecules, motes and atoms, washed down the throat of the ocean by Adam's sweetest ale. Aqua blue.

Ilse smiles at bright yellow tang as they swim boldly close to her, only to be caught up in her descent and down they all go, spiralling and tumbling, until at last, together, they hit the deep coral reef below. A florid cloud of fish mushrooms around her and, furious at the imposition, the little surgeonfish flex their tails, exposing their white spines and, blade sharp, they slash at Ilse from every angle, even as the jagged coral scratches at her legs, bright red blood pearling at every touch, with every move. Ilse realises the water had numbed her but the heat of the ichthyic attack revives her and, as she tries to fight her diminutive aggressors off, even as the greyness seeps into her vision, flowering up from the reef, something of the pain thrills her. She knows she must change but for a moment she relishes feeling so alive at last. Real. Corporeal. Even through the tearing at her flesh, the scorching of her senses, as the grey rises around her, she knows she has seen that colour before, that tone – scarlet against the fog, red against the night – she remembers… she remembers…

The wardrobe is oddly cool against Ilse's cheek when she wakes again. She had not expected to wake up there, but beggars cannot always be choosers, so they say. She wonders if the water pushed her up onto the island of the wardrobe, off the reef and onto safer ground. It does not feel much safer, to be sure. Every inch of her stings and Ilse wonders how she will get down without hurting herself. Her skin still bleeds from the tangs and the coral, and her hair is sopping wet. She touches one of the wounds carefully, the bright red leeching onto her fingers, making small puddles on the tips. She touches them to her mouth, her tongue slipping from between her lips to taste. It is salty, not metallic at all, and she savours its warmth, imagining her own bright red being absorbed back into her body, recycling, restoring, the wounds slowly healing shut. It is a drug like no other, a closed system of repair and repeat, and Ilse shuts her eyes tight against the sudden rush of euphoria, too much, that threatens to throw her from the wardrobe, her body seized in its exultant, healing grip, muscles spasming as she cries out and slips into a blackness that welcomes her with an adventurer's hand, a place where wonders rise and fall and rise and fall again.

When she returns to herself and opens her eyes, the bleeding has stopped and the wounds are nothing but red smears on her legs. Her hair is dry and she no longer feels unsafe. Maybe this is her place after all, here on top of the wardrobe. A crow's nest looking down upon the tiny kingdom of her hotel room. She has always liked heights, liked to climb onto the roof at night as a child and feel the rush of vertigo course through her veins, making her feel more frightened and more alive than anything else she has known since. Back then the fear had always won of course, but knowing she had been that close had seemed enough. She'd never wanted much, just a taste, had never thought to ask for anything more, yet here she is, in her prison, as though she had taken it all. Still afraid, still half alive. If the moon had been in the sky, she would have howled. Again. Forever.

For now, she swings her legs over the side of the wardrobe and looks down. It is further than she'd thought it would be, a vague sense of that childhood vertigo making her scalp and the backs of her knees tingle, her breath quicken. The grey is encroaching, it has become so much quicker now; perhaps her desire for more has affected it, finally tested its limits and accelerated it. It knows it is losing and this is its last offensive. All or nothing. Excitement flares like a long-forgotten beacon and, even as a long ingrained wail of caution warns of dangers to come and reminds her of her fears, Ilse embraces it, allowing it to fuel her. Finally trusting in her true nature, she leaps from the wardrobe… and plunges into the bright blue sea below, her body seal sleek and undulating through the waves. She rolls and flips, dives and then breaks the surface, over and over, barking with the joy of her freedom.

At last, she thinks, at last I am me. And she forgets about the girl in the red coat, forgets about the ferryman and the room as she rolls and flips, dives and breaks the surface over and over, on and on until she is but a speck on the horizon, and then is gone with the setting of the sun.

The room is quiet. The cabs honk their horns as they come and go on the rain-slicked street outside. Charon bears his charges, dashing in and out of the rain, his top hat a grey sail against the tide. The azure blue carpet is still, the curtain tucked in place, and on the bed, pressed and laid out neatly, is a bright red coat.

THE STONE LION

PART I

There was a certain turn of phrase that Agnessa's manager used. When something bad happened to a member of staff she would say, '*I'm sorry, you didn't deserve it.*'

It stuck with Agnessa as a quirk, but when the manager said it after the death of Agnessa's husband Ivan, a shiver coursed down her spine and it seemed that all the clocks had stopped about her. Agnessa wondered at the simplicity of such a phrase; that bad things should only happen to those who deserved it, and that if you were good enough then your husband wouldn't die in a motorcycle accident on an icy morning in December.

She returned to the farm outside Samara where she'd grown up, leaving the two-bedroom flat on the outskirts of the student quarter in Moscow and choosing not to think about the mortgage payments, the lump sum of life insurance, the casseroles and pies in the freezer and especially not the motorcycle, chained and left in the garage below the Soviet-era apartment building.

Returning had been the idea of her mother, Marfa, and Agnessa didn't dare reject the offer of spending her compassionate leave on the farm, knowing her mother would come up to Moscow in the glory of her sixtieth year and drag her out of the house herself if she had to.

Agnessa's mother had long ago decided that suffering each time something bad happened

C
A
T
H
E
R
I
N
E

A
D
A
M
S

was a waste of time, and so had spent one year when she was sixteen consolidating all her pain into a twelve month period. She had dressed in black and taken to her bed, crying twice a day and eating only crusts of bread, and emerged at seventeen like a butterfly from her chrysalis, resolved to never again feel such a deep level of disconsolation. As a result, she remained stoically cheerful through the death of Agnessa's grandfather, and even on hearing of Ivan's death managed no more than a sympathetic tut.

The train was delayed leaving Moscow due to a problem with the station clock, which was not running. Marfa had been waiting for the train at the local station and then once she arrived drove her to the farmhouse in the Lada Niva.

The house appeared over the rise of the road, a blur of darkness under the cover of the thickly falling snow, windscreen wipers working frantically to keep Marfa's view clear. It was the only building for miles, a squat two-storied wooden thing with a pointed roof to keep the snow off and decorated windows which Marfa repainted herself every spring.

A front door existed, but was so rarely used that Marfa had forgotten its exact location, and instead the half-door into the kitchen was the main entrance. In floorspace the kitchen was only a small part of the house, but due to the time spent there, it had rejected the borders the bricks had placed upon it and so expanded, with red floor tiles and a huge stove above which clothes dried and beside that a hand-hewn table that sat twelve, marked with acrylic paint and wine stains and a thousand other things that bore testament to Marfa's fierce determination to be happy, always.

The kitchen door was constantly left open, no matter the weather outside; the stove was warm enough to heat the red space and more. A little stone lion reclined on the concrete step before the kitchen, curiously covered with only a light sprinkling of snow against the white backdrop of the rear garden.

Agnessa slumped at the great table, filled with happiness, and allowed her mother to place a slice of warm bread and butter at her elbow. Marfa pulled out a three-legged stool and sat beside her, feet up on the bench, and waited for the three sheepdogs to come to the kitchen searching for food.

Marfa had made a stew from beef chuck, carrots, and floury white potatoes pulled from the cellar. The gravy was thick and dark, thickened with the same flour used to make the bread. She carved another two slices from the warm loaf, thick as the table, and allowed the butter to melt into them before she spread it.

"You don't have to go back," Marfa offered. "You can stay here as long as you want, until you feel better."

Seated at the table, eating bread and stew as the snow fell outside unifying the land and the dark sky, Agnessa considered the promise in the offer. She dipped her spoon into the stew and ate while Marfa filled a bowl for her husband who took his meals in the book room, where he lived.

The dogs were asleep, the stove burned hot, and the stone lion on the doorstep was now almost obscured by snow. In a perfectly natural movement, he arose and shook the snow from his mane, padding into the kitchen much like a house cat would. He observed Agnessa sitting at the table with her supper, wandered to the dogs' water bowl, lapped from it, then curled up beside the warm stove and closed his eyes.

～≈～

The clock on the mantlepiece in the formal living room was suspended at a quarter to the hour. Agnessa banked the fire and took a place on the flowered sofa with the album of wedding photographs she had sent her parents after her marriage to Ivan. Flicking over the heavy grained rice paper, Agnessa traced the photographs with the pad of her index finger, reliving the sensation of joy, of being so weightless she could float away.

She turned the page and there was another Agnessa, with Ivan on her right, her parents flanking them. Marfa's sun-wrinkled skin was like creased paper, out of place in pale Moscow. Agnessa bent her head to the photograph, placed her nose against the cool print as though she could push her way inside it, fall through the lithograph paper and be back there, at Ivan's side. If she closed her eyes, the snowflakes outside the window could become thrown rice, the crackling of the fire the clapping of their guests.

The door shifted and the stone lion appeared. A night indoors had done him good, and colour had bloomed in his eyes and paws. He regarded Agnessa balefully, then leapt onto the sofa beside her, tucking himself into the space formed by her bent knees. Turning another page, confronted with a full photograph of herself and Ivan beaming from the front steps of the courthouse, Agnessa reached for the lion as some small comfort.

His mane was warm.

Marfa returned to the house for lunch, and Agnessa offered to take a tray to her father, leaving it outside the door of the closed book room. He had not answered her note, slipped beneath his door, and did not respond when she knocked.

At first, he had read every book in the house. While Agnessa studied at university she sent him books in parcels every week like a mother sending sweets to her child at summer camp. His latest obsession – reading all the works of Dostoevsky – had emerged only after her marriage. Agnessa had suggested intervention, but Marfa insisted it was the only way she and her husband could happily co-exist. It was not so unusual. There was a distinguished tradition amongst some - the English, for example - where the man of the family disappeared bit by bit into his library, until he was absorbed into the fine print text of the *Sunday Times* and discarded his earthly body entirely.

On returning to the formal living room, Agnessa discovered Marfa had not left the house. She stood by the fire with the poker and the book of wedding photographs, feeding them to the flames and banking the logs until the heavy grain photograph paper bubbled, twisted and blackened.

"The snow is too fierce to finish mucking out the cattle," she said. "It will have to wait until it settles."

The stone lion had disappeared from the room.

Agnessa watched Marfa finish burning the pages of her wedding album without speaking.

When Agnessa had taken a class on Russian literature at university, they had studied folklore. It was impossible to avoid superstition in the country. Sensible Marfa eschewed the old traditions, preferring to trust in the work her hands produced, but old neighbours would sit in silence before a journey and kill chickens that crowed three times before noon. Agnessa's elegant Moscow classmates had dismissed such things as children's nonsense, but she had argued strongly that the opposite was true.

She had never been more sure in that assertion than now, when she entered the red kitchen to find her stone lion at the stove again. Deep amber had bloomed across his back, and when he rolled to expose his belly, his face was fully coloured tawny gold. The guardian of her house, a *domovoi*, a grandfather who lived in the stove and protected the family, undoubtedly.

Agnessa filled a dog's bowl with milk and pushed it over to the stone lion. He ambled toward it, bending over it, getting his whiskers wet. Why had he been left in the snow on the back doorstep when she arrived, when it was so clearly good for him to be warm and well fed?

She knelt beside him and stroked his back as he drank the milk.

∽PART II∾

Some limited and waning memory of Daughter's husband still remains, though in truth he's been long since swallowed up by cows and sheep and the dogs which are constantly underfoot in a house such as this. I dimly remember a tall man, with cheeks scarred by an adolescent acne and a strong sensation that he smelled often of leather and motorcycle oil. He had impressed on me the understanding that he was an unassuming man, but his death had retroactively transformed him into the most good-hearted individual anyone had ever met.

Like all women, I understood that my lot would be the birthing bed. Hadn't I helped half a hundred calves, kneeling on the floor of a hay-covered barn, coaxing the lowing heifer until she did what all of her sex did best? I knew it would fall on me. Sons and daughters, enough to move the cows and shear the sheep when it is required.

Instead there had only been one. Daughter, a girl of the threshold, born on the cusp of two decades, two countries, the Wall coming down in fits and bursts of noise and static on the car radio as I drove myself to the hospital in the snow, contractions making me low like one of my own cows.

Husband took the incident of her birth to mean she would do well in life. Then, he had been taken with astrology, and he plotted the heavens at the moment of her birth on a large sheet of paper which he took into the book room when he withdrew there to join his other sacred scriptures. Shaking off such prophecy, Daughter married the tall man and moved to the city and worked at a university and I stayed with the farm.

I dislike the past and tolerate the future. It is the present which I enjoy the most, the simple reality of what occurs around me. For this reason I eschew calendars and timetables, and will have nothing whatsoever to do with curios, keepsakes, mementoes, museums, photographs, pictures, and stories told in the past tense. It is why I name all of the sheepdogs by the same name, so when one dies I can continue without grief and without reminder of what I have lost.

This has had a direct effect on my memory. Names such as Daughter's husband's have disappeared into the barbed recesses of the forgotten. If asked to make an educated guess, I could perhaps sketch the broad features of Husband's face, but I would not trust the accuracy of anything I produced. Snow in winter takes me by surprise, as does the thaw in spring. The passing of time is not important, but I appreciate the sun rising each morning.

Yet this is enough, and it brings me joy in times when others might find cause to be unhappy. Why wallow in the past and what happened in that strange, savage place?

For this, I burned the photographs.

Daughter sits in the dingy kitchen, at the table in the small nook. She is pressing her finger into a scald mark left by a too-hot pot, but she draws herself upright when she sees me enter.

She is not pleased I burned the photos. Her frigid demeanour burns me while I pour the tea and greet the dogs who lie at the foot of the stove, hot in their coats. She recalls – as much as I do not like to use the word – my lack of grief following Father's death. Apparently that is some sin. It is not enough for me to say that floundering in misery and tracing the face of a loved one with fervent fingers until the glossy coating of photographs is worn smooth and blurred by constant touch will only hinder the enjoyment of the present.

My eyes are drawn to the stove while she speaks, something flickering at the corner of my vision, but when I look there is nothing.

The fields will wait, but I will not. I leave Daughter at the table and return to the chugging Lada.

Daughter has gained a shadow in my house, a padding four-footed beast that follows her from room to room and feeds from her. I sense it is growing stronger and more dangerous, but I have yet to see it with my naked eyes. It appears only at the fringes of my vision, when looking directly at something else, when I glide quickly over a scene and glance away again. I wonder whether it has revealed itself fully to her, whether it is too late and she is already in its clutches.

At dinner we are silent, eating together in the kitchen, crammed into the small table with our elbows jolting each other. Three dogs cower at the half-hung door despite the cold, watching the shadows grow long around the stove. I sense the beast is there but looking yields no answers, only a surge of frustration that I recognise in myself and restrain like a sheep struggling at the shearing.

Still, the itch stays in me like a tick in flesh. There is something at the stove that Daughter has welcomed into my house. I propose a drink, *in vino veritas*, and fetch cold vodka and two cheap glasses. Daughter remarks they are not the ones she remembers from her childhood. They were hand-carved, engraved with mine and Husband's names, she claims. I have no method of discerning whether this is true and so I merely shrug and pour her a measure.

She raises a toast to my health and I accept it in silence, bowing my head and lifting my glass. I drink. Daughter drinks. The vodka is cold in my mouth and fire in my throat. It slips to my chest and I wait for the glow it gives me, like a sunrise warming from within. Daughter coughs and covers her mouth.

I broach the subject of my burning the photographs. I want to impress on Daughter just how terrible the past is. At first it is like the shallow end of a pond – yesterday, the day before, last week. Below the surface are roots and slime and weeds, waiting to tangle you and make you lose your balance and you step deeper and deeper into it, until the water is at your waist, your chest, your neck, and then your nostrils are below the surface and you cannot breathe. The days become decades in the blink of an eye, centuries and eons spreading back as long as women have been giving birth to other women and suddenly you realise it's not a shallow pond at all, it's an ocean and you're drowning in the weight of all that has come before, all the remembering and the indescribable pain that humans have wrought on other humans and if we think about the past and we let ourselves live in it then it will take over us, take over our lives until we can no longer see what's in the present, can no longer be surprised by the sun rising every morning.

Daughter pours another measure for both of us and tells me I am old and scared of forgetting things. Little does she know how much I have already forgotten. Perhaps it is the measure of vodka that makes me tremble as I speak to her, or perhaps the shadow of the beast at the stove that puts me off my words. She drinks her second drink and leaves the kitchen. I cannot look at the stove until she is gone, until the sheepdogs come forward to put their heads in my lap and tell me in their silent way that there is an intruder in their space.

I smooth their hackles down with soft words and my palms.

In the light of day I am ashamed of myself. When I look at the stove I barely remember the fear I felt during the dark hours, unable to believe that only a shadow stirred up such feelings in me. My work takes me to the far reaches of the farm, reviewing the fences which shift when the water freezes in their foundations and dislodges them. I have a hammer and the act of driving them into the hard earth to keep them from shaking in high winds brings heat to my cheeks and chest.

On returning to my house, there is nothing within which has changed compared to the morning. However, in the kitchen, a slow and gentle sensation of despair settles upon me. For a moment I am the shadow, lurking at the threshold of my own house. I understand the beast, this four-footed demon who stalks Daughter, and I know he is coming for me, too. He will swallow us both whole and leave my house empty.

What is this? A touch of madness.

I cross the threshold and find Daughter upstairs, unwashed and undressed, lying beneath the covers in her bedroom. Her hair is matted and I comb it and braid it for her, with fingers sore from wielding the hammer. She complains of a sore throat and I promise hot water, honey, while stroking her back. She cries that she has lost her husband and the back of my neck prickles. Without turning my head from Daughter's face I swivel my eyes to the left and to the right and it is there against the wall that I see it, like a shadow cast from hands before a lamp.

It is huge, the size of a black bear, shoulders rolling as it pads across the floor of Daughter's room. One loping paw is placed upon the bed and I freeze where I sit. First, my mind turns to the shotgun on the wall of the kitchen, but I do not believe this is the sort of beast who can be hunted and shot with lead. Second, I think of Daughter, who is soft, unlike me, with my callouses and my wrinkles. The beast envelops her and she sinks, her shoulders sagging, taking a breath to encompass the beast in the spaces of her ribs.

The despair permeates me as it did in the kitchen and I hate this beast for the constant comparisons it causes me to make between now and the before. I am up to my knees in this pool of yesterdays.

I must save Daughter. She must understand what I have done with the past.

I take her hand and together we walk to the door of the book room.

Daughter looks at me curiously as I take hold of the door handle and open it. She claps her hands over her mouth as the room is revealed.

It is empty.

~PART III~

Marfa did not believe in graves, so there was not one for her husband. She did not even remember the date of his death, but had merely understood it to be another occurrence in the never-ending cycle of rising and setting suns. His final resting place was the soft ground in a far field, and after placing the last clod of soil over him she had continued to bring him his meals and new books as she had done before his death.

This routine became so familiar to her that she continued it long after the memory of his burial faded, and she continued full conversations through the closed door of the book room. The forgetting was her way of dealing with the grief, of closing herself off from the past and seeing only what was there and not what lay beyond.

It was why Marfa did not recognise the stone lion, who had grown as big as the sheepdogs and now padded beside Agnessa wherever she went, keeping her company. Fearful of forgetting, as Marfa had, she recounted stories of Ivan to him, starting from the first day they had met in a club off Moscow's Revolutionary Square, to the day he had brought her coffee in bed and kissed her forehead before skidding off his motorcycle and colliding with a moving car.

Not just the past. She spoke about the future. How she had found her first grey hair before he died and plucked it out from the scalp and he had kissed the hair and wound it around his finger in delight. Now she would grow old alone, her face becoming more lined while his would always be frozen, preserved in her mind exactly the way he had looked at thirty-two. It was her who would feel the aches of old age, the regret of not having done more in her youth, the fear of forgetting as the years tumbled into a spiral of oblivion behind her, while Ivan rested, perfect, unimpeded and unhindered by pain or regret or fear.

Just as he had been, just as he was, just as she had loved him.

The stone lion took her grief and swallowed it and he rewarded her by growing, fur turning a deeper shade of gold, the detail in his mane strengthening until every hair was visible.

Sleeping became more difficult in the cold nights before the change of year. The stone lion had taken a place beside Agnessa, his mane tangling with her own dark hair on the pillow. She threaded her fingers into his fur and lay there holding him as once she might have reached for Ivan's hand in their Moscow flat.

Agnessa would have insisted to Marfa – if the two had been speaking – that the reason she could not sleep was the isolating silence of the farmhouse. In the Moscow Khrushchyovka the walls had been paper thin. Every sound made by the neighbours, every rev of an engine outside, every shout from the street – it was all audible in the bedroom. Years of living there had deadened Agnessa to the sound.

The truth was that the dark ceiling of her childhood bedroom became the perfect backdrop against which to play out the happiest scenes of her life with Ivan. With the lion's head on her chest she whispered the stories to accompany the scenes, as if he were the only audience member at a silent cinema and she the pianist desperate to play.

When the lion moved his head and nuzzled at the crook of Agnessa's arm she let him do so. He opened his mouth to reveal lines of white teeth like needles and he dug them into the top of her forearm, breaking skin and drawing blood.

Agnessa did not hesitate, only continued to recount the stories to the lion until the scenes on the ceiling clicked over to the last slide, the morning of Ivan's death. The lion had taken his fill of her blood, he rolled away from her and quickly slid into sleep.

Marfa marched into the kitchen with the shotgun broken over her left arm. Agnessa sat on the floor beside the stove, the lion in her lap, sated with blood taken from the same bite as the previous day. She looked up as Marfa slipped two shells into the barrels and snapped the shotgun closed.

"The beast goes," she said.

Agnessa's arms instinctively surrounded the lion. He was hers, he was her *domovoi*, the guardian of this house. He shrugged off her embrace and stood, rolling his shoulders and shaking his mane. Marfa trembled. Her eyes were not fixed on the lion but rather a spot behind Agnessa's shoulder.

She could not see him.

The lion bared his teeth at Marfa, blood-soaked where he had fed from Agnessa. He was larger than the sheepdogs, large as a lion of the plains, his tail flicking in anticipation of a fight, of more blood. Agnessa scrambled to her knees, her feet, as Marfa levelled the shotgun. Standing between her mother and her lion, Agnessa begged.

Marfa had forgotten the *domovoi* with the rest of her past. That was why she didn't recognise the lion, why her eyes simply refused to see him at Agnessa's side, from which he had not departed since she first began to feed him.

"He is no protector of this house, he is grief and sorrow and only madness lies at the end of that path if you follow it."

Agnessa saw herself in the house long after Marfa had gone, closing and bolting the door behind her, winding the shadows of her life with Ivan into a shroud, woven tighter and tighter until the home became a tomb, allowing herself to wither gossamer-thin until she could join him, the lion grown fat and bloated the more she fed him.

She saw herself as that woman: like a stick insect

with soft bones and a matting of hair that covered her balding scalp, sucking the spaces between her teeth and peering into corners of the deserted house waiting for Ivan to reach a hand out to her and pull her into his realm.

The lion would only take, and could never give. Marfa's eyes saw only truth and left grief at the kitchen door, refusing to step into the past for fear that she would wither there. Agnessa had let the lion grow too strong, and now she barely had strength to stand.

"Mama, help me," Agnessa said.

∽PART IV∾

It gives me great pleasure to know that I am the only person within hearing of a gunshot. That this house and the great acres of white that surround it are all my own and I am the one that lives here. If my boot makes a print outside my kitchen door, it stays there until fresh snow conceals it or the wind drags it away.

I walk as far from the house as I dare, until it is nothing but a smudge on the horizon and I let myself look back at it, white fields around it matching the emptiness that is a constant ache between my ribs. With my hat and hood over my ears I can hear nothing except my own breathing and when I close my eyes snowflakes fall there, too.

When I am inside the house I hear the wind again. It picks up and howls like some beast trying to get in, rattling at the doors and windows and drawing darkness against the glass. The sheepdogs cower beside the stove and bark at the noise.

I am silent.

Grief is so often a woman's lot. We bear it and nurture it and are testament to it long after others have driven it away. In every woman there is her sadness and her mother's sadness and her grandmother's sadness and it stretches back through the eons to the first woman to experience grief and harbour it, letting it grow in the deep desolate spaces we have hidden.

We hold the grief of all the women in my family. The lost children, fathers, husbands, lovers.

The wind is rising again.

There is an animal in the book room. It lives there with the door locked and a shotgun hanging on the wall outside, in case… Well, in case. It leaves no prints and makes no mess, but in the dead of night I sometimes hear it growling and I open my eyes and look up at the dark ceiling to see if it will scratch at the door.

It never does.

So we have lived in this way, peacefully cohabiting in this house of stopped clocks, except for the nights where I've woken up sweating, knowing that I simply must go and look. I know where the key is hidden, palms growing damp as I've imagined holding it in my hands, the creep across the landing, the satisfying click as I open the door and step into the book room to see my animal, my beast, my grief. Usually the urge passes and I return to sleep.

I know that one night, with the wind beating at the roof and the windows, and the snow sealing me inside this house, I will be too weak to resist that dangerous urge and I will do it.

I will open the door.

INERT ALIGHT

I peer through the keyhole of my room at the dimly lit landing, waiting for our newest boarder to appear. I watch the salesman leave his room, wearing the unofficial uniform of his kind. Trenchcoat and trilby, his shoulders squarely set. A new hire, he still looks hopeful. By his second stay with us he will have acquired the world-weary stance of someone used to having doors slammed in his face. He rattles the handle of the door to ensure it is locked before pocketing the key and walking away. I smirk. No room in the house is safe from me. This is my home not theirs. They are the invaders. Plus, I'd stolen Mother's spare master key. This is her fault. Strange men stamping through my memories, through the one place that should feel safe.

I creep down the corridor, my feet hit the floor softly in worn-thin slippers. I pause to listen as the salesman enters the dining room. Upon hearing Mother greet him, I slip the key into the lock and steal into his room. I close the door behind me and lean against it as my eyes adjust to the dimness. No point in trying the light switch, the ceiling light stopped working months ago. The room smells of boiled cabbage wafting up from the kitchen, dashing my hopes the boarder has perfume samples I could pilfer. A pity, they always sold well to the older girls at school. I know the exact location of the furniture in all the rooms. Hours spent helping Mother clean them had burned the arrangements into my memory. However, the shadows in this

S
E
L
I
N
A

L
O
C
K

room are wrong. Something has been moved, but I'm unsure what.

I dislike coming into this room, but I always need extra cash. It had once been mine, filled with toys and joy. One wall had been covered by a collage of magazine clippings, postcards and any type of picture I could scrounge. I cried so many tears when my mother tore the collage down. Once she would have hugged me close and dried my cheeks. Times change. Her face had hardened at my distress. Her voice was rough as she told me as a young woman I had to accept reality, that we had to take in boarders to survive. I was relegated to the tiny box room. Those mementoes of childhood all disappeared as she whitewashed every wall in the house. Our home vanished under layers of cheap, sharp smelling paint.

I venture forwards into the room, sliding my right foot ahead, feeling the space before me. Then I plant it firmly and repeat the process with my left foot. Further into the room something thin and cold trails across my calf. I stop, feel the hairs on my legs stand up. I imagine tentacles sliding up my leg, ready to pull me into the underworld. Sometimes, I wish that could happen; nonsensical thoughts. I carefully move my leg and whatever is touching it snags on my clothes. It drags along, and I hear a muted click. I turn towards the noise and a light appears, hovering halfway up the wall. As I stare at the light, I become aware of a low insistent hum. My heart beats a little faster, and my breathing becomes shallow. This guy is selling something far more interesting than perfume.

I drag my gaze away from the light and let my eyes wander over the shapes around it. Slowly, familiar patterns resolve from the gloom. The outline of a chair, that normally lives across the other side of the room. The glow is not hovering. It is leaking from a suitcase perched on the chair's seat. I reach my hand down to unsnag my clothes and feel the rubber of an electrical lead. The suitcase is plugged into the single socket in the room, normally reserved for one of the bedside lamps my mother had acquired off the back of a lorry.

I shuffle towards the glowing suitcase, the hum increasing slightly as I near. I reach out and gingerly unsnap the case fasteners, the cold metal smooth against my thumbs. Breathing deeply, I gently open the lid. The light is so unexpectedly bright I nearly lose my grip, so I squeeze my eyes shut until I've pushed the case fully open. Once I hear the lid thud against the back of the chair, I open my eyes, just a slit. My overlapping eyelashes protect me from the worst of the glare, as my eyes acclimatise and the lights resolve into a pattern of coloured lines. The suitcase contains several connected glass tubes, each sporting a different coloured light. I'm used to the sickly yellow glow of electric bulbs, but this is a revelation in illumination. One of the tubes contains a yellow as vivid as the skin of a lemon, another resembles a pale blue sky, and yet another the green of a succulent leaf.

I reach out hesitantly to stroke the blue tube. It feels surprisingly cool, until I touch the metal curve at the end. I jerk my fingers away as the metal burns. Even so I feel myself reaching out again to stroke the green cylinder. Part of me yearns for such luminescence. My hand returns to the blue tube and I grip it tight. Closing my fist around the pale, pulse of light. The hum from the suitcase grows louder in encouragement. I squeeze and feel the cylinder give way against my palm. The sharp scratch of glass makes me loosen my grip. The hum rises in volume and the pastel blue light leaks from its container, mingling with my blood. Tingles rush across my hand as my veins pulse with an unnatural gleam, prickles surge up my arm as the glass vessel empties itself into me.

I snatch my hand away from the suitcase, but the light infuses me. I hear a muted tone inside my ear drums harmonizing with the humming from the case. I run out of the room, slamming and locking the door behind me loud enough to disturb the conversation in the dining room below. A clink of cutlery against plate, and I hear my mother hiss up the stairs, "Clara, be quiet!", before a murmured apology to the house guests. That's how it is now. I must be quiet, unseen, a ghost in my own home. I want to run to her, for comfort, but I can imagine her shock and anger at me breaking into a guest's room, destroying their belongings. Dots of blue light pulse across my skin, betraying my crime. I run across the landing into my small box room and lock the door, sinking onto the bed and staring at my hands. The flat tone in my ears starts to vary in pitch as the lights seem to relish my attention. They break into intricate dancing patterns, like a synchronised swimming routine. I push my sleeves up as the light dances along my arms. Spikes of pleasant warmth follow their movements. They are happy to be free, to express themselves.

I lie on my bed for hours, watching and feeling the radiance that possesses me. I'm vaguely aware of the sounds in the house, as the guests retire to their rooms. I hear my mother ascend the stairs. She knocks lightly on my door, and when I don't respond she lays the supper tray outside without a word. I realise that I don't feel hungry. I feel lonely; no, more like a part of me is missing. The lights stop coursing through my body and gather in my right hand. They swirl like creamer through coffee. The buzz in my ears impinges on my awareness, pulsing in tandem with my feelings of isolation. My thoughts and the noise reach a crescendo. I feel an overwhelming urge to free the rest of the coloured illuminations from the salesman's case. Before I can stop myself I retrace my steps to his room, use my master key and tiptoe inside.

The salesman is a snoring lump on the bed. I know I should stop. Turn around and leave, but my body doesn't listen. The salesman's breath reverberates through his nose. I slip over to the suitcase and carefully unlatch it, muffling the noise with my body. I open it but it's inert. No bright lights, luminous colours, or muted hum. For a moment I don't understand, then I realise it's unplugged. They need power to come to life. I lean over, using the now steady pale blue glow from my right hand to locate the plug. I hear the bed creak as the man adjusts his sleeping position. I wait for the creaking to stop and then I push the plug into the socket. The suitcase comes to life, the lights slowly strengthening as electricity crackles into them. It is bound to wake the salesman but even so I smash my palms down on to as many glass tubes as I can. I hear a noise of confusion from the bed, then a yell of surprise as I scream in pain and ecstasy. Glass shards pierce my hands as the green, red, yellow, orange and pink lights surge into my body. I feel the salesman drag me backwards, away from the ruins of the case. He's shouting something, but I can't hear him over the thrumming tones of triumph in my ears. They are free and they are happy and now I am we.

Mother and two other guests burst into the room. Mother shrieks as we turn to face her. Our face is alight with a glowing rainbow. We smile a luminous smile and reassure her we're fine, in fact we're wonderful. We push past their shocked faces. We strip off the last remnants of humanity along with our bloodstained clothes.

We shine, as we have always been meant to shine.

PAIN IS A LIAR

In the dark forest, there is fear. But the fear is really in the sun glaring above you, in the touch of the others' gazes around you.

"Remember the old days, when it used to hurt?" they tease him.

"Not really," Anton answers the coterie, forgetting about the voice, and he stretches his ankles out a little on the bed, hoping that the movement is imperceptible.

But they are distracted, talking among themselves, and it is very gloomy and he finally dares to let his eyes dart sideways to the windows that extend down to the floor. The wind is blowing the cherry blossoms hard against the panes. In the deepening dusk they have a quality of something. Something important. He can't explain it. And does it even matter?

Yes, says the voice, *it matters.*

He pretends the coterie's incessant whispering is the wind outside. He imagines each fall of blossom driving one of them from the room.

They finally say they are going for ice creams or a beer or something, but they don't invite him.

In any case, he doesn't like ice cream, not after somebody else has licked it, anyway.

He is left alone with impressions of soft pink crushed against glass. It's not quite enough to stop him shivering. He balls his fists, careful not to leave any marks. He keeps his fingernails short. They are not the least bit interested in how he looks, as long as he doesn't hurt himself.

"It's voluntary," they tell him.

He lifts his head and studies his toes. All there. But they are bent, broken.

"Pain is a liar," they say.

So why doesn't he just get up and go?

Pain is in the brain, pain is in the brain, he thinks. He slides his leg up the bed. "Holy little fucking gods, it hurts!" he shouts at the trees.

They've left painkillers, but if he takes them they'll think he's weak.

He imagines arms closing round him, the arms of a long-dead father. *Shush, little monkey, shush*, the imaginary father says.

And then he is part of the darkness.

He wakes and calls Jen, one of the remaining members of his herd, to come and pick him up. He knows it's over for today, that they won't return. Of course, they are much cleverer than him, hard to predict and easily distracted.

Jen bustles in. "Anton," she says, and smiles at him in a way that makes him feel he is weak. But this is precisely why he called her: she spends a lot of time in the gym and she is strong enough to support him to a car.

She probably assumes he's taken the painkillers, but he's hidden them in his undershirt pocket. His imagination is not strong enough to dull the pain and he'll need them for later.

He wants to ask her if she's ever done such tests, but he can't bring himself to. If she has, he bets she wouldn't have used painkillers.

"Come on, you big bub," she says, placing her arm around his back and helping him to sit up sideways on the bed. He squeezes his eyes closed, and opens them to see his toes dangling at odd angles like soil-less roots.

He bites his lip.

She hoists him onto his feet. The strength of his scream surprises them both.

She lays him back down and digs in a pocket. "I was saving it for later, but you better—"

She pushes the pill into his mouth. For a moment, before he passes out, he feels as if she could be the arms.

I have been in the gaps of your sleepless hours.

Anton wakes to the voice. There is no one there. He lies on the bed in his little attic room, staring at the curve of yellow moon, bright against the dark square of window. Jen's pill has almost worn off and the pain is seeping back. He is contemplating taking the hidden painkillers, when the coterie enter without knocking, stand around his bed staring down at him like excited children.

He can see they have been shopping: they are barefoot, with crowns of thorns and torn white loincloths, splotches of red deliberately staining the finely-woven fabric.

They are dressed like their fashionable little god, Jesus Christ. The one who hung and suffered there. "For all of us," they say, and giggle. "Except for you."

And Pocock bends and wiggles Anton's big toe.

He can't help grimacing.

Sometimes this expression makes them happy and they stop. But he tries not to grimace again. Sometimes they don't like the fact that he is more like Jesus than them, that he can suffer.

He wishes he were a lot more like Jesus. Why is his pain threshold so low?

Shush, little monkey, shush, they'll get bored.

"Pain is a Liar," he says, with a controlled wince, and they are satisfied. Thank their little god!

He stares at their beautiful faces and wishes they could feel pain, that he could watch their faces contort in agony.

Don't be mean, Anton, he tells himself. It isn't their fault.

The moon wavers in front of Anton's eyes. Pain is a Liar. Pain is a Liar.

They leave soon after, to go sightseeing or something.

Ha! He's fooled them. They've left him alone because they think he's taken the pills. He's no fun.

Their lack of interest bothers him. He knows they are right: he's weak. His hands reach into his pocket and he finally swallows their pills. They work fast and he sits up and wrenches his toes back into place one by one. He is quite expert now. He has done this before.

He wishes he had the coterie's stoicism in the face of pain, but it's like beauty, he tells himself. They were born that way.

He remembers the blossoms falling against the panes. Thank their little Jesus they forget about the herd sometimes. Despite being so clever, they think that the members of the herd are all alike, although they would never call themselves a herd because they are individuals.

In the dark forest, there is fear, but the fear is really...

Patterns of cool leaves swim in his head; soft moonlight ripples over his aching body, soothing him with gentle threads of light and dark.

He feels as if he has been in this house forever. Long ago, there were some happy days among the herd, until the coterie began to take a special interest in him.

"He's so sensitive, he feels everything," Pocock used to say, stroking his head, giving him treats. Before the tests started.

Now the herd is thinning. Some of them disappeared.

"Gone to pasture," the coterie told him, when he asked. And they laughed. As usual. They find a lot of things funny.

And Dad? Was there a Dad? He can't really be the strange voice. Can he?

Either way, he'll never tell them about it. If they knew, they'd notice him for longer. Hopefully, they will soon grow bored. If he can just manage to work out what it is they want.

He often wishes they would put him out to pasture, wherever that is. But he has to make them happy first. And he wants to please them, he does. It's just that he wishes he knew more tricks, stuff that didn't hurt so much.

It's the fingers again this week. He might have known. He understands that they need to do the tests, but why the fingers, why the toes? Why not his back or his stomach? Somewhere else so that he can still walk and pick things up, as well as keep them happy.

They tell him it's important. And voluntary. But if there's yet another round after this one, they'll have to rejuvenate his tissue. They promised him that they would. And they will, won't they?

They start with the bending back and the pain scale of one to ten. He can see the determined look in Pocock's eyes.

"We have to establish an objective measure of pain," Pocock says, "before we can realistically assess its extent."

Pocock is the most rational. He picks up a hammer and before anyone can stop him he seizes Anton's wrist and brings it down hard on his finger.

"Was that a ten?" asks Pocock.

Anton's face is white from not screaming.

"Oh, Pocock, why do you always have to be so extreme," says Marj, the smallest of the group. "Why do you always have to break everything so quickly?"

They have not blocked their ears. Your cry simply passes them by; they cannot hear it.

He doesn't know where he is. He runs towards the voice. He runs towards the arms. Dad? Dad?

He regains consciousness, feeling sad and alone. What if the voice is like the pain: only in his head?

And the coterie is still there. He holds up a damaged hand; he dares to signal that he can't do more today, and they grumble, but they are smiling.

"Pocock, you ass," says Tarquin, but he is smiling too.

Pocock administers painkillers, unbidden. "Well done, you," he says, and Anton can't help feeling pleased. It's the first time Pocock has praised him.

Pocock smiles down at him. He looks young, like himself, but it's impossible to tell; they all look young. "Later, write down what you feel," Pocock says, passing him an electronic pad. "Note down how much pain you're experiencing, on a scale of one to ten."

Anton nods, woozy.

He sleeps after they have left, waking in a state of bliss, his head fuzzy. He knows he has to do it now, before the pills wear off. Only one finger today. He sucks in a breath and pulls it straight. No pain, but he doesn't like the click.

The pad is lying next to him on the bed. He notices something has been typed.

Why? Why try and try and try. Why be? Why me?

He stares and stares, feels uneasy. Did Pocock write it? A practical joke? Or was it the voice?

Either way, they better not find it. But why does he care? It is all voluntary. He can do whatever he likes.

Before the pills wear off, he limps next door to Jen's. She has a bigger attic room than his, with a private entrance.

He can't decide whether to tell her about the voice so they sit in silence for a while. In the end he holds out his hand. It doesn't hurt now, he thinks, so why do I want to cry?

"You've got to get through. If you show too much pain they'll carry on," she says, and then he can't hold back the tears.

He's worried she'll be disgusted by his weakness, as she reaches under her mattress and then hands him a pill. He feels a strange longing to throw his arms around her, but swallows the pill instead.

"They have everything," he says. "Why do they need me?"

"It's a sort of retro thing for them," says Jen.

He doesn't understand, but the pill works fast and soon he doesn't care.

"I've only got a few pills left," she says. "You have got to try harder."

The coterie has gone on a trip. He has the house to himself for a few days. Time for his fingers to heal, although they haven't left any painkillers.

The house records everything except the attic, though they don't usually bother to watch the recordings because they have new things they'd rather do.

In any case, they know they can trust him not to run away, they know how loyal he is. And, after all, it's voluntary.

Nonetheless, he can't sleep and the voice grows

louder in the night. He lies on his bed, trying to overcome the pain. "Pain is in the brain. Pain is a Liar. Fear is a Liar," he mutters.

But he's weak and the pain persists. He worries that it will worsen. He's not good enough for the coterie. He can't make them happy. He can't work out what they want. They need someone stronger, someone like Jen.

His fingers and toes are lumpy. They will make them better after they've finished the tests. They will, won't they?

When he first arrived at the house, they used to fuss over him in their own way. He misses their little pats, their treats, their admiring laughs. He has a strange longing for the past. A side effect of the memory erasures, he supposes. The coterie is always telling him that he is full of side effects, that he is just one of the herd.

The pain persists into the second day and he longs for the voice, for the arms. He doesn't know what would happen if he ran into them, but maybe the pain would cease. He knows he is thinking these things because he is irrational. He is weak. Not like them. And perhaps they are simply attempting to make him stronger.

In the afternoon he reads the message again, still not understanding. He places the pad on his chest and dozes fitfully on waves of pain.

He wakes to the sound of cherry blossom branches hitting the window. For a moment, he thinks the coterie is leaning over him and he is terrified. He remembers that he is in his bedroom and there are no blossoms here. The pad has slid off his chest and he picks it up.

Me free. Whee! Want to be. Now. Ow! Can't. Can't be. Own, alone. Pain. See?

He stares at the screen. What is this? He doesn't know anything other than that he should erase it.

In the early evening when the pain becomes unbearable he limps over to Jen's.

She has to help him ascend the outside stairs. "Pretend," she whispers, in case they're recording.

But even with her strong arm around his waist, he can't stop grimacing.

Once they are safely in her room, she offers him a pill and pats his back until it takes effect. "They'll get bored," she whispers. "You just have to get it right."

But he does not understand how, and he is too sore and too tired to ask.

He hears their laughter, the slam of the front door downstairs, and he feels unhappiness followed by guilt. They are only having fun. They are made that way. He erases the words on the pad and feigns sleep.

And today, they forget him. A part of him feels sad he'll never belong, yet, as he starts to drift, the voice calls to him and he runs towards it into a forest of cherry trees, their soft blossoms caressing his broken body.

"Imagine it hurting," they say, and Pocock bends back the big toe on his left foot.

They know he can feel, so why does he have to imagine? He keeps his mouth tight, straight.

"Does it hurt now?" they ask, more anxiously. "Try to imagine the pain," they say, and, "Pain is a liar," they say.

He concentrates hard on the forest and the line on the machine remains stable.

"Imagine harder," they plead. "Imagine! Imagine! Pain is in the brain."

They look so desperate, it's hard to know what to do. Jen said that you have to get it just right, but do they want him to scream or not? He bites the inside of his cheek until the soft flesh holds the texture of a bloody rag.

"Look at his eyes," says Tarquin. "You can tell from the eyes."

And they finally smile. "At this rate, you'll be like us one day," they joke.

Pain is just pain, thinks Anton. It's not real. It's all in the head. Nevertheless, it is making me feel unwell. It is making me want to scream.

"Let me have a go," says Pocock.

"Always so impatient, Pocock," says Marj.

Anton braces himself, but he can't stop the yell.

"Superb," says Tarquin. "You're the most sensitive we've ever had."

But Pocock looks displeased.

"Sorry," Anton says.

Pocock ignores him. "Pain, on a scale of one to ten?" he asks.

"Eleven," says Anton.

"Clever little bugger," says Pocock, and hands him a pill.

Anton glances at the line on the monitor. It is almost ten.

He thinks he might tell Jen about the forest, but when he is settled on her bed he can't find the words, although he can almost feel the blossoms touching his skin, smell their scent.

When he cries, Jen says, "Don't you see, bub? They are not brave like you. They just have no fear."

"I can't. I can't—"

She puts her arm around him and strokes his back.

Jen slips him two pills as he leaves. "Just pretend it's hurting," she whispers.

Anton lies in his room, confused and guilty. He's too weak, he can't go on, but it's important to the coterie and he wants to help them. He starts at every sound. It's hard to predict when they'll come for him. You can never tell what they'll do.

In the afternoon, he hears their footsteps on the stairs and he swallows both the pills. He is hurting all the time now; whatever happens, they won't be wasted.

"Anton," they call. "Come down! Tests today." They sound so cheerful, it almost makes him happy.

He lies on the table and pretends to wince, only a little. Sometimes, they like it when he doesn't complain. He's worried about his eyes. Will they be able to tell from his eyes?

They start on his fingers and he decides to scream immediately, although he is actually half in the forest, running towards the voice.

Marj is angry. "I told you, Pocock! You have to take it slower. He's too tender now."

The look Pocock gives him – hatred – makes him want to cry. Anton is terrified Pocock will notice his eyes.

And then he is weeping.

They are delighted.

"Have an extra pill today," says Pocock. "We don't need them."

And they burst into pleased laughter.

"Come on, let's leave the little baby to recover," says Marj, and they trail out, excited. "Crying! Actual tears!" they say. "Can you believe it?"

Their delight reminds him of when he first arrived at the house, when they loved him more.

I have pleased them, he thinks. But I? I?

He asks Jen to meet him at the herd café. The coterie would never come here; there is nothing much for them to do.

He's not like them. He loves the simplicity of a cup of plain tea and a slice of cake. He nods to the members of his herd as he enters and they nod in reply, though there are few of them left and the atmosphere is subdued.

He sits with Jen at a corner table.

He feels ashamed about the crying, but Jen has seen it before and she still likes him. And the coterie seems to like it too, so maybe it's OK? He takes a deep breath and shows her the latest writing on the pad. She reads it, frowning.

> *Pain gone. Pain away. Be. Be free. Pain come back one day. Not free, small, not really here at all. Edge, ledge. Jump. Whee! See? Free!*

"Oh, bub, bub," is all Jen says, and she squeezes his hand tightly.

Relief floods him. "Is there a forest, Jen?" he asks.

Jen looks angry. "Bub," she says, "we used to have dogs."

"Dogs?" he asks.

"You know, bub, those furry creatures. Not wild, tame. Pets."

"Yes, pets," he says. "I've seen pictures."

"And cats," adds Jen. "We used to say 'It's raining cats and dogs'. Of course, that part never happened. It was just an expression."

"What happened to all the dogs and cats?"

"Don't you see?" says Jen. "To them you are like a cat. Or a dog. They are just having fun."

"Did we love the dogs?" he asks.

Jen slips off her shoes and shows him her crooked toes. "They'll forget to make you better," she says. And then begins to cry.

If I jumped, I'd break my ankles, he muses as he thinks about the strange messages on the pad. This almost makes him laugh. Jen managed to obtain stronger pills and the coterie seems distant, as if they are standing behind glass. He forgets to pretend.

Tarquin bends over and stares into his eyes. "He's not responding. He can't feel it."

Anton can see the panic in their faces.

"Of course he can, you idiot," says Pocock. "All of them feel pain," and he brings his hand down hard in a karate chop on Anton's stomach.

Before Anton can stop it, his hand with its broken fingers hits out at Pocock, hard, right across his stupid laughing mouth.

Despite the painkillers, Anton screams.

Pocock laughs. "Now we are finally getting somewhere."

They are satisfied and leave.

He has only hurt himself. He doesn't cry, he sobs. He sobs about his lost father and the forest he will never see, that is probably all in his head. He sobs because he loves the coterie, though they do not love him. And because he cannot bear to hurt them, although they hurt him. It isn't their fault, really. They just don't understand pain.

He sobs most of all because he would like to nail each fucking little Jesus Christ god one of them to a cross. He would like to make them scream.

Jen and Anton sit on her bed and read the pad together.

In the dark forest, there is fear, the blossoms barely breathing, but they do, they still do. I am, I am, they sigh in the trees, in the branches.

Jen set down the pad and they lie next to each other on the bed.

"Do you mind?" Anton asks, and he settles into the circle of her arms, held firm, his broken fingers splayed against her chest. The new pills are working splendidly and he feels no pain.

"If I can just make them happy, maybe they will let me go," he murmurs. But he forgets that he wants to go; he is lost in this dear moment of cherry blossoms and warm arms.

He pretends that his father is watching over him, he pretends that Pocock and the coterie love him, that he belongs to them and they to him. He imagines that Jen is his mother as she rubs his back.

"You mustn't be afraid, bub, you won't feel a thing," she tells him once he's fast asleep, as the gaps between his breaths increase.

BECOMING HOME

When she woke, she didn't remember anything. She stared at the ceiling. It was a white sea of plaster with hairline cracks for waves. The electric lightbulb had cobwebs hanging from it but no spiders.

How can there be cobwebs and no spiders? Did they die? Did they die and the flies ate their decaying bodies?

She sensed movement at her side and turned her head. There was a woman present, her face anxious, her hands in her lap, the fingers fidgeting. She wore a dark green cardigan which had two of its seven buttons missing. One sleeve bulged with a tissue. Behind her was a window, the net curtains rippling in the breeze. It looked like the blazing light from the window was being sucked up by the figure, who seemed gloomy against such a brilliant backdrop. Only her hair shone, a golden halo about her shadowed face.

'Lily?' the woman asked hopefully

Lily. This had to be her name but it didn't sound quite right. It was familiar, as if the name of a sister or close cousin, but not her own. Yet since she couldn't remember her name, this one would have to do.

'Do you remember anything, Lily?' the woman asked, leaning forward just slightly. Wrinkles clustered around her mouth and eyes.

Because she smokes. She sucks on those little sticks and her mouth wrinkles with the effort while her eyes wrinkle with pleasure.

CHARLOTTE BOND

Why does that seem more familiar than my name?

Lily started to sit up then stopped as the woman bolted from the chair and backed away. Fear blazed in her eyes and the hand that clutched her cardigan was trembling. Wanting to reassure her, Lily went to speak but found that her lips would not part. Frowning, she touched them. She knew what lips should feel like. Buried deep down inside her, like the knowledge of the smoking wrinkles, was the idea that lips should be fleshy, plump, and parting. But she felt only smooth, unbroken skin.

'Lily?' asked the woman, creeping forward. 'Is it really you?' One hand darted quick into the other sleeve, pulled out the tissue, wiped her nose then stuffed the soggy mass back where it came from. She reached out to touch Lily's face, but Lily shied away, thinking of the snot coating the tissue. The woman hesitated, almost drawing her hand back, but then she extended her trembling fingers a little further and Lily forced herself not to recoil.

The sensation was strange, as if Lily's cheeks were numb and could only sense pressure rather than hot or cold, soft or hard.

Or is this how it always felt and I never noticed?

The woman let out a stifled sob and then suddenly gathered Lily into her arms.

'Oh, my precious daughter! My darling! I thought I'd lost you. But you're back, and that's all that matters.' The woman kept hugging her tightly, and Lily started to feel uneasy. She wanted to ask the woman to let her go, but how could she, without lips?

Eventually, in her own time, the woman pulled away, dried her tears and smiled. She sat down again and Lily could see that the tremble in her hands had grown to encompass her whole body.

'Now, he warned me that things wouldn't be quite the same as before. We'll have to adjust. That's why I've bought this new house. It's nice and secluded. No one will bother us while we come to terms with your new...' She licked her lips nervously, clearly unwilling to say whatever word rested on her tongue. 'Would you like to see?'

Lily nodded.

The woman guided Lily to stand in front of a mirror, and Lily thought, *This is a dream. I am a dream. How can I be what I see I am?*

She stared at her reflection, and what caught her eye most was the paleness of her face. Her skin might, with a brief glance, simply look incredibly pale. But anyone who took a moment to look closer would see that it was in fact satin. Lily tilted her head, her cheeks shimmering as the light danced over them.

Her gaze travelled down over the patterned summer dress she was wearing. Against her skin, the light, floaty fabric seemed dull. Lifeless. It held merely garish colours, while her skin held glorious light.

Lifting the hem of the dress, Lily saw that her legs were smooth and pale too; the ends of her feet, where her toes should be, were perfectly rounded. A seam ran up the back of her calves, invisible except when the light hit it just right.

Like the women in the war, drawing lines on their skin instead of stockings.

How can I remember that but not remember myself or this woman?

She inspected her fingers, which were dainty and well-formed, the digits flexing when she willed them. Placing one fingertip against her arm, she waited for sensation to filter through – either her arm telling her she was being touched or her fingers telling her she was touching, but nothing registered in her mind except a gentle pressure.

Part of her recognised that she should be panicking. This was not her body, not her skin, not her not-toes. But all she felt was bemused.

I'm a doll. A creature of satin and stuffing. How? Why?

She turned, searching for answers in the eyes of the woman who claimed to be her mother. But she saw there only a hundred questions, waiting to be asked.

Lily put her hand on her chest, waiting for the tattoo she knew should be there. When she couldn't feel it, she took the woman's hand and pressed it against the curved smoothness of her breast.

'No heartbeat,' the woman murmured, slightly awed. Then she pulled her hand away and gave a brittle smile. 'Still, no heartbeat, no heartbreak, so that's something. And it means you can't die again.' Her eyes widened, her lips pressed together as if to restrain any further words from leaking out.

So I died then.

Again, Lily felt the absence of shock. On instinct, she tried to give a wry smile at the thought that she should be shocked at this lack of shock, but even though she felt her cheek muscles clenching, that only served to pull her skin tight. Leaning closer to the mirror, she examined her face in more detail. Her eyeballs glistened wetly. When she breathed in, her nose twitched and her chest moved in a corresponding rhythm, but she had no nostrils, only dark smudges where emptiness should be. Lips had been painted on above her chin so that she wore a permanent, enigmatic smile.

Who determined that I should always be smiling? What is there to smile about? I'm a doll with a mind, and lungs apparently but no nostrils, and no mouth and no toes and no memory.

At that moment, she felt something akin to anger; she had a vague notion that it should be hot and sharp whereas she felt something dull and achy, prickling along her skin.

'Do you remember anything?' the woman whispered. She'd crept closer while Lily examined her face and now peered over her shoulder, looking into Lily's reflected eyes rather than her real ones. 'About dying, I mean.'

Lily straightened, and the woman scuttled back like a nervous mouse that had just flicked the cat's tail. Lily thought hard, wondering if the memory would come to her in a burst, like that of the drawn-on stockings. But she could recall nothing beyond waking up and staring at that ceiling. She shook her head. The woman's shoulders sagged.

'Well, that's something then. Let's start, shall we? I'll serve tea and cake in the parlour. Come down when you're ready.'

The woman hurried out. Lily stood alone for a moment, then went over to shut the door. Her silken feet made no noise as they crossed the carpet. She took off her dress and examined every inch of her body. It was made of the best silk, with finely stitched seams, real craftsmanship. Every part of her was smooth, unmarred by hair or moles or even a navel. But like her eyes, the hair on her head seemed real. She ran her fabric fingers through it, not able to detect whether it was smooth or wiry, soft or rough.

Is that my hair? I mean, was it from me, my other body, before I died?

'Lily! Come along, dear,' called a voice from downstairs.

Lily pulled the dress back on then went downstairs to sit in a chair while the woman she had to believe was her mother poured tea and ate cake and talked about all the wonderful things they'd do. Lily wished she'd talk instead about who Lily was, how old she was, how she'd died, and how she'd come back. But without lips, Lily couldn't ask such questions; she could not eat cake either. Her mother didn't seem to notice.

For a week Lily, wandered round her new home, examining the details, trying to feel something. Now and again, she'd have a flash of memory. The photo of a little girl with ice-cream around her mouth made her think of white sand, hot beneath her bare feet, and the scent of vinegar on chips. A candle holder with a little snuffer attached to it brought to mind an image of watching the magic of a flame being alive one moment and then dead when she lifted up the snuffer. But all these memories were ephemeral to herself; they didn't define her or give her a sense of who she was (or is? Or could be?) She looked at the walls, their paint as fresh and unmarked as her satin skin, and wondered whether she would remember more if her mother hadn't moved them to a new house.

She liked the willow tree outside best. The previous family had left a tyre swing there and Lily loved to sit on it, being gently blown to and fro by the wind. The first time she tried the swing, she'd come away with a black smudge of dirt on her arm. Her mother had fussed and tutted, and tried to scrub it away with soap. When that didn't work, she'd gone to the cleaning cupboard and retrieved some liquid detergent. She'd applied a smear to a scrap of muslin and bound it round Lily's arm. They'd left it there overnight.

She's leaving me in to soak, Lily thought as she lay awake in the darkness, staring at the ceiling, watching for any sign of spiders.

The next morning, her mother carefully unbound her arm and rinsed it with warm water, leaving Lily's silk skin clean and bright once more.

'You must be careful on that swing,' she'd admonished, but she'd not forbidden its use, for which Lily was grateful. Swinging on it made it seem like the world was made of wind and motion and nothing else. It was the only time that Lily felt at peace.

After a month of wandering round an empty house

with a head full of questions, Lily became increasingly restless. She was vaguely aware that strong emotions like anger, hate, joy, and terror could exist, but she felt things only in a diffuse way. She knew people (should she call them real people, or other people?) had strong emotions because she could read them on her mother's face. There was joy there, a lot of the time, but now and again there was a momentary glimpse of terror that went so deep, Lily thought you could probably find it written on her mother's bones if you peeled the flesh away.

That had led her to explore her own body. Did she have bones? She couldn't tell. There were no toys in this house, but Lily held the vague notion that a doll's arms should bend in every direction. Hers didn't. But she also couldn't feel the solidness of bone in the centre, or the definition of muscle.

She had so many questions, but no way to ask them. In those early days, her mother had given her pencil and paper, hoping she could write something, but the pencil had not responded the way Lily wanted it to, and she'd succeeded in making only a wiggly mark on the page. So one night, when her mother was asleep, Lily crept into the drawing room and retrieved her mother's sewing scissors. Sitting in front of her bedroom mirror, Lily cut along her painted lips. When she'd cut the full length, she parted the fabric, hoping for a sound, but instead a snowstorm of stuffing came out.

Lily swiftly clamped her hand over her mouth, stopping the flow. It had felt strange and unpleasant as that stuffing had tumbled from her lips.

Like being sick.

She gathered up the stuffing and tried to force it all back in. It was a struggle since every time she opened her mouth, more stuffing fell out before she could push the old stuff in.

When dawn came and her mother found her, the woman stifled a gasp of horror and sank to her knees. 'Oh, Lily,' she murmured, staring at the pile of crumpled stuffing in Lily's lap. She parted Lily's fingers just enough to see the ragged line of her severed mouth. 'My darling, what have you done?'

She traced a line across Lily's cheeks and frowned. 'Your skin is wet like... you've been crying. But that's not possible. What on earth were you trying to do?'

Instinctively, Lily opened her mouth to speak and more stuffing fell out between her fingers. She turned away, hiding her face. She could sense her cheeks becoming wetter.

Her mother left quietly and it was some time before she returned, carrying her sewing basket and a bundle of scraps. 'Let's see what we can do, shall we?' she said tenderly.

It took the rest of the morning and a little of the afternoon to finish Lily's mouth. When it was finally done, Lily stood before the mirror and tentatively parted her lips, defined and plump thanks to her mother's needleworking skills. No stuffing fell out. Inside, her mouth was lined with red satin and a pink chenille tongue lounged at the bottom. Experimentally, Lily waggled it. Then she smiled.

'Is it alright?' her mother asked.

'Yes.' Lily took time and effort to form the word, but it felt wonderful to do so. Her voice was accompanied by the soft hiss of fabric rubbing against fabric. She turned to her mother. 'Thank you.' Suddenly, her mother's cheeks were as wet as Lily's.

It took several weeks for Lily to master using her lips and tongue. The words in her head arrived perfect and fully formed, but trying to get them to come out of her mouth the same way was difficult. She restricted herself to only answering questions when in her mother's company, waiting until she was in the privacy of her own room before she tried to create words from nothing.

Eventually, when she was ready and her mother was pouring them both tea, Lily asked very carefully, 'Is Lily my full name?'

Her mother started, sloshing some of the tea into a saucer. Without looking at Lily, she mopped it up then sat and stared at the lemon drizzle cake for some moments. Lily instinctively understood this woman was taking just as much effort to form her words as she herself had.

'No. You were named Lilian.'

Lily considered this. 'Then I think I would like to be called Lilian. It seems... better. You are very nice, and I don't want to offend you, but it sounds wrong when you call me Lily. It sounds like you're thinking of someone else.' The woman raised her hand to her mouth, holding back a sob.

'I think I look like her, the Lily you knew,' Lilian went on, 'but I don't think I can *be* her. I am myself. I think calling me Lily would only confuse things.'

Tears were pouring over the woman's lashes, cascading over her fingers. Shaking with emotion, she turned away, those fingers darting into her sleeve again. There was a rustling, then wet noises, and then after a few more minutes scrubbing at her face, the woman turned to face her.

'Lilian it is then,' she said softly. 'I had always hoped you'd call me... if you had a tongue that you might...' her eyes flicked down and up again, 'but you'd better call me Sylvia. If you're not my Lily then I guess I'm not your... well, never mind. We shall be Lilian and Sylvia and muddle on as best we can.'

Lilian reached out to take Sylvia's hand, but the woman snatched it away. 'Thank you, Sylvia,' Lilian said gently, placing her hands back by her sides.

Sylvia nodded, and so the next stage of their lives together began.

❦

Lilian and Sylvia existed in a strained harmony. While Lilian remained calm and reasoned at all times, Sylvia went through wild swings of emotions. On the good days, they'd sit and talk about the world that they'd seen on the television or read about in books. They'd often laugh at the same things, which gave Lilian a warm feeling in her chest.

Lilian didn't go out much for fear of her skin drawing attention, and Sylvia didn't go out much due to some secret fear that she didn't share with Lilian. Instead, they pottered around the garden which was screened from unfriendly eyes by a high hedge. They had their shopping delivered once a week, which was plenty given that Lilian didn't eat or drink anything. While Sylvia ate Battenberg and biscuits, washing it down with mineral water, Lilian would sit with a cup of Earl Grey positioned just beneath her nose and breathe in the delicate scent of it. That was nourishment enough for her and she was content.

But when the bad days came round, Sylvia would lock herself in her room and scream with rage. Lilian could hear books being thrown and pillows punched. Sometimes the door would fly open and Sylvia would shout, 'Why aren't you like her? I paid him, god damn it! I paid him! I want my Lily back and you're nothing but a rag doll.'

Lilian felt little emotion, but she did feel a prickling inside her when Sylvia spoke like this, as if her stuffing was filled with ants.

Yet even the worst of Sylvia's rants didn't last beyond sunset. After an hour's quiet, she'd appear downstairs with puffy, red eyes; the first few times this happened, she'd begged Lilian's forgiveness. But as the fits became more frequent, more often she said nothing when she came downstairs and instead the two of them merely moved silently about their business, like two birds hopping about in the wake of a thunderstorm.

When Sylvia's fit was bad enough to involve screaming accusations, Lilian would sit down at one end of the sofa and Sylvia would lie the length of it, her head resting on Lilian's lap. Lilian would stroke Sylvia's hair and hum some tune or other she'd heard that day, and they'd remain like that until Sylvia got up to fix tea.

The strangest thing about Sylvia's rants, though, was the rainbow. Lilian had first noticed it during the third screaming fit. She'd looked out of the window and there it was in a clear, cloudless sky. Lilian had thought it strange and beautiful, but had attached no further significance to it than that.

However, when she saw it a second time, coinciding with the next screaming fit, she began to get curious. The sky was dark but the rainbow was just as clear as it had been during that bright day three weeks ago. Furthermore, it was in exactly the same place.

As each new fit brought a new rainbow, Lilian felt more and more curious about where they came from. They couldn't be the same as normal rainbows because they appeared in all weathers; and if they weren't normal, then what was waiting at the end of them in place of a pot of gold?

Lilian began to feel less and less at home in Sylvia's house. She began to feel a sense of dislocation, as if she was somewhere she wasn't supposed to be.

It was a rainy afternoon in September when Lilian made up her mind to leave. While Sylvia first raged then slowly calmed down in one room, Lilian started packing in another. Lilian felt little connection to objects in the house, since they either belonged to Sylvia or had once belonged to Lily. So she packed only clothes, some washing detergent to keep herself clean, and a photo of Sylvia.

By the time Sylvia came out of her room, Lilian was standing by the front door, wearing a raincoat, holding an umbrella in one hand, with her suitcase by her feet.

Sylvia stood at the bottom of the stairs, her face white as the moon, her eyes round and sunken like craters.

'You're... going?'

'I am. I don't think I belong here anymore. I feel out of place. And I do not think *you* want me here either, do you?'

Sylvia looked taken aback, but Lilian could read the truth in her eyes. 'You're right,' Sylvia said eventually, 'I don't want you here. I can't stand you looking so like my Lily but not being her.'

Lilian felt a crumpling in her chest, as if someone had reached inside and crushed all her stuffing together.

This must be what pain feels like.

They stood there in silence, looking at each other. Then Lilian bent down and picked up her suitcase. She opened the door but just before she stepped out, Sylvia called out to her.

'Wait. I want you to know...' She twisted a tissue between her fingers, her face a picture of misery. 'I want you to know that you might not be my Lily, but I want you to remember that you can come back, if you ever want to. I've... grown fond of you since you've been here. I wouldn't like you to think you would always be unwelcome. That was never what I intended.'

Lilian smiled. 'Thank you.' She stepped outside

and started to close the door behind her when Sylvia rushed forward, panicked.

'Wait! Don't go! Stay! You're better than no Lily at all. Please, stay! I—'

Lilian closed the door behind her. She could still hear Sylvia shouting and banging on the door, but those sounds faded as she walked down the steps and onto the road.

The rainbow hung bright in the air and she started towards it.

With no real concept of time away from the house and its ticking clocks, Lilian couldn't say how long she followed the rainbow before she reached her destination. All she knew was that it had been raining when she'd left Sylvia's house, and the wind had been light; as she stopped before the boarded-up Victorian mansion, the air was sharp with the promise of snow.

Lilian took a moment to examine the house before her. She'd walked down a friendly street with modern homes lit by electric lights until she'd come to this forbidding building. Situated at the end of the road, it towered high and dark, a relic left forgotten while the rest of the world moved on around it.

The garden was a jungle of weeds. Every flagstone on the path leading up to the porch was broken or cracked. When she reached the door and lifted the knocker, Lilian expected it to screech with rust, but it moved as smoothly as if it had been oiled only yesterday.

She knocked three times, the sound echoing inside the house. She waited for some time, listening for footsteps, and was surprised when the door suddenly opened without anyone behind it.

She hesitated for a moment, wondering if it had truly opened for her or whether it was just a gust of wind, when a voice drifted through the empty hall. 'Don't just stand there.' It was a man's voice, authoritative but tired.

Lilian stepped inside and closed the door. The floor beneath her was spongy with decaying carpets. She stepped lightly, trying not to brush against any of the walls for fear that the black mould might rub off on her. The unsettling idea lodged in her mind that not even the strongest detergent could free her skin from such a stain.

Reaching the middle of the hallway, she stood there, looking around, trying to decide which way to go. A wide staircase rose ahead of her, curving round at the top to turn into a balcony that ran along the first floor, closed doors hiding unknown rooms. The ground floor was filled with shadows, except for a doorway on her right, a sliver of light indicating it was slightly open. Walking carefully across the rotting floorboards, she tried not to wrinkle her nose at the scent of decay that rose around her. She imagined invisible spores puffing into the air with every step, lodging between the silken strands of her face and neck, nestling there until mushrooms staring growing out of her skin or between her fingers.

The door had a patina of grime over its peeling paint, and she covered her hand with her coat before pushing it open. The room revealed had a high ceiling and a musty yet earthy smell to it. Lumps of plaster had fallen off the walls and there were large rectangular patches where the paint was a deeper shade, as if a painting or mirror had once hung there.

Dusty drapes were pulled tight across the tall windows, allowing not a pinprick of light to sneak through. A miniscule fire crackled in a huge fireplace, and a row of unevenly placed candles on the mantlepiece illuminated very little beyond their immediate surroundings. There was a man sitting in a tattered armchair, reading a newspaper by the light of an oil lamp on the table next to him. He lowered it as she walked towards him. He had olive skin and features so finely chiselled they looked ethereal. His hair was dark but streaked with grey and it fell to his shoulders in a greasy tangle. One eye was a normal blue, but the other was pearly white except for the black pupil. He wore a pinstripe suit and smart, polished shoes.

He looked her up and down. 'You have all your limbs intact?' His voice was soft and rich.

'Yes. Should I not?'

He put his newspaper on the table next to him. 'Quite often when your kind come to me, they have an arm torn or missing. Their loved ones cling onto them, you see.'

Loved ones. Like Sylvia.

'No, my mother let me go.'

He raised an eyebrow. 'She let you go? Or cast you out?'

'Let me go, although she didn't look happy about it. I think she changed her mind at the end and wanted me to stay.' The echoes of Sylvia's cries from behind the closed door bounced around Lilian's mind. They made her stitching feel too tight. To break the tension of her thoughts, she said, 'If you knew I would come, then you must know what I am.'

'I know *what* you are, but *who* you are is more of a question.'

She waited, but he didn't elaborate so she countered with, 'And who are you?'

'I am Ballah.' He cocked his head. 'Where did you get your lips and tongue?'

'I cut my mouth and Sylvia sewed them in for me.'

He stood up and walked over to her. With his dishevelled appearance, she had expected him to shuffle untidily across the floor, but he moved with the grace and poise of a dancer. She tried to shy away when he reached for her, but his fingers were too quick; they grasped her chin and pulled it down so he could inspect the inside of her mouth. 'Crude, but effective,' he said, stepping back. 'I'm impressed, with you both. It would seem a shame to destroy something that has advanced so much.'

'Destroy? Why would you destroy me?' His words evoked puzzlement, although an idea scratched at her mind, like a dog wanting to come in, that she should be afraid of someone who spoke so casually of destroying her. But something about his dusty room and this faded man with his bright, mismatched eyes made her feel more at ease than she ever had at Sylvia's.

Ballah looked at her curiously. 'Is that not what you want?'

'No. I don't think so, anyway.'

'Strange. That's what the others normally want.'

Her head suddenly felt light. 'Others? There are others like me? With satin skin?'

'I have made others like you,' he admitted, 'and plenty have come back to me, always with the same request: that I take away the life I gave them.'

'Why would they ask for that?'

He shrugged. 'Loneliness? Regret? Rejection?'

'Don't you ask them why?'

'I do, but they cannot tell me. They don't have lips or a tongue like you do.'

'Then how do you know they want to be destroyed?'

'I can see it in their eyes,' he said, his own eyes glittering. 'That's why I always leave the original human's eyes in. And when they come to me, they lay down on this table here,' he gestured to a long table that was at the other end of the room, 'and I know then that they want to go to sleep.'

Lilian looked at the table. She tried to imagine lying down on it, curling up like a babe ready to nap or an old woman ready for her eternal sleep, but such an image skittered out of her mind as abhorrent. 'That's not what I want at all. I don't want to sleep. Or die. Or whatever it is you do to them. I want...'

'Yes?' Ballah folded his arms and stared at her.

'Something. I don't know what. May I have a moment to think about it? I followed a rainbow here and now you're asking me what I want instead of death.'

'Think, by all means,' he said, returning to his armchair and picking up his paper. 'Time is the one thing this house has plenty of.'

There were no other chairs in the room, so Lilian returned to the hallway and went back outside. Placing her coat carefully down on the damp and rotting steps, she sat, listened, looked, and thought.

The light was fading and the end of the day was bringing everyone back to their homes. Lilian watched men in suits get out of cars, chattering into phones; she saw a little old lady exit a taxi, reaching back in to haul out four bulging bags of shopping. As the taxi drove away, another car drove up and two women got out, laughing and chatting as they locked the car and went inside. Soon, every house had a light on in at least one window. The sounds of babies crying to get out of the bath and cats crying to come into the house drifted softly through the still air.

Everyone has somewhere to go, something to do. Where have I to go? What have I to do?

She tried to imagine entering a house while talking on a phone, being filled with the business of the day while also ready to let it go. She thought about carrying heavy shopping bags into a kitchen, then taking out each item she'd purchased one by one, putting it in its rightful place, standing back and seeing full cupboards. She considered how she'd feel sharing a house with someone – not Sylvia, maybe not even a human, but someone like her, someone she could talk to and laugh with. Although such ideas seemed so remote as to be impossible, Lilian realised they were easier to imagine than lying down on that table and asking to be put to sleep.

Getting up, she retrieved her coat and walked back inside, straight up to the man in his chair. 'I have thought about it and I want a purpose in life.'

He looked up, interested. 'What purpose would you like?'

She hesitated. 'What purpose did Lily have before me?'

'Humans think they have one purpose, but they actually have many, and they usually work themselves into a great state of unhappiness trying to figure out which one is the most important.'

'And which is the most important?'

He shrugged. 'All of them. None of them. Would you like some more time to think about this as well?'

'I... yes. Please.' Suddenly a hundred thoughts filled her mind, all clamouring for her attention.

Ballah walked into the shadows at the far end of the room and pulled another chair up next to his, leaving a groove through the rotted carpet. Then he picked up his paper again as Lilian sat and pondered this next problem.

I am sitting with my creator, and he wants to know what I want to do with my life. He and I will agree, here and now, what I should be and how I should be it. How many humans get such a chance?

Yet try as she might, she couldn't decide which purposes were better than the others or which would make her happy. In the end, she asked a thought which kept jostling aside those around it.

'Why did you give me life?'

Ballah looked over his newspaper. 'I'm afraid I did not give you life for you, but for her. The woman who calls yourself her mother. I could not bear her sadness and I hoped to ease it for a while. But I always leave the rainbow to guide my creations back to me. When the living tire of having a reminder of their dead loved ones, the beings I have created know how to find me.'

'She did not tire of me. I tired of her. I left.'

'So you told me,' he said, and went back to his paper.

As the moon rose outside, it found a chink in the curtains and cast a silvery dot onto the floor. Lilian watched as it moved, infinitesimally slowly, and thought about all she had learned since her first sight of that cracked white ceiling and the empty cobwebs.

'I think I have decided,' she said. Ballah put his paper down and looked at her politely. 'My purpose will be to live, like they do. Can you give me that?'

'Alas, little doll, I cannot. That is too much for me to grant. Like I said: too many purposes all crammed into their heads. But don't fret, you can get this for yourself.'

'I can?'

'Why, yes. You need only watch them. Go out, be among them. Humanity is like something sticky – if you spend enough time brushing up against it, the essence of it rubs off on you. That's why my wife and I live so far from them. To avoid such corruption.'

'Your wife?'

'Yes. Come. Meet her before you go.' He rose and she followed him to a closed door, different from the one she'd entered through. He opened it and bright colours spilled over them. In the centre of the room was a huge black cauldron, its rim higher than Lilian's head, and the colours of the rainbow that brightened the walls around them were coming from inside it. Standing on a stepladder next to the pot was a large woman, a hair scarf wrapped round her head; her gaze was fixed on the contents of the cauldron as she stirred it. She completely ignored her audience.

'My wife creates the rainbows,' Ballah whispered, 'some just for pleasure, some to bring my creations to me.'

'Creations like me.'

'Creations like you.'

'How should I—?' Lilian began, but she turned to find the place where he had been was empty except for dancing motes of dust. Then darkness surged around her as the rainbows were snatched away, and she found herself in an empty room and an empty house, feeling empty herself.

Lilian got a job in an underground bar. It was frequented by goths and punks. Everyone assumed that her shiny skin was some kind of body paint and her seams, which showed up more under the UV light, were artistic tattoos. With her first month's wages, Lilian rented a little flat. It was small and clean but it wasn't home. She couldn't find anyone to share it with, and she didn't have a phone that she could talk into. She bought one, then realised she had no one to call and felt too shy to ask those she worked with for their numbers. Luckily, unpacking her shopping was the joy she thought it would be.

Yet as she lay in bed at night, staring at the smooth plaster ceiling, she would often think of a cracked white ceiling with cobwebs, the smell of Earl Grey, and the laugh Sylvia would give sometimes when she truly forgot her sorrows. In those moments, her eyes would drift to the picture she'd brought with her and put on a shelf, high up so she didn't catch sight of it by accident.

She wanted me to remind her of her daughter. I'm supposed to be Lily. But I'm Lilian. I don't remember Lily's life. I don't have Lily's memories – only my own.

She wanted me to be someone I'm not.

Some nights, Ballah's words would race around her head. 'I did not give you life for you, but for her. I could not bear her sadness and I hoped to ease it for a little while.'

My only purpose was to be Sylvia's happiness, she thought, and the idea made her cry. She couldn't live for other people, she knew, but didn't know how to live for herself. And the thought that Sylvia was out there, suffering, and that Lilian could ease that suffering, made her toss and turn late into the night.

One day, a young boy with satin skin and tightly stitched lips entered and took a seat at the bar. He hung his head, looking up only when she approached him. She saw fear in his eyes.

'Did Ballah send you?' she asked.

He nodded.

She stared at him for some moments as the truth dawned: it seemed Ballah had found a purpose to give her after all.

<hr>

Lilian bought them both a bus ticket back to the small town where Sylvia lived. As she and the boy walked up the long drive, she caught sight of the tyre swing and felt pure joy in her heart – for the memories she had and the ones she had yet to make.

This must be what coming home feels like.

Only as she was climbing the steps to the front porch did it occur to her that Sylvia might have moved. That's what humans did when they wanted a fresh start, or to distance themselves from their memories. But when she knocked on the door, it was opened by a tired, familiar face that took on an expression of surprise.

For a long moment, the two of them stared at each other. Lilian had written down the words she wanted to say, had spoken them over and over in her cramped little flat, but now they seemed to stick against her chenille tongue. With great effort, she said, rather haltingly, 'Hello, Mother. I have met Ballah. I have thought about things. It occurs to me that as he is my creator, then he is my father. And that since you asked him to create me, that must make you my mother.' Sylvia's eyes widened then filled with tears. Lilian hurried on, eager to finish before they could spill over. 'I cannot be Lily for you, but maybe I could still be your daughter. Your daughter Lilian. In my own way.'

Sylvia stared at her for a long, long moment, then she lurched forward and drew Lilian into a tight hug that almost permanently rearranged her stuffing. Lilian returned the embrace, feeling something inside her starting to glow in a way it never had before.

Pulling back, Sylvia wiped the tears from her cheeks and said, 'I would be pleased to be your mother, Lilian.'

Lilian took Sylvia's hands and in a soft voice said, 'I don't know if I can bring you happiness, like you wanted, Mother. But Ballah has sent me a task, and perhaps, if we work together, towards the same purpose, we can bring happiness to those around us. And maybe we'll find happiness with each other too, at the same time.'

For a few moments, Sylvia seemed unable to speak, then she took a shaky breath and said, 'I only ever wanted Lily to be happy, but whether she is or not is out of my hands now. I can – and I *will* – do my best to help you be happy.'

Lilian smiled so broadly that she felt her stitches start to pull.

Sylvia's gaze drifted over Lilian's shoulder to the boy standing behind her. She scrubbed the tears from her eyes and asked, all brisk and full of business, 'And who is this?'

Lilian gestured for the boy to step forward, which he did, with an anxious expression. 'He cannot talk but for now I have named him Joaquin. He's my friend, maybe even my brother. With your help, I thought we might teach him to speak. I can't sew but perhaps that's something you can teach me. I'm sure there will be others who follow him. We could help them all.'

Sylvia smiled and embraced Joaquin, whose eyes widened in shock before filling with tears of his own. 'Come inside, both of you,' Sylvia said, beaming broadly, 'I bought some new needles just the other day.'

THE GEMINATED

I am walking past the guards when it dawns on me. It's a realisation, knowledge that sits so deep in my spine that I can't help but believe it.

I know it started with a rather innocent trip to the supermarket where I bought milk and a six-pack of beer. One of them tasted funny and I remember scowling as I drank it, but I did so nonetheless because I wanted the full buzz. Then I fell asleep over an old episode of *Stargate*, the one with the giant aliens, and when I came to I was so out of it and so surprised that it was like waking to a new universe, one that looked the same but didn't feel the same. Now nothing really feels the same as before.

The guards are looking my way. I stand still, letting this bizarre feeling set in. I can only compare it to full-blown déjà-vu, the kind that makes you certain you'll be knee-deep in the snake pit in a matter of minutes.

One of the guards keeps looking at me, even when the other one starts to walk away. Maybe he suspects something because he raises an eyebrow, stops walking, and then he smiles at me. The first guard is smoking a cigarette. He extinguishes it on his shoe and places what is left in his shirt pocket. The second guard pats him on the back but as they leave I notice that the smiling one is still keeping an eye on me over his shoulder. There's a look in his eye, one I would interpret as interest if we were sitting on opposite sides of a badly lit bar, but here in the

EY GLÓ KARLSDÓTTIR

shopping mall it must mean something else entirely, though I'm not sure what.

My purse is full of cheap jewellery and low-carb chocolate that I haven't paid for. My heart is beating way too fast. The thrill is like nothing I've experienced before.

I don't know exactly what compelled me to do a thing like this. I haven't stolen anything since I took a new dress for my Barbie doll when I was ten years old. When my mother found out she became so furious that I thought she would never forgive me and when I told her that I couldn't help it, that my doll needed a new dress and that I couldn't afford it, she sat me down and lectured me for what felt like more than an hour about just how evil it was to take what didn't belong to me. I never did anything like it ever again.

Until now.

I put my hand inside my shirt, push the finger underneath the bra to feel the lump.

It's still there. It hasn't gone anywhere. Not that I thought it would, but it's become a habit to check it whenever something strange happens, as if one strange thing would automatically cause another.

My doctor wanted me to undergo chemotherapy. He looked me straight in the eyes and said that it wasn't an aggressive cancer and that we would "probably be able to sort this out," as if he was talking about a minor credit issue, or a sore throat, rather than my life.

I turn to leave. The guards are almost out of sight and the exit is right in front of me. I could just walk right through the swing doors and force myself to enjoy the low-carb chocolate that usually makes me cringe.

And if this was life as usual I would have, but it isn't. This is something else entirely, a place where the illuminati might be conspiring against me, a world where Donald Trump is president, men leave their wives to live with their sex-robots and I find a lump in my breast.

So, I turn around, follow the guards down the hall of the mall. It's eerily quiet. A lot of shops are closed, it's not the place it was a few years ago. Instead, there are giant posters hanging over the walls where there used to be storefronts. Enticing advertising about how wonderful this space is for your store. The clerks in the stores that are still open all look slightly paranoid, or so bored they can't be bothered to look up when you enter.

It's ideal to steal from this place. No one seems to care.

The guards walk at a slow pace and I can follow them easily, but when the one who gave me that look turns around and sees me following, I begin to get cold feet. I almost turn back, but then I raise my hand and call him.

"I'm sorry," I say, and pick up my pace to join them. "I don't usually do this," I tell them in my most sincere voice, "but I noticed a woman fill her purse with things from the supermarket and head down to the parking lot. I don't think she paid for any of it."

"What did she look like?" the man who had given me the look asks. He has dark hair, kind eyes and a smile that would look cheesy if he was wearing a suit, but looks rather charming in this situation. I feel my heart thumping again, this time from a different sort of excitement and I make an effort to look him in the eyes, relentlessly, without pulling away.

That kind of behaviour doesn't come easily to me.

"The supermarket hasn't complained," the other guard says rather grumpily. He's obviously in need of some coffee.

"Well, you do as you see fit," I tell them, and start to turn around when the dark-haired, handsome one raises his voice.

"You go ahead Paul, I can take a look at it myself," then he turns towards me and cocks his head ever so slightly and blinks with one eye. Is he flirting? There is something inviting in the gesture and I smile back.

We have an understanding.

The other guard just hums something and leaves while we slowly walk back down the corridor.

"What did she look like, this woman?" he asks. He is walking so close that our hands almost touch. I could reach out and stroke his finger if I wanted to.

I start to describe myself in not so many words. A woman in her forties, a green purse, long brown hair, brown boots, a desperate look on her face. The man stops and looks me up and down, and then he raises an eyebrow, but he doesn't say anything, just smiles and continues walking again. When we reach the elevator that leads down to the parking area, he hesitates before pushing the button.

"She's probably long gone," he says.

I don't say anything, just shrug my shoulders and make an effort to look him in the eyes.

"I guess there's no harm in looking," he says, and we enter the elevator together. I raise my hand to push the button, and he does the same, our fingers meet on top of *-1*. I push it, and then I move my finger slowly to the one in red.

"What happens if I push this one?" I ask.

"A silent alarm will go off, Paul will be notified, and at his own pace he'll check the security camera."

"And when he sees you in here, what will he do?"

"Nothing unless I signal him," the man says.

I push the button.

"What's your name?" I ask him. It feels important.

I notice an immediate look on his face, one of surprise or maybe hesitation. Then he let's the thought go.

"My name is Mark," he says, and I can see he's struggling with something, but whatever is on his mind gets tangled in this thing between us, this soft feeling of quietness. "Why?" he whispers, just before I kiss him.

I mumble between the kisses. I mumble that I don't know why, and it's true that I don't. I just know that this is something that needs to be done, something that I want to do and in this world it's alright to act on impulses that I otherwise wouldn't act upon. It's alright to do things I otherwise would never do. These impulses aren't something I've ever acted upon before. I've had them, but I've let them lie, let them rot in the basement of my inner sorrows and die.

In this world they don't have to become regrets, or mistakes never made, mistakes you'd rather *have* made when you are lying on your deathbed thinking about what has been.

I want to feel for the lump, but my hands are busy elsewhere.

He is slow at first and it isn't until I see him glancing up at the security camera that I realise why. He's worried about his friend watching. I look up and smile. "Does it bother you?" I whisper in his ear.

He shrugs his shoulders and kisses me again. The moment is vulnerable and he realises that. It could so easily be broken by doubt. I open his zipper with my right hand and ease my fingers inside.

"Are you sure about this?" he asks, again glancing at the camera. I say nothing, just put my hand around his penis and stroke gently.

"You aren't married are you?" I whisper, feeling that doubt prying into my head.

He shakes his head.

"My purse is filled with goods I didn't pay for," I tell him.

"Is this your way of paying?" he says.

"No," I tell him. "This is me getting caught."

"You came to us," he reminds me.

But I don't answer. I need to get caught and that was my intention, but this got in the way and is something I need to do. Yet another impulse to follow, just like stealing cheap jewellery and low-carb chocolates.

"Can you feel it?" I ask him when our pants are down.

"Yes," he says simply, as if it's clear what I'm talking about; that this is as right as rain. I realise that such things only happen in dreams, in worlds where those dreams come true, miraculously, and where other things break apart and vanish into thin air at the drop of a hat. This isn't the world I used to live in, but a new one. One where I've got a lump in my breast and have strange impulses I can't help but act upon.

When we've sweated it out, worked for it in a way I've never worked for it before, when we've reaped the fruit of our effort, we get dressed, slowly. Mark glances at the camera, but not in a worried way. He seems more amused.

"I think I'll have to let you go this time, but don't do it again," he tells me.

"Don't do that," I say. "I'll keep returning to get caught."

"Is that right?" he asks. He looks happy.

"It's an impulse," I tell him honestly.

He looks at me for a long time and I see such gentleness in his eyes. "It's alright," he says. "You'll be fine."

And his words seem to unlock something. I feel tears start to well up inside me, and then they start streaming down my cheeks. These tears seem to ease the tension, then the fear starts to build that my world will suddenly click back to normal again, as it was before, that I won't be in this story anymore, but in my previous life, and I suddenly realise that I would rather have the lump and these strange impulses than that. The thought is simultaneously frightening, sad and invigorating.

"Will you see me later?" I ask him, and he quickly nods his head.

"I don't do this to all the shoplifters," he says. "I wouldn't normally."

"I know." I stroke his cheek. "This world is different," I tell him.

Later, as I walk away still holding my purse filled with cheap jewellery and low-carb candy, I realise that I paid no penance for my crime; instead I gained something new, and a surge of guilt washes over me again.

The guilt dies a sad death, however, when I leave the mall. The sky is such a spectacular shade of red that it leaves me breathless. I walk up a steep slope and take in the view of the city. It looks like the horizon is on fire and is about to devour the buildings. It's such a sight that I call Mark to tell him. It's so instinctual that it doesn't feel like this is the first time I've ever called him. Each time I encounter something extraordinary, or even not so extraordinary, it feels like I've been doing it forever.

"You should take a look outside," I tell him as he picks up. "The skyline is on fire."

He doesn't sound surprised when he asks me what I mean and I tell him to find a window and look outside. When he does, I can hear the awe in his voice.

"That's incredible," he says. "Something awful must be happening somewhere for something so beautiful to happen here."

His words echo through my head as I walk home.

Something awful must be happening somewhere for something so beautiful to be happening here.

I push my hand into my shirt, my fingers find their way inside my bra.

It's been so easy to find the lump lately. For several weeks I've just pushed my finger inside and it's been there, unwelcome and relentless. I know exactly where it is and I know exactly where to find it. How to push to feel the hardness of it underneath the soft skin.

But now I can't find it.

The sky is on fire and I can't find the lump.

An old man is standing underneath a skyscraper looking up. He looks distraught.

"Is something wrong?" I ask him.

"They're coming," he tells me.

"Who?" I ask.

"I don't know, but it's not good," he says. The fear in his eyes is real, his fingers tremble as he grabs the sleeve of my jacket and pulls it lightly. The look in his eyes scares me a bit.

"I'm sure it will be alright," I tell him.

He just shakes his head. "They're coming," he repeats.

And I see the planes in the distance as he says this. Their black hulls contrasting beautifully with the red in the sky, and I know what they are, just as I know the old man knows.

"Bomb planes," he whispers.

And I know what they are carrying.

My hand is still underneath my bra trying to find the lump. I almost wish I *could* find it, almost wish it was there, hard and terrifying underneath my skin. But it's not. I can't find it. Instead, these planes are coming closer, the speed at which they approach is beyond comprehension and there is nothing to do but stare and witness the atrocities.

I see the first bomb drop well outside the city. It lights up the ground and pushes a pulse through everything at an incomprehensible speed so that when the second one drops in Fools Park I feel sure that we're about to be boiled off the face of the earth.

The blast is considerable, but it does nothing to hurt me or the old man. We stand still for a long time before registering that whatever these planes dropped didn't actually hurt us – or anything around us – but instead sent some form of pulse throughout the city instead.

"What the hell was that?" the old man cries. The horror in his eyes has only increased.

"I don't know," I tell him. "Maybe a dirty bomb?"

We wait, staring at the sky for a while as if it will provide all the answers. The red has become orange, yellow and dark.

I shake my head. "Can I help you in any way?" I ask him. "Do you have people inside?"

The man looks at me as if he hasn't seen me before, "Who are you?" he says and shakes his head. "What's happening?" and I can see that the fear in his eyes has diminished, as if he's forgotten what just happened.

A young woman exits the skyscraper door and smiles at me.

"I'm sorry," she says, "Grandpa has the tendency to wander. Was he any trouble?"

"I don't think so," I tell her. "There were bomb planes." I feebly point at the sky.

"He talks about them all the time, sees them every week. He used to be a soldier," she tells me. "The feeling sometimes infects others."

"But I—" I don't follow through. I don't tell her that I also saw the planes, that I felt the energy of whatever they dropped go through me. I don't tell her anything about that. I just look at the old man, watch as she puts her arms around his shoulders and heads inside with him.

The walk home is slow. When I arrive, I empty my purse on the kitchen table and look at the contents. Five low-carb bars, two pairs of earrings, a necklace and a bracelet. It's the biggest proof of today's oddness. There's a small ornament on the bracelet in the shape of a hexagram. I open one of the chocolate bars and take a bite. It's as disgusting as I remember. I place everything in the rubbish bin except for the bracelet, which I strap around my wrist, fiddle at it with my fingers.

A proof of life. That's what it is. A proof that things can be unpredictable, difficult, strange and wonderful at the same time. I go to the mirror, take off my shirt and bra and feel my breasts properly. There is no lump anymore.

It's gone.

I feel relief, but I want this proved properly, so I call my doctors' office and ask for new tests. The receptionist is reluctant, but in the end she puts the doctor on the line.

"We can do the scans again," my doctor tells me. "But you know it's useless, the tumour will still be there. You really should come in, so we can discuss what to do about it."

"But I'm telling you, it's gone," I repeat, urgently.

"How can you tell?"

"I can't feel it anymore. I knew where it was and now it's gone."

"You can't feel it?" I can hear doubt in his voice.

"I'm telling you my breasts are fine," I tell him.

There is a long pause and then he sighs.

"Diane," he says, "You never had breast cancer. You have a tumour in your brain and it's not going to magically disappear."

I sit down once I've hung up the phone. He reluctantly agreed to do one more scan, but told me that such things rarely if ever take care of themselves. He also told me he was worried about the state of my mind, which I guess is why he agreed to do the scan.

When I hear a key turn in the door I get so startled that I stand up and grab a candleholder that's on the table beside me. This isn't quite the way I expected my day to end, but I'm ready for whatever monster is about to walk into my apartment.

It's Mark.

He is grinning at me.

"We gave Paul quite a show today," he tells me. "He didn't mind."

I stare at him, and he stares at me as I'm holding the candlestick.

"Diane? Are you alright?" he asks. I see sadness in his eyes.

"Mark?" I whisper.

And I'm no longer in the story, but stuck in my own stubborn reality. He walks towards me, takes the candlestick away and holds me in his arms.

"What's wrong?" he asks, genuine concern in his voice.

It's natural, we've been married fifteen years.

"I have a brain tumour," I whisper. "I might die."

"The hell you will," I hear Mark say.

We fall asleep in each other's arms, not with our backs turned like so often before, and when morning comes he calls work and tells them that he's taking the day off. He takes me to the slope above the mall, and we watch the sun come up. The sky is as red as the previous day and then slowly it clears to blue.

"Tell me what you see," he asks me after a while. He is sitting beside me on a large stone. I can feel the heat of his body. It's familiar and it's foreign to me at the same time. As if I know him and don't know him simultaneously; as if both realities are true: the one where I just met him and had sex with him in an elevator, and the one where we have been married for fifteen years.

"I see the city skyline," I tell him. "The sky is blue and I can't see any stressed people," I add.

"And the mountains in the distance?" he asks.

I look to my right. It isn't in my direct line of sight and the angle is a bit awkward as I am leaning towards him. I see something approaching, and for a moment I'm afraid it's another set of fighter planes coming to drop more bombs, but then I notice that's not the case.

"It's a dragon," I tell him. "No, two of them," I sigh. "They're beautiful."

"And when they get here, what will happen?" he asks me.

I turn back to look at him. His beautiful brown eyes look concerned, but focused. I know there is something I should remember. Something I should never forget, but I also know that it sometimes slips my mind.

"I am…" I hesitate and continue to look into his eyes. They hypnotise me, keep me alert, but ecstatic at the same time. I kiss him. It's all I want to do.

He returns the kiss before he insists on an answer.

"I'm going to ride back with them, vanish for a while," but I can't remember where back is.

"And when you've been there for a while?"

"I will return and I will be fine. I will continue doing my job, like I always do."

"And what is that? Why are the dragons here?"

"The worlds need to be kept separated," I answer, proud of myself for remembering.

"And who makes sure of that?"

"I do," I say, and I kiss him again.

I feel my mind merging too quickly. I desperately need to return otherwise the two worlds will collide; I will collapse and both worlds will be thrown into chaos. The dragons are made of iron and steel. One of them lands in the slope behind us. The daisies are in such stark contrast to the silver dragon that I can't help but to laugh.

"I thought you left me for a sex-robot," I tell Mark. "I thought you were someone else."

"They can be enticing," Mark grins, "but you have nothing to worry about."

I sit on the dragon and wave Mark goodbye. "I will see you on the other side," he yells at me, true sorrow in his eyes.

I can feel my mind slipping. Slowly seeping into nothingness, imploding as I take the ride back. It's not a world of dragons and wizards I belong to, though one might easily think that. It's just advanced editing, the illuminati making sure that the world doesn't slip into chaos. It's all very complicated, but the iron dragons do their job well. I am back in the core before my mind slips entirely.

Tomorrow I will know if I will ever see Mark again. If the dullness of the day will be mine or if I was too late in realising what was happening.

I put my hand underneath my shirt and push it inside the bra. I feel for the lump.

It's there, thank god, it's there. It's supposed to be. It's how I know when it's time to recharge.

When they're finished, if they succeed, I will be recharged with so much normalcy that it will contaminate the entire city. Everything will be as it should be and I won't be going to Mark's mall to shoplift earrings and low-carb candy.

The bracelet is still on my wrist.

I feel my mind slipping away further.

I can't remember my name.

The lights go out slowly. I can see Mark's worried eyes, his brown hair in disarray. He's been crying. Why is he crying? There are tubes, and people around me that I don't know. I don't feel any fear, just sadness.

I slip away slowly.

I will come back later. Recharged and fit. Mark reminded me.

"I'll see you on the other side," I hear him whisper as my eyes close.

"I'll see you on the other side," I repeat, though I'm not sure my mind is allowing my mouth any movement.

Then everything blackens and all I hear is the heavy beat of dragon wings.

It will all be fine.

SHARED
ENDORPHINS

I was out on a date with a man who had an insomniatic parasite. He was very embarrassed, as he confided within the first ten minutes: 'I think you should know, I have an insomniatic parasite.' Charles was a Cambridge boy with shoulder-length blonde hair, pushed back in a way that seemed to defy gravity. He was *so* clean-shaven that I wondered if he had in fact ever shaved, despite being in his early thirties. I had scouted him out on Bumble, as a talent agent does a Hollywood actor or cruise ship entertainer. While not my usual tortured-poet type, my housemates had persuaded me to go out with this slightly older, corporate sort. 'What have you got to lose?' they had said.

'A what?' I remarked, sipping my cranberry and vodka, which I'd paid £15 for the privilege of. He went on to tell me a little, but not a lot, about the parasite that inhabited his brain, and how it tortured him every night with sleeplessness.

'I didn't know parasites could cause insomnia,' I stated, inquiringly.

'Oh yes.' Charles nodded, enthusiastically. 'It's the worst sort of insomnia imaginable. Completely debilitating.' He then pointed at a small cut on his cheek, just below his eye, that I hadn't noticed before. 'This was from the beast, during a midnight brawl.'

⚒

I met the insomniatic parasite a few weeks later. I lay awake next to Charles because he was restless, and I could never sleep next to someone who was restless.

All of a sudden, Charles let out a massive snore that made me jump. He was *asleep*. I turned my head towards him and met the insomniatic parasite, strolling out from under Charles' ear and across the pillow towards me.

It wasn't quite how I'd imagined. It resembled a caterpillar, but with yellow, marble-sized eyes on the end of its antennae, and bat-like wings that were folded into its sides. Slithering across the white bedding, it left a trail of slime behind it, glistening in the moonlight that trickled through the crack in the curtains. It was all very David Lynch.

It looked around inquisitively for a moment, smiled briefly, and then swiftly launched itself towards me. I had barely a chance to breathe, let alone move, when I felt the slithery demon wiggle into my ear, down the canal and into the auditory centre of my brain. Here, I felt it set up camp, promptly beginning its work.

For several unrelenting, torturous hours, I was at the mercy of my sadistic parasite. I lay awake, but with my eyes closed, unable to move. My body burned as the parasite engulfed it in flames, the skin melting away from the bone, dripping onto the cream carpet like an accidental fondue. Bald vultures flew through the open window, landing on my paralysed face and pecking ferociously at my exposed eyeballs, eyelids long flaked off. Body still burning, and vultures still pecking, masked soldiers stormed the doors and began their gruesome tactics. They ripped off my fingernails one by one, they broke my bare bones as though they were candy sticks and they launched rats upon my decaying carcass to mop up the remnants of my fried organs. I was awake for it all. I felt it all. It was the insomniatic parasite, playing with my mind, but it was real. And it was hell on Earth.

When I woke the following morning I was confused and surprised, as I hadn't remembered falling asleep. Looking over to Charles, who was shaking and sweating,

I realised that the parasite had evacuated my body during the early hours, returning to its former host and leaving its holiday home to collapse with exhaustion.

'I feel amazing.' Charles beamed, munching down his bacon and eggs while I scowled at him, nursing my woozy head with cheap instant coffee. 'Okay, hear me out, hear me out.' He continued. 'What about if we shared the parasite? Every other night, we'd take turns. Then we'd both get at least *some* decent sleep. And I tell you, after last night, it's totally worth it.'

I stared at him in disbelief.

'Charles, before last night, *every night* was a decent night's sleep for me. This is *your* parasite, don't bring me into it.'

At this, he scoffed and shook his head, and then the conversation was over and we moved on to discussing Artsakh and global politics.

I didn't see Charles the following night. I was out for a friend's birthday. Over more vodka mixers, I dished the dirt on my parasitic night to my dearest girlfriends. They empathised with both mine and Charles' situations. 'How terrible for him,' they remarked, 'dealing with that every single night.' They all understood my unwillingness to share parentage of the creature, 'You've only been dating for a few weeks, far too soon to take on that sort of responsibility.' I left the bar feeling secure and proud of my actions from the previous evening, but with a renewed understanding and pity for the tortured soul of Charles.

I returned to his flat the following evening and we had a wonderful time. We ate and we laughed and the insomniatic parasite didn't come up in conversation even once. I forgot all about it, which was a mistake.

I woke in the middle of the night tied to the bed, with Charles looming over me. To the right of my head was the sadistic beast, salivating over my untouched dreams. Before I could speak, Charles did.

'Look, I'm really very sorry to do this. But I've had to put up with this for almost ten years and it's really not very fair. You don't understand what it's like.'

'Ch-Ch-Charles.' I whimpered, struggling against the straps which secured my hands and feet. 'What are you doing?'

'It's hell, it's complete hell. And what wouldn't *you* do to escape hell? This isn't my fault. It's, it's that *thing's* fault. I haven't slept in a *decade.*' He rubbed his hair, troubled and panicked.

'Please, whatever you're doing, just stop, just stop,' I cried, straining hopelessly once again.

'I've made a bargain with the insomniatic parasite. I've made a bargain with the devil. My body, for yours.'

I cried, because I had no words left.

'Unfortunately, the parasite wanted a better deal. Something more exciting to make it pack up and leave its faithful old home.' He sat down next to me.

'You see, it's been rather kind to me. Letting me go about my daily business, only plaguing me in the solitude of night. But it's lonely and gets bored during the daytime. Understandable, right? And so, I've promised it residence in your brain, day *and* night. There'll be no break, as such. I'll keep you here, tied up, so the parasite may thrive as I've promised. You needn't worry, you won't get ill or die or anything drastic like that. I'll wake you for feeds, for showers. I'll look after you. I promise. It's the only way I could persuade the *thing* to leave me. You see, it's really not that bad. And just, I really just need this, you know?'

Before I could say another word, the insomniatic parasite launched itself like a rocket, straight down inside my ear. And my hell on Earth, the hell that existed in my brain and my brain alone, began.

GIRLS' NIGHT OUT

We are having an evening off. It is a necessary respite from work and our roles as caregivers, which we perform day in, day out, twenty-four seven. It is also time away from our Significant Others, who tell us that an evening out will be good for us. It is, overall, A Good Thing. Good Protocol. In the long-term the odd break will make us more effective at work; it will also make us feel more human again. They tell us to enjoy ourselves. *Relax.* Who are we to argue with them?

It takes us a moment or two to transition from one reality to the other and to truly believe that we are *there* and no longer *here*.

⤙⤚

We ready ourselves for the evening; agonize over what to wear. *What will the others be wearing? What dress would* he *like best?*

We leave our homes and cross the twilit city – anticipation, like the perfumes we are wearing, on our necks, our breasts, between our thighs. We travel on foot, by bus, by taxi.

We arrive at the restaurant, instinctively on the lookout for *him* (although we know he will not be here until later) and greet one another. We kiss, we hug, we make showy displays of giving each other compliments while making a critical assessment of each other's appearance.

The hostess shows us to our table – which, thankfully, is close to *his* piano – and provides us with menus. Well-dressed waiters fuss around us. This is probably because of Francoise's online following. *What would we like to drink?*

We order several bottles of white wine, and a jug of iced water. We continue to study each other while scanning the menu.

Gita has lost weight. She looks lean, well-toned, and she tells us she feels fantastic, so full of energy. For the past six weeks she's been doing that new training regime. You know, the one that's all the rage at the moment. And she's going to do a run for charity. Will we sponsor her? *Of course!* we say. *Of course. Send us the link.*

Adele has gained weight, but appears to be pleased with this. Her dimples seem secretly satisfied. *She couldn't be pregnant, again, could she? Surely not? However did she get permission for that? Must have been expensive. Then again, her husband is an Elite.* We say nothing and steer clear of the topic of babies.

Francoise, in her designer dress, diamonds at her throat, is as beautiful as ever. The diamond choker is on loan from one of the companies who advertise on her YouTube channel. We cannot help but marvel at her success, at the sheer number of her subscribers, her Instagram followers. The book deal. *How do you do it?* we ask. And, as usual, she laughs and says she has no idea why people are so interested in her. She's just a normal person. *Yeah right.*

Suzie looks drawn, and we each know that this is due to the ongoing divorce. *You'll get through this,* we say. *You're strong. And when it's over we'll order champagne. Okay?* She nods and manages to keep her tears in check. She tells us in a brittle voice that Amy's been great about it all. *She's such a fantastic kid,* she says. *We're going camping next week. It's something she's always wanted to do but, you know, her father never wanted to go.*

Nichelle's unruly afro is threaded with grey. *Work,* she explains, adjusting her glasses. *Of course,* we say. *It must be stressful.* We do not ask anything more. The less said about her distasteful scientific research the better. Still, Francoise, who is sitting next to Nichelle, puts an arm around her and takes a selfie of them both. *Loving hanging out with the girls tonight,* she writes on Instagram. *This is Nichelle, one of my oldest, bestest friends. This woman will change humanity forever. Isn't 'Nichelle' a gorgeous name? It means "like God" in Hebrew.*

We groan and tell Fran to put the phone away. Thankfully she doesn't, and we each find ourselves on her timeline too. The comments and likes begin to roll in.

The waiters arrive and take our orders. We continue to gossip, and giggle, while nibbling on buttered rolls. The loud twenty-somethings two tables away gain our attention and we make disparaging comments about them, although, in secret, we envy them their smooth skin and lack of responsibilities. We worry, too, that they will draw *his* gaze.

The food the waiters bring is delicious, simply perfect, and we each comment on how it's such a welcome change. We have become tired of the taste of the meals that we cook for our families and ourselves.

We have just finished dessert (our third course, and Adele has barely drunk a drop of her wine – we must be right about her being pregnant) when *he* comes in. He is wearing that aftershave again – the one that is rich in notes of cedarwood and bergamot. The scent, full of potential, diffuses through the air, and as it reaches us we sigh inwardly and sneak conspiratorial glances at each other. He sits at the piano and begins to sing.

His voice seeps into the cracks of our arid good sense – who knew it was this porous? – and makes us realize how thirsty we have been for the sound of desire. We are entranced by the melody and do not understand its power; it twists its way into the very core of our being, pulsing its way along our neurons and dancing with our hormones. For each of us, he is the ideal man. We want him to make love to us. We each want him to sing to us in private, we each want to be the only one for him.

Sometimes he looks at us, and when he does it is as if the song has taken hold of our spine and begun to slither around it, like a sine wave.

It takes us a while to acknowledge the waiter who asks us if we'd like some coffee.

Nichelle says yes, we would like coffee.

And all the while we sip our coffee, he sings his way into our souls.

Later, when he is gone, and the other, older, singer has replaced him, we pay the bill. Francoise gets us a discount for simply mentioning the restaurant on Instagram. We secretly think that what she has done is tacky. And yet not.

You know, says Suzie, *this has been the perfect evening. Don't you think? Good friends. Good food. Good wine.*

Definitely, says Adele.

If only we could somehow capture it, Gita says, *and bottle it and…*

Sell it, adds Francoise, with a laugh.

Fran! says Gita. *Honestly. What are you like? But if we* could *bottle it somehow, we could then get it out from time to time, couldn't we? And take a great big whiff of it when we needed to, you know, remember, and be comforted.*

Now there's a thought, says Nichelle.

And we begin to tease her, telling her that maybe she should forget about her work on those horrible hybrids (she ignores the slur) and does as Gita suggests.

She laughs good-naturedly and Francoise takes a last group selfie before we leave the restaurant.

Until next month, we call to each other. *There's always Facebook, of course, but real life is best.*

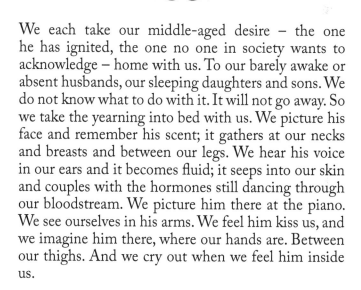

We each take our middle-aged desire – the one he has ignited, the one no one in society wants to acknowledge – home with us. To our barely awake or absent husbands, our sleeping daughters and sons. We do not know what to do with it. It will not go away. So we take the yearning into bed with us. We picture his face and remember his scent; it gathers at our necks and breasts and between our legs. We hear his voice in our ears and it becomes fluid; it seeps into our skin and couples with the hormones still dancing through our bloodstream. We picture him there at the piano. We see ourselves in his arms. We feel him kiss us, and we imagine him there, where our hands are. Between our thighs. And we cry out when we feel him inside us.

It is at this point that our Significant Other releases us from that reality.

"Wakey wakey," says Frank, extracting the memory beads from our heads. We are at the Hybrid Farm. In our replenishment pods.

"Enjoyed your night out?"

"What night out?" we say.

"It's always the same," he says with a sigh, placing the beads in a jar labelled: *Adele, Gita, Francoise, Nichelle, Suzie: 2027 [collective memory] #46-5 (Evening at a London restaurant.)* He runs a hand through his grey hair. "You never remember it afterwards," he says, "but I always like to ask. Just in case."

"Just in case, what?" we ask.

"In case you're more human than you look. Or can remember." He suddenly laughs as he places the jar on the shelf where it usually lives. Amidst the thousands of other jars. "Donated decades ago," he mutters. "Those girls are long dead now, bless 'em."

More loudly, to us, he says, "Or in case you ever want to rise up against the Elites who made you this way. Figure out that you're really individuals, with your own destinies."

We ask him to elaborate, but he never does. So we get up, out of the pods, and return to our work. Some of us look after the humans, the other humans, the Elites have rejected – those that will likely become hybrids, like us. And some of us do the unpleasant, unsafe and tedious jobs that the Elites refuse to undertake.

We think about what Frank has said, but we do not understand what he means. Sometimes, though, when we catch Frank cleaning our pods, humming a tune to himself, we experience a pleasant sensation. The oldest humans call it *a memory*, and it makes us pause for a moment as it snakes its way through our neural networks, making us feel as though someone, an "other", is inside us. Within our fleshy, metalloplastic bodies. But no, we say to ourselves. That cannot be. That cannot be. And so we return to our work.

THE NIGHT PARADE

Airi sparks up a cigarette. Summer night air lies blanket-heavy across her bare shoulders. She grew up in rural Itakura in a house without air conditioning. On those stifling nights, all you could do was sweat, listless on a stripped-down futon, the futile drone of oscillating fans pushing hot air around. A sluggish breeze through the windows, if you were lucky. Here in Osaka the whirring cicadas compete with main road traffic to produce the most noise, and the humidity is laced with diesel fumes, the stale heat pumped out by a thousand air conditioners. Sweat-dappled forehead, the persistent cling of damp clothes. The musty scent of unwashed bodies in too-small apartments.

She exhales. It is not yet full dark; the apartment blocks are hazy silhouettes against a sky the hue of a fading bruise. Grey smoke rises from her parted lips, hanging still in the air for a long moment. The complete absence of a breeze feels like punishment, and yet she persists. Summer in Osaka is yet to defeat her, and remaining outside is an act of defiance, breathing smoke into the soup-thick night. To retreat to her tiny air-conditioned apartment would feel too much like failure. Not that she has anyone to prove herself to; her friends are scattered across the city, and the luckier ones are probably embracing the chilly relief of their own aircon; skin gleaming rather than glistening, the deliberately cultivated glow of the young and the beautiful, while she sweats punitively on her tiny balcony.

Down on the darkening street, something small and quick darts across the road. Sometimes, in the height of summer, the rats move in. They chew on the electric wires and cables, build nests beneath the vending machines. They scurry through the children's park, feasting on the remnants of dropped snacks, the detritus of small children. The ripe trash bags left out by her less disciplined neighbours, improperly sorted, marked with lurid red "rejected" stickers and left to rot.

For a long moment, she sees nothing; everything is still save for the maddening dance of mosquitos, insubstantial as heat haze. And then it emerges from behind a parked car. A fox, russet hide blood-dark in the gloom. It is strangely unhurried as it enters the children's park, incongruous against the sand-pale gravel. Every few steps it pauses, looks around, as though surprised to find itself here, surrounded by looming apartment blocks. Airi nestles her chin in the cup of her palm as she watches it, this well-fed beast with its full, thick tail. She has seen foxes before, but never here, deep in the heart of urban Osaka, and never once such a regal-looking creature.

The skitter of sandals on sun-warm concrete, loud in the still silence. On the other side of the road, a small child; a tiny girl clutching something small and white, dark hair cropped short. She is surely no older than three. Airi frowns. The streets are peculiarly deserted; not even the ubiquitous bicycles are out tonight, and the roads are conspicuously quiet, as though the entire city has collectively and secretly agreed to remain inside tonight. Airi leans over the balcony, scanning the street below. Surely there must be a parent in tow. Perhaps they have been distracted by their cellphone. Perhaps the child has wandered out onto the street while they browse the chiller cabinet in the Family Mart, entranced by the fox. Any moment now some harried-looking mother will burst onto the street, calling after their little darling.

The child bolts into the road. Instinctively, Airi flinches. The girl does not look before she runs; she is so small, eggshell-fragile in wisteria blue. That there is not a single car on the road does not register to Airi as she stubs her cigarette out on the bricks. She leaps up, pushing the screen door aside and into the apartment, weaving through that narrow, cluttered space, pausing to grab her keys from the dish and tug on her sneakers as she scrambles out the front door. The frantic pitter-patter of her feet on the stairs. Out past the bike racks and onto the pavement, squinting in the serene blue glow of the streetlamps. The child is gone.

Her heart thuds with exertion as she crosses the road – so empty, so *eerie*. The harsh rasp of her breathing sparks a recurring memory. Mizuki's voice, insistent, exasperated: *you really ought to quit smoking, Ai-chan, you're not supposed to have lungs like an incinerator at our age.* Rich coming from Mizuki, who subsists on the pizzas she delivers on her hellishly noisy Honda scooter, and who swoons at the thought of walking further than two blocks. The child, Airi realises, is not there. Impossible; a child so small could not have disappeared completely in such a short space of time. She turns in a useless circle, peering down the road; small birds sit silhouetted and static on the power lines, gradually blending in with the blooming dark. Into the children's park, where there is no child, no fox, no living thing at all save for the languid summer bugs circling the streetlamps. The swings cast spindle-limbed shadows across the gravel. A breeze kisses the treetops; dry leaves whisper conspiracies. A plush rabbit toy, abandoned.

Scrapemarks in the gravel indicate movement. A thin pall of yellow-gold dust lingers in the still air. She has missed the child by mere moments. But this is impossible; there is no path beyond the low bushes, nothing but wire fence and brick wall. A single exit and entrance. But both fox and child are nowhere to be seen. She follows the marks towards a cluster of bushes, a low-hanging tree. She kneels, tentative. "Hello?" Hesitant, so as not to startle. She knows well enough that a cornered fox might bite. A cornered child might, too. There is no sound from the bushes, no motion; a strange, pregnant silence, as though something is holding its breath. As though something is poised and ready to strike.

Ridiculous. She'd grown up on farmland, curious and wary in equal measures of the mamushi snakes, watchful for suzumebachi nests; there is nothing in the city that can scare her quite so much. She is unfazed by drunks, will glare at subway gropers until they back away, cowed. She reaches a slow hand out, brushing back foliage. The warm-wood scent of temple incense rises up. The space between the leaves is dark. Her hands are wet when she pulls them back, dappled as though with rain. She turns her wrists, examining her skin, the rivulets running down her forearms. And there, inside the bushes, the distant echo of footsteps on stone, the low hiss of rain in the trees. Airi glances back into the still Osaka night, at the cloud-curdled sky and the bone-dry gravel, the perfect stillness of the strange, empty roads. Deserted balconies and darkened windows. The sound of rainfall echoing, impossibly, from deep inside the bushes. A plush white rabbit, abandoned in the middle of the park. All of these things are true.

A firefly flicker of gold catches her eye, a flutter of motion as something turns, disappears into the deep shadow. She follows before she realises what she's doing. She is a child again, chasing frogs into the reeds, incurably curious. Headlong into the bushes, into a darkness so full and profound that it feels, just for a moment, like she may never see the sun again.

The patter of rain shocks her summer-warm skin. Instinctively, she ducks beneath an outstretched bough; her damp hair clings to the curve of her forehead. She blinks slowly, adjusting to the deep, sudden gloom. The rich odour of leaf mulch and damp moss and incense, somewhere close by. The air is thin here, sharp with pine-scent; there is a narrow path creeping steeply upwards, choked with thick foliage, a carpet of ferns. Innumerable torii gates burn vermilion in the moonlight, lining the path, disappearing into the blue-dark wilderness.

She has seen this before, in a different space, a different time. Stone foxes dappled with bright moss, eyes weathered and watchful. A child's tired legs, and the seashore murmur of a thousand tourists, a hundred unfamiliar tongues. The sweet-salty scent of fresh yaki dango. But this is not that vibrant, sacred place. These paths are unlit, choked with ferns, untroubled by human feet. A lost, moonlit wonderland. The torii gates are weathered and crooked, listing at broken angles like a long and twisted spine. A severed shimenawa rope dangles limp from the lintel, a length of damp, weatherworn twine. The forest has crept in, wrapped lush fingers around pillars, and the paths are engulfed in its mossy gullet.

A sudden rustling in the undergrowth. She turns, curious, afraid. What silent, dark-dwelling creatures might live in this forgotten place? What has scented her strange flesh, is watching her from the shadows? So many places to hide up here. So many places to watch, and to wait. But when it emerges at last – slow, careful, perched in the branches of a black pine – it is only a calico cat, rheumy eyes gleaming jade-green in the dark. A thin creature, pitiful flesh stretched tight over sharp ridges of bone. It regards her with feral suspicion; she remembers these too, the half-wild beasts who haunt the Inari shrine like sleek ghosts. The cat descends; it slips from branch to branch as though half-liquid, all serpentine spine and whiplash tail. In spite of its thinness, it is enormous. It is bigger than any cat she has ever seen, and its claws are half-sheathed sickles, teeth like slivers of bone. Its eyes meet hers, incurious, unthreatened.

"I'm sorry," she tells the cat, quite sincerely. "You look so hungry, and I haven't got anything to give you." Her bare legs feel exposed, vulnerable; the cat could close its jaws around her ankle, drive sharp teeth into the meat, shredding tendon and bone. There are food carts at the bigger shrines – thick, glistening skewers of grilled beef, cloud-soft mochi – but this shrine belongs to the forest, and this cat is nobody's pet. It must sustain itself on the small creatures that scurry and hide, that cower in the long grass, so still and quiet. Pickings must be lean of late; up close she can count each vertebra, see the undulating topography of its ribs.

She thinks of the child, then, wandering deeper and deeper into the twilight forest. Might a hungry cat stalk a lost child? Might it follow them through the trees, into the enveloping darkness, waiting for them to stumble? Might it scent blood, sense the terrified adrenaline, the weakness of exhaustion? There is no sign of the girl here, but she must have come this way, and she cannot possibly have travelled far. She must be within reach.

The cat turns its hungry gaze towards the gate-tunnel, into the distance, where the path is swallowed by shadow. And in that shadow, a cluster of distant lights like bright eyes, the flicker of flame, white-pale as they pass through the forest. A late-night pilgrimage to the shrine, perhaps, though there is no sound, no sense of motion. It seems the lights are travelling of their own accord, like obon lanterns buoyed on a gentle current. Surely a child would be drawn to those lights.

Wet ferns brush at her ankles as she ascends, passing beneath the severed shimenawa. The dark unnerves her, the way it bleeds through every gap, every fissure, ebbing like a gentle tide. Like black water at the mouth of an unseen river. The relentless hiss of rain and her exposed skin rippling with gooseflesh. Into the gate-tunnel, in search of the girl-child, alone and vulnerable. A lost and sodden pilgrim following the procession of lights.

The gates are infinite. They are a parade of arthritic limbs held at abject angles, a gallery of dilapidation. Her feet ache miserably; raw skin and damp bones, and still she treads with caution, for mamushi make their home in places like this. Uneven ground underfoot, the sway of loose ankles. She is dressed for hot weather, but the sweat in her hair has long evaporated, the weight of Kansai summer cut loose and drifting; the damp cold permeates her flesh like a fever chill. It feels as though she has been walking for days, and still the lights remain maddeningly distant.

She could turn back, still. She could leave the child and return to that quiet threshold, that black and empty space between spaces. It is not too late to go home. But when she turns, footsore and rainslick and tired, the path is swaddled by pale, impenetrable mist, the road lost. She cannot go back. The only way out is through, like a sweltering fever-dream; she is all aching bones and empty, growling stomach and the mist mocks her, accuses her: *did you really think...? are you actually that stupid...? would you truly leave that child to die...?*

And no, of course not, of course she would never, but the lights are as faraway as ever, and the girl is nowhere. No child so small could have travelled such a distance so quickly. She must have wandered off the path, somewhere. She must be lost in the deep woods, or asleep beneath a persimmon tree, or perhaps she is warm meat in the stomach of something enormous. Perhaps she is close by, weeping softly in the green-black dark. Airi does not particularly like children. She wards off questions of dating and marriage with blunt force, leaving a string of disappointed relatives and nonplussed friends in her wake. This is not some frustrated maternal crusade but a sense of obligation, of responsibility; no other soul saw that child disappear but her. Nobody would ever think to look for her here. She imagines those small bones couched in bright moss. A scrap of wisteria blue like a flag in the breeze.

"You're lost."

She looks up. A tall, thin boy, or perhaps a girl, long in the limb and fine-boned, narrow face and summer-dark skin. Underfed and cautious. Thick hair snarled and knotted as though it has never known a comb, half-hidden beneath the hood of a grey cloak. And those eyes, as sharp and green as sea-ice.

"It can't be."

Lips part in a wide, bright grin. The teeth are needlesharp. "Can't it?" The voice is half a purr. A glimpse of a thick, heavy tail flickering between narrow ankles. Airi recalls childhood stories of the weird and the monstrous, her ojisan's insatiable love of folklore; tales of bakeneko, old and wily cats who shift shape, who dance wild jigs with napkins draped over their heads. Who might lead a man to his doom, if the fancy takes them. "You underestimate what is possible. But then, I'd expect nothing less from a human."

There is no obvious hint of threat in the bakeneko's voice, but cats are capricious beasts; their whims change with the direction of the wind. "You're right," she says. "I don't even really know where I am right now. I came here to find a lost thing and now I'm lost myself." A small, frustrated laugh. "Could you tell me how to get out of here?"

"Well, that depends," the bakeneko purrs. "Where exactly do you want to end up?"

"If I can at least find a way out of the torii…"

The grin widens, a flash of garnet tongue. "Why do you suppose I'd help you?"

"Either you've come here to kill me, or to help me." She looks the bakeneko in the eye, tries not to flinch at the way its pupils dilate. A bear might let you live if you play dead; a cat will only make a toy of your corpse. Mizuki would call her insane, and perhaps Mizuki would be right, but Mizuki is not here. "If you've decided to kill me, there's nothing I can do to stop you. And I've nothing to offer you to convince you to help me. But I hope you will."

The hollow drum of raindrops on old, rotting wood, a maddeningly familiar rhythm. Somewhere out in the forest an unseen animal calls out, low and eerie. Her heart thrums loud in her ears. The bakeneko's eyes are bright jewels in the shadow of its hood, unblinking, watching her with what might be suspicion, or admiration, or anger. Her heart plummets into the depths of her gut; her body stiffens, taut-muscled, ready to run, but she is so tired, so lost.

"Follow the lights," the bakeneko says at last. "And whatever you do, you must not let them see you."

"I've *been* following—" But the bakeneko's grey cloak melts into the surrounding darkness, dissipating with the smooth ease of ink in water until nothing remains save for a hint of pale green iris, watchful even in its absence. She turns back to the path, to the lights, which have progressed no further, drawn no closer. Their steady distance infuriates her. On aching feet she walks on.

The bakeneko, at least, is true to its word. Further up, the path forks. One leads upwards, a steep track carved into the hillside, slick mud glistening; the other leads down. Here, the gates grow sparse, blasphemous in their disrepair. The loamy smell of rotten wood. Fragments of red-painted pillar nestle in the leaf litter. And between the trees, glimmering in the near distance, the procession of lights. So close, now, that she can almost make out the shapes of the lantern-bearers; indistinct, a slow-flowing river of half-lit figures meandering through the forest.

The way down is a gauntlet. Thick roots grasp at her ankles; the thin moonlight of the upper slope barely reaches down here, in this deep green gully. If there are snakes she will never see them. The forest floor is cut through with shallow streams, rocks gleaming with wet moss. The descent looks endless.

She wonders if they can sense her, if they are possessed of keen hearing, a sharp sense of smell. If her flesh carries with it the sour tang of gasoline and cigarette smoke. The bakeneko's warning nags like an old ache. What will they do if they find her? Their lamplit silhouettes are vague, varied; they look motley, misshapen, but light plays tricks, and so do cats. Are they keen-eyed and fierce-clawed? Are they strange beasts at all, or merely quiet, solemn men searching for some long-forgotten shrine?

Unpainted torii sprout from the mulch as though grown spontaneously from seed. Enormous sugi trees marked here and there with shimenawa; here, the kodama dwell, the tree-spirits who, her ojisan claimed, would curse any man who dared to fell the trees in which they lived.

"Steady, now." A whisper from the trees. She looks

up, startled, but it is no kodama. The bakeneko peers down at her from a low branch, thin cat-body poised as though to strike. Its ears swivel, tracking sounds too fine for her dull human ears. "You're almost upon them. If you are truly determined to save the child – well, then you're an idiot, but that's no problem of mine. If you must go, go in disguise. If they sense that you are human, they will show no mercy."

Airi frowns. "I never said anything about a child."

The bakeneko smirks. "And yet, why else would you be here? Strange enough that one human might happen upon the parade. But for you to stumble in after her on those great, clumsy feet, well… Coincidences are so lazy, aren't they?"

"The parade…?"

"Did you not think it strange, human, that your realm would be so empty, so *quiet*? Didn't you ask yourself why?" The bakeneko stretches; sickle-sharp claws graze old bark, and Airi knows this is a deliberate reminder; it could still turn on her, if it wanted to. "The night parade is coming. They will leave this forest and pass through into your world. Any human who looks upon them will drop dead on the spot, such is their power. Did you not feel it? That terrible unease, like a sickness, warning you to stay inside?"

The lanterns hover. The parade has stopped. Her skin prickles. They are so close. "But who are *they*?" she whispers. The sudden stillness unnerves her; even the rain seems to have stopped, and she feels the hush deep in the fibres of her muscles, a terrible pressure like the moment before a storm breaks. They are waiting, she realises, and she is late.

The bakeneko's voice echoes, a faraway song: "Perhaps you should go and find out."

When she looks up – the glow of the lanterns seared pale into her retina, ghostly in the branches – the bakeneko is gone, and its cloak hangs from a bough like a shed skin. She pulls it down, slips it on; it is warm against her damp skin. The fabric smells strange; a musty animal odour, yes, but something else. Temple incense and old ash. The sweet-fragrant scent of cedarwood. She pulls the hood up over her head, obscuring her face in shadow. It will have to be enough. The night parade is waiting for her.

The first thing Airi realises is that the lanterns are not lanterns at all, but flickering orbs drifting between the trees, awash with flame. Kitsune-bi; fox-lights, red-gold glow and deep shadow, casting the monstrous procession in sharp relief. They are *everywhere*; beside her, a fur-covered beast in scarlet hakama trousers, black-lacquered teeth bared in a grin, or perhaps a snarl. Bird-beaked tengu, their eyes bright and keen as crows. An elegant woman, long white neck and sleek-silk hair and smooth spider legs erupting from her kimono, splayed and skittering. And there, on the very edge of the parade, the child. She regards the beastly circus with benign curiosity, the way a child might regard a room full of relatives.

She moves through them with care, barely daring to breathe as she weaves between the squat, slick-skinned kappa, a cluster of chittering tanuki. The low murmur of inhuman voices forming peculiar words. They are legion, these yokai. They choke the forest path with their numbers, astonishing in their variety; monsters plucked from her ojisan's tales and still others, anomalous but oddly familiar: the corpulent caterpillar smoking a pipe, the raggedy-eared hare sipping deep green sencha from a chipped cup; creatures from another tale, another place, yet they too have joined the procession, and it seems all beasts are welcome here. The night parade, the bakeneko had called it: *they will leave this forest and pass through into your world.* And still the child sits among them as though none have noticed her obvious humanity.

The child looks up at her as she approaches, unafraid. Airi kneels; the cloak pools around her, swallowing her feet and ankles. She extends a hand; her exposed fingers feel vulnerable, the slender bones of her wrist, the veins pulsing just beneath the skin. "Let's go," she whispers, and the child's eyes widen a little at the sound; those words, that language, the sound of home. She reaches out, hesitant, one grubby palm unfolding, the dirt-caked crescents of tiny fingernails. The call of familiar skin.

A hand on her shoulder. Rank fox-stink strong in her nostrils, sweet carrion-breath. "She is not one of yours," a voice says, barely a murmur. "If you leave now, I will let you go. I will tell nobody you were here. But if you persist, I will tear off your head and throw your body to the oni."

Airi swallows hard. She is aware of the carnival of beasts gathered behind her, around her; of the nervous sweat beading her skin, pungent with adrenaline. The flimsiness of her disguise.

"Do you doubt me?" The brush of skin against her neck, smooth and hot; sharp-tipped fingers tighten around her shoulder. In the corner of her eye, the bright gleam of teeth. "Oh, but you shouldn't. Leave the child and go while you have the chance. You don't belong here, girl. They'll sniff you out soon enough, and they will not show you mercy as I have."

She speaks between clenched teeth, a furious mutter: "She's just a child. What use is she to you? Why won't you let her go?"

"She belongs to *me*." A hand at her throat, now, grasping her chin, the wrench of taut muscle as the kitsune twists Airi's head around so that they are face to face, eye to eye. She is beautiful, long-limbed and powerful, skin like burnished gold; dressed all in red silk, an arterial queen. Claws rake Airi's neck, playful as a lover. "Her coward father cast me out. He sent me away from my own child. Ashamed of his fox-wife. But she has my blood. I carried her and I gave birth to her and she is *my* daughter."

The kitsune releases her grasp. Airi staggers back, rubbing at her chin, her face, the bright sting of ribbon-thin lacerations. Her breath comes in shallow gasps. The kitsune's eyes are black diamonds; a carnivorous gaze. When she turns back to the child – so soft and vulnerable – there is a glossy beetle caught in her clumsy grasp. Her eyes light up in delight, enchanted by her treasure. She beams at Airi, white pebble-teeth and bright girl-eyes, unmistakeably human. The girl crams the beetle into her open, smiling mouth. Teeth crunch against carapace, spraying fragments like black glitter. The hint of a gauzy wing melting on her pink tongue.

"She has my blood," the kitsune says, and there is such pride in her voice.

The terminal dance of black matchstick legs as the girl chews, open-mouthed, unselfconscious. Airi's gut roils; the kitsune snickers as Airi backs away, choking down her repulsion. It proves nothing, Airi tells herself, fixing her nauseous gaze on the undergrowth, the lazy drift of a wayward fox-light; children eat worms and dirt all the time, if you let them. It does not make her half a kitsune. Somewhere in Osaka a terrified mother and father are searching frantically for their daughter. Isn't that all that matters? Isn't that why she came all this way?

Green eyes bloom in the air before her. "It would be easy to distract them," the bakeneko says, disembodied. "Can you run? If they catch you, they will kill you."

They are moving behind her, this seething, monstrous mass; they are a dam on the verge of bursting. The parade is about to begin. "I don't know," Airi says. She is so tired, so hungry. The forest gloom is pervasive, monotone; she dreams of the human clutter of Shinsaibashi, awash with the white noise of a hundred conversations. The neon headache of Dotonbori, comforting in its permanence. It feels as though she has been lost here for weeks. "There're too many of them."

"Chaos makes them stupid." The floating mouth curves upwards, a Cheshire grin. "What other chance do you have? Join the parade? Your disguise won't last that long."

"Why would you do this?" She tries to meet the bakeneko's gaze but its eyes are maddeningly evasive; its grin remains static even as the eyes dance lazily in the dark. "Why help her get away?"

"Oh, it's not for her." The eyes close, blinking out of existence. "It's not for you, either. They were gods once, did you know that? They were powerful deities. But an unworshipped god decays over the centuries. They still dream of godhood, these yokai, even as your kind turn them into mascots and trinkets. I could feed you to them, certainly. They would make short work of your flesh, chew your bones into powder. But it's over too soon. Chaos is so much more fun. Get ready to run, girl. Don't stop until you see daylight." The grin dissipates. "Don't stop until you're home."

The bakeneko's gambit reveals itself in a mad flourish; the manifestation of a human form in among the monsters, screaming as it holds the child aloft. It howls in the language of the yokai, a strange and lilting dialect fit for the gods they once were, and never will be again. The child's chin is speckled with beetle shell, her eyes wide and confused as the yokai turn, first confused and then enraged; this human intruder in their midst, who dares address them in their own sacred tongue, who dares hold in their mortal grasp the kitsune's own child. The bakeneko's approximation of human skin is uncanny; it is too smooth, too perfect; beautiful and androgynous and utterly false, but the parade converges upon it with ready anger, a monstrous tide sweeping in, engulfing the bakeneko's faux-human body. And Airi, on the periphery of the crowd, watches as the child is buoyed along by hands and paws and wings; one by one, towards her yokai-mother, conveying her so carefully; *all must have prizes,* she thinks, as they visit their savagery upon the intruder in their midst. How, Airi wonders, can she join the throng, intercept their false fox-child? How can she insinuate herself among them with their blood so high, their senses incendiary?

"Quickly," the bakeneko's voice echoes. "The illusion will only keep for so long."

The yokai writhe and thrash, hunting for a trace of the insolent red-garbed human. Airi turns to the bakeneko; no floating eyes or half-moon grin, but there, sitting precisely where she had been before, is the child, unruffled by the chaos unfolding around her. Airi scoops her up quickly, tucks her beneath the folds of her cloak; the girl is heavy in her arms, but she is still, and quiet. She does not protest as Airi moves, slowly at first, tiptoeing away from the parade; the irony of skulking fox-like into the forest, the human turned trickster.

Don't stop until you see daylight, the bakeneko had said. A pinprick of pale green light glows in the distance, between the trees. That way must be home, she thinks; where the sun rises, the night parade cannot follow. She is exhausted, but she is so close. The girl presses her face into Airi's shoulder, arms too tight around her neck. She runs, and as the air is torn ragged from her smoker's lungs, the burn of acid flooding underused muscles, she realises dimly that the forest is quiet. There is only the sound of her own laboured breathing, the rhythmic thud of feet on wet mulch. Could she have outpaced them so soon? She chances a look over her shoulder, back into the depths of the forest, where no motley shadows lurk in pursuit; but there, close by, three slow-drifting fox-lights burning blood-gold in the gloom, and that is enough. She clutches the girl tighter, forces herself to keep going. To run where they cannot follow, these kitsune-bi, these bright, watchful eyes: *I will find you. I will come for you. I will destroy you.* Into the light. Towards the rising sun.

Osaka hits her in the face like a clenched fist. It is barely morning and yet the sheer sensory overload is paralysing; thick petrol and the rumble of engines and people, so many people, like brightly-coloured flags in the breeze, smoking and talking and knocking back hot, canned coffee. The sun, migraine-sharp in a sky so blue it makes her teeth hurt. She made it. She is home.

The gravel gnaws at her knees as she sinks to the ground; so warm, so solid and dry. The bundle beneath her cloak is still; sleeping, perhaps, or scared stiff, but safe. With trembling fingers she pulls the cloak from around her shoulders, peeling the wet fabric back like a shed skin. The sun feels so good she wants to weep. It has only been one night, she scolds herself, but it feels as though she has been gone for days; it feels as though she walked those torii-lined paths forever.

"Mummy, is that lady okay?"

She looks up. A young boy in crisp school uniform stands at the mouth of the park, flanked by his well-dressed mother. She regards Airi with wide-eyed dismay, her discomfort evident in the stiff set of her shoulders. Airi looks down at herself; her grubby legs are tattooed with glistening lacerations, her shoes clotted with thick mud. Wet hair and sodden clothes and skin so cold she almost looks blue. The girl in her arms, so still, so quiet. She must look insane, a mad scarecrow of a parent.

"It's okay," she says, because it *is* okay. There is warmth, and there are people, and the child is safe. The yokai cannot come for her here, where the sun burns so brightly. This is not their world. "I just… I need to find this little girl's parents. She got lost and I brought her home, and her family must miss her so much. Please, will you help me?" She holds out her arms, her precious cargo. A flash of wisteria blue. The boy's mother utters a horrified yelp as the child disintegrates into wet leaves, fragments of bark, crushed-twig limbs dangling limp from empty sleeves. A scattering of glossy black beetles disappearing into the bushes, away from the light.

The boy's mother tugs at his hand, urgent, hurrying him away; Airi feels the weight of his gaze upon her as she turns, still clutching the bundle of twigs to her chest, back to the bushes, the infinite forest hidden within. The smell of temple incense filtering up through the leaves; the barest flash of jubilant teeth fading into the dwindling shadows like an afterimage a grin without a cat. The leaf-girl, scattered and withering in the sun. A plush white rabbit, abandoned in the middle of the park. All of these things are true.

HOMECOMING

The leaves had begun to fall, a shy rehearsal for the denuding of the trees by the storms that would surely follow. Ellie found it hard to believe summer was over. It had rained frequently, fine days had been few and far between, and she spent most of the season indoors, watching for signs that the clouds would lift and the sun burst through the gloom. The garden was a soggy mess – she had not found the courage to go out and cut back the straggly stems of the foxgloves which had colonised the beds, their seed pods green and swollen. Honeysuckle, studded with scarlet berries, swamped the trellis. Blackbirds, sparrows and other wildlife were profiting from her absence from the garden, along with the weeds.

There was no reason to be so timid, so wary of going outside. Her neighbour's children were noisy, but well-meaning. They played outside every day, sometimes in the rain, racing their bikes up and down the road, kicking a football about. Once, on a fine day, Ellie had steeled herself to walk to the top of the village and back, nodding to acquaintances in their tidy gardens. Back home she found she was cold and clammy, her hands shaking. She told herself she was turning into a silly old woman. What could be more natural than a stroll along her village street? Why, then, was her heart still thumping in her chest?

Her work as a technical writer did not require her presence in the office. They were

ROSALIE PARKER

very much leaving her to her own devices: she was
not sure when her supervisor had last been in touch.
It was possible to spend day after day indoors and not
go outside; to see no one. This dread of the outdoors,
this malaise, had been with her only a few months.
It was difficult to believe that, in her late fifties, with
nothing obviously worrying her, she had succumbed
to so disabling a condition.

More leaves were falling. From her study window
Ellie could see them detaching themselves and
floating down from the tall beech tree at the bottom
of the garden. 'Leaf litter is good for insects,' she told
herself, as the leaves settled on the shaggy grass of
her unmown lawn. 'There's no need to rake them
up.' For a second or two, the sun broke through the
grey clouds, illuminating the scruffy flower beds
and still unpainted shed. Ellie turned back to her
computer and the interminable technical manual she
was writing. So far, her work was not affected by the
malaise, although she had begun to notice that it was
difficult to concentrate for long periods of time. She
found herself going to the kitchen frequently to make
cups of tea or coffee, or to eat biscuits from the tin she
kept in the Georgian corner cupboard Belinda had
bought. 'I'll feel better when Belinda returns,' Ellie
thought. 'Or in the spring, whichever comes soonest.'

The children were outside, standing on the road
next to the low garden wall. One of them, the girl, was
holding a toy bow and arrow, the arrow pointing at a
blackbird perched on top of Ellie's trellis. Ellie rapped
her knuckles on the window in warning, but the girl
had already fired the arrow. It swooped half-heartedly
into the garden and nose-dived onto the lawn. The
blackbird bobbed its tail and flew off, unharmed.
Nonchalantly, the girl climbed over the wall. The boy,
seemingly losing interest, got on his bike and rode
away. Having stooped to pick up the arrow, the girl's

attention was caught by something in the long grass. She reached out her hand and grasped what Ellie could clearly see was the silver bracelet she had lost last time she went out in the garden. The bracelet had been given to her by Belinda. It was engraved with images of elephants. The girl, stealing a glance at the window where Ellie stood, fixed the bracelet onto her wrist, climbed back over the wall and rode off on her bike.

Perhaps the girl intended to return the bracelet once she had finished her bike ride? Surely she knew Ellie had seen her pick it up? Ellie felt hot tears prick her eyes. Was it not more likely that the girl knew Ellie was agoraphobic – she would have heard her parents talking – and realised that she would not come out and confront her? Ellie knew she should phone the girl's mother and tell her what she had seen. It was probably the only way she would get the bracelet back. The bracelet was very precious – it was unique. Belinda had commissioned it, the elephants signifying never forgetting. When Belinda returned, she would wonder where it was.

On the other hand Ellie didn't want to make a fuss. Having to meet the mother to discuss the situation was out of the question. Ellie was too upset by what had just happened. Even the thought of going outside was enough to bring her out in a cold sweat. She would have to pull herself together for Belinda's sake. Being some years younger, Belinda had, at the beginning of their relationship, looked up to Ellie. It had been part of the attraction.

There was a small pile of leaves under the beech tree. The summer flowers were long gone, only the blowsy pink pompoms of the hydrangea brought a touch of colour to the garden. Last year, Ellie had grown strawberries in the now weedy fruit plot, carefully netting them against the depredations of

the birds. The luscious fruit had been a favourite of
Belinda's, doused liberally in thick cream and sugar. It
was dispiriting to note how quickly nature could get
out of hand and run to seed, how rapidly neglect set
in. Ellie could see that oregano had seeded itself in
the cracks between the paving slabs of the path. How
long would it be, she wondered, before the garden
reverted to woodland?

She was seldom hungry at meal times, her appetite
lessened by the malaise and the biscuits she ate during
the day. More often than not she simply opened a can
and spooned the food straight from it, a habit she
would have to forgo when Belinda returned, along
with staying up half the night. Her inability to sleep
more than a couple of hours had worried her at first.
Tonight, as she pulled back the duvet, she was puzzled
by the neatly folded, red satin pyjamas that lay on
Belinda's side of the bed. They were Belinda's, she
was certain of it. Belinda had bought them in Paris
on one of their weekend breaks. Ellie thought that
Belinda had taken all of her clothes with her when
she left, so the mysterious presence of the pyjamas
was troubling. How long had they been there? She
couldn't remember the last time she had changed the
sheets, although they looked clean.

With the morning came further mysteries. There
was an alien toothbrush in the holder in the bathroom;
a bottle of shampoo in the shower. The kitchen
cupboards and the fridge had been stocked with
groceries. Outside, autumn breezes swirled the fallen
leaves in lazy pirouettes. Ellie sought explanations that
were not forthcoming, traipsing forlornly through
the rooms, noting further signs. A window had been
opened in the conservatory, a newspaper discarded
on the coffee table in the living room. Perhaps, she
hardly dared think, Belinda had already returned and
was hiding somewhere in the house. Perhaps it was

supposed to be a surprise for her, although it was a funny way of going about things.

Ellie returned to the kitchen. The kettle was hot, although she had yet to make her morning cup of tea. She called out, 'Belinda? Are you there?' In the silence that followed, Ellie noticed a pair of muddy wellingtons standing on the doormat in front of the back door. Rain began to pitter on the window. Looking out into the garden, she could see that the path had been weeded, the oregano seedlings removed. All of the foxgloves had been cut back tidily and the lawn mown. Was it possible that she had engaged a gardener and then forgotten about it? But that wouldn't account for the boots on the doormat.

All through the morning Ellie waited for Belinda to show herself. She sat in the conservatory, attempting to read the newspaper that had been left on the coffee table, although it was difficult to concentrate on anything other than thoughts of Belinda: Belinda in her shorts and halter top striding along the beach at Barcelona; Belinda presenting Ellie with the elephant bracelet, charmingly pleased with her own cleverness; Belinda in their bed, tousled and sleepy, smiling her special smile. The newspaper proved a poor distraction; it was all too easy to let yourself get out of touch with world events. Some of the stories were quite frightening. It was better simply to wait for Belinda to show herself.

The grandfather clock in the hall struck twelve, which was something of a surprise, as Ellie had neglected to wind it since Belinda left. It woke her from a light snooze – she'd been dreaming that Belinda was driving them to the seaside, only when they got there the sea had disappeared and the sand was littered with distressed, floundering sea creatures. Ellie went to the kitchen; the wellingtons were still on the mat. Outside, it had stopped raining, but heavy grey clouds hung in the sky. The girl from next door was standing by the wall, looking at the house, fiddling with the elephant bracelet around her wrist. After a minute or two she opened the gate and walked up to the back door, took off the bracelet and pushed it through the letter box. It landed next to the wellingtons. As the girl let herself out of the gate, Ellie found that she had been holding her breath.

The bracelet remained in good condition, untarnished despite its sojourn in the grass. Ellie placed it around her wrist and fastened the clasp. She was now completely ready for Belinda's return.

She was too excited to eat lunch. The afternoon dragged on and still Belinda did not show herself. Ellie sat in her study and gazed out of the window. The pile of fallen leaves under the beech tree had been raked up and the honeysuckle trimmed. Once, the garden had been her domain, and she had kept it tidy. A robin hopped about on a patch of freshly-weeded bed.

Ellie walked through each room but did not spot any new signs of Belinda's presence. Perhaps she had gone out for the day? There was no car in the drive. Belinda enjoyed driving; she was good at it. Ellie tried hard not to think about what Belinda might be doing. Everything would be all right as long as she came back home at the end of the day. At least, it had nearly always been all right. Looking through the bedroom window, Ellie could see the boy and girl on their bikes next to her garden wall. More leaves were falling, forming a new pile on the shorn grass. The boy threw back his head and appeared to be laughing at the girl, who thrust out her arm angrily and pushed him hard. He wobbled but just managed to save himself and his bike from falling over. The girl rode off. It was the first time Ellie had seen them argue. Before she went downstairs she checked in the bed. Belinda's pyjamas were still there.

In the kitchen the boots were by the door, further proof that Belinda was... or at least had been... in the house. The kettle was cold, though, and the food in the fridge untouched. The sun broke through the clouds and a shaft of brightness illuminated the kitchen. Ellie took a deep breath and turned the handle of the back door: it was locked. She realised that she did not know where she had left the key. How would Belinda get into the house when she returned? The front door was also locked. Searching fruitlessly for the keys, Ellie found, at the back of the Georgian corner cupboard, the gold ring she had given Belinda on the day they moved into the house. It was set with opals and diamonds; an expensive gift.

Ellie slipped the ring onto her finger. Both the ring, and the garden – still damp from the earlier rain – sparkled in the sunlight. She watched the blackbirds pecking at the lawn, the pair of doves that lived in the beech tree billing and cooing. Everything was tidy, ready for winter, the work carried out as she would have done it herself, if she had been able. Everything except for the growing pile of leaves under the tree.

She could hear a car in the lane. It would be Belinda coming home, perhaps with a present, bought on her shopping trip in town. Ellie reached into the corner cupboard and took out a bottle of champagne. Untwisting the wire and popping the cork, she filled two glasses, ready to toast the renewal of their union, the rekindling of their love.

Ellie watched the champagne bubbles rise to the top. The car stopped in the drive. A few seconds later, she heard a key in the lock and the front door opened.

SEA HEART

There is a memory, or a dream of one, of being nine, of poking a stick through the wrack on the high-tide line on the shingle beach, of being determined to ignore arguing parents, of being even more desperate to avoid the awkward silence of the car ride home.

"What's this?"

The argument doesn't stop. Neither parent turns to look.

The Thing sits there, a wooden heart, shining like the French-polished mahogany table that Gramma insists must remain untouched by cups and glasses.

"Mama? Mummy?"

Still neither turn and look. They don't care.

The Thing is picked up, larger than the palm of the hand and an uncomfortable fit. It's warm and smooth and perfectly dry, but it's midday and it has been hours since high-tide. Young legs struggle to run across pebbles that roll and slip beneath trainered feet.

"Mama? Mummy?"

It takes several sleeve-tugs to make the argument pause and both parents turn.

"What's this?"

The Thing is held out, an offering.

"A sea heart," Mummy says. "They're lucky. You should hold on to it."

"A magic bean," says Mama. "They grow on giant beanstalks thousands of miles away."

"Like Jack and the beanstalk?"

Mama laughs and the curl of her mouth is beautiful. "But without the giant at the top."

J
O
M

T
H
O
M
A
S

Mummy frowns.

"What? It's true," says Mama, but the way she has to defend herself causes doubt.

And the parents are arguing again, their focus no longer on their child or the found Thing except, perhaps, for it being yet another thing to disagree over.

The Thing still sits uncomfortably in one hand. It's a little large to grip properly and the smoothness makes it difficult for stretched fingers to hold. The other hand is clenched into a fist to compare sizes.

Human hearts are supposed to be the size of a clenched fist, Mummy said so, whenever that was. The sea heart belongs to someone or something larger; if it really is the Sea's heart then the Sea must have many of them. Human hearts ache. Do sea hearts? If the Sea has many hearts, does it feel any one of them aching? Does is care about one heart or what happens to it? It would be nice not to care.

A human heart lands on the pebble beach with a soft wet thump. Blood droplets spatter against bare legs but these are wiped away quickly and easily, the smear marks rubbed away with licked fingers. The human heart itself is hidden by pushing it under the wrack with a stick, possibly even the same stick used to find its replacement.

The rest of the memory is warm spring sun on a face held up to the sky, light salty air that ruffles hair, the tang of not-quite-rotting seaweed, the cries of gulls, the gentle rub and roll of pebbles beneath feet. The parents still argue but it is no longer the centre of the memory.

"That's stupid," he says and that's the end of the matter.

It takes too much effort to argue otherwise, despite feeling as if the ever-growing beanstalk could shoot tendrils from a wide open mouth and prove him wrong.

It isn't worth it when the reward will be to watch him walk – no, run – away. The desired outcome is for stability, for those tendrils to wrap around his heart slowly and hold him as surely as the sea heart has vined and twined itself where a human heart should be. He needs to be held in this life, not lost beyond grasp. He is too good a match to lose.

Not that there's anything more to him than the other schoolmates, really. He certainly doesn't provide the "chemistry" the girls gossip about. But everyone says he's smart and presentable and they pay attention to him. He is expected to progress, to grow straight and tall above mediocrity, to succeed. He's the sort of student everyone else gets compared with. He's the sort of boy mothers love, both of them, all four of them if current partners are counted. He is the kind of boy to tie the future to. It makes sense. All his response means is he's not the kind of boy to share secrets with. But it could be considered the first sign that things will not go as well as hoped.

The rest of this particular memory is embarrassing. Wet, sloppy kisses mingled with insistences that *someone* is doing it wrong. Those kisses never got any better, at school or at college, despite considerable effort. By the time the next stages of life were being planned, it was easier to let him slip away. The fragile but flexible vines unbound from him with minimal effort and without pain.

❧

There is a girl at university. A young woman. At graduation, her eyes shine with pride and she hugs tightly. Another tree that will stand tall in the forest, a great oak to be part of the canopy not hidden underneath it. Another who can help support the weight of the vines.

"Partners in crime," she says with a smile.

Her parents laugh politely.

The after-graduation flat is small – "bijou" – and the jobs are just space fillers for the intended careers, because the market is poor and there are so many other recent graduates chasing the few choice roles.

"It'll work out," she says with confidence.

Hours at the space-filling job are long. Days drift by, summer fades.

"I still want to follow my dreams," she says.

The "well, so do I," is entirely defensive, a wish to have self and desires recognised. There is money coming in and even businesses renowned for hosting dead-end jobs must have managers, so there's a possibility of reaching some height, if not the originally planned kind. Only her ambition is still true.

When a job offer for middle management over the stop-gap roles is made, the reply becomes, "That's fine. You can do that. I can do this. We'll get there together."

Dreams are not as important as a roof over heads, a bed beneath backs, food on the table, available funds to go out with. Why waste time and effort holding out for another, imagined career ladder that probably won't be all that different. These are just minor trappings, minor changes. The fragile vines of the sea heart are growing thicker and stronger regardless of uniforms and job titles.

Her kisses are soft and warm, her hugs are tight. She has hope, she has dreams and ambition; she's also not stupid enough to walk away from one job without another to go to. The money will continue to come in and will increase with time. This is partnership, this is being bound together.

"I love you," she says.

Is it "love"? Does it matter if everything else is there? No, but it is close enough.

"I love you, too."

The woman has become a ghost of her proud, smiling self. Her face is taut, her smile hides poison.

"About the child support," she begins, many times.

"You wanted children."

There is only one salary coming in and one person on their own is always penalised. The new flat is too small, there will be no more big cars, food shopping must be carefully considered. Resources are few and need to be protected, not shared out to people who wanted to be free so badly that they cut away the unseen tendrils and broke the vines that had grown fine and strong.

"I thought we wanted to be a family," she says, just as she did before the separation.

"So did I."

But the children were to keep her happy, to keep her within the grasp of the sea heart. Now she's gone and the kids have, too. The only hole left behind in the thickened vines is hers; the shape of a second, partial, intermittent income. Filling that empty space is going to take time.

If she wants to be restricted to part-time hours with gaps in her working history because she chose to have kids, that's her problem. It's no longer a shared burden. It is not a weight the vines can carry.

"They're your children," she says. "Our children."

"And who took them from me?"

"You talk about them like they're *things*," she

sometimes says with disgust. "You're only upset because the *things* you think you own are no longer in your possession."

Other times, she says, "I should have seen it sooner. I can't believe I didn't. You never wanted to take on any of the work or responsibility for them, did you? You only ever cared about the good things, the fun things, and making me look like a bitch in front of them."

The arguments are echoes of the parents' on the beach, so many years before; words that have recycled through the mouths of every partner they've had since and now inhabit the mouth of their daughter-in-law.

"I could take them to the beach, some time."

And perhaps the nine-year-old would find their own sea heart, their own magic bean, their own promise of finding gold at the top of the beanstalk if they just keep focussed on their future.

"No," she says. "I'm not letting you wind them up and tell them lies about how it was all my fault."

He smiles and loosens his tie.

Why this memory? He's not important. It's just an affair.

It started on a shared project, a cross department thing. That work policy forbids this kind of relationship at all is spice and ensures that both parties regularly mouth platitudes about it being a minor thing.

It's easy to agree with a whispered, "Sure."

He works late most evenings, it's easy to drop by his desk on the way out when there's no-one else left in the office. His idea of flirtation is to tell his lover-to-be colleague about the gorgeous wife and mother of his children he will never leave, and the nanny who's so understanding about how much stress that causes, and the mistress who accounts for something like a third of his business trips. It only creates envy over the lack of understanding people in life.

It isn't love. It isn't a partnership. It isn't a life together. It doesn't solve the problem of one income but it's entertaining and it doesn't distract from the daily ladder climbing.

In the morning, it feels like a lose-lose situation.

In the evening, it feels like a win-win.

It makes working all day easier, just like the pokey flat that's supposed to be home.

"Nonononono."

This is life flashing in front of eyes. This is chest pain. This is sweating like a racehorse. This is the room spinning. This is feeling sick with some unknown mass caught high in the chest.

And he isn't working late tonight because of some child's birthday.

And he wouldn't care even if he was.

And the woman is probably wishing for it.

And her children probably don't even remember.

And that boy is long grown and gone into his own life.

"Are you okay?" the cleaner asks.

The mass seems to be moving. This is no longer feeling nauseated, this is retching.

A breathless, "No."

Does a heart attack come with vomiting?

"Is there anyone I can call?" the cleaner asks.

There's the biting taste of stomach acid in the throat.

Gasping, "No."

And there's the mass. It splash-shatters on the desk.

A groan. "Oh, god."

Tired. Eyes closing.

There, shining wetly, are several sea hearts, without the blessing of the sea, without being wrapped in seaweed and travelling unknown miles. Magic beans for someone else to find the treasure at the top of the beanstalk.

MARI LWYD

The family go into the field behind the farmhouse to dig up the skulls before the ground freezes. Their youngest boy goes with them. He knows it's an important day. They are the keepers of the spirit of Mari Lwyd.

Mari Lwyd. *Grey mare.*

They work along the markers, slicing into the earth carefully for fear of damaging this final, most precious harvest of the year. When they locate the skulls, they use trowels as if excavating ancient remains.

The boy remembers how the last one died. Screaming and a shard of bone puncturing skin, then the gunshot. There's no shielding him, no sentimentality. If a chicken's neck is wrung, the boy bears witness without silliness or squeamishness.

Afterwards they'll carry the skulls inside and together they'll clean out every crevice and suture with soap and water. They'll sit around the kitchen table, sleeves pulled up over the heels of their hands, nursing steaming mugs.

But that's for later. Now the sweat of their labours is fast cooling on their skin in the morning chill. For all its brightness the day is cold. This light won't last; the shortest day is coming.

∽≺∼

The boy is allowed to touch the stallion's skull before it's decorated.

Their father names each part. He insists that the children, those old enough, wrap their tongues around the words and learn the proper terms for things.

Orbit. Zygomatic arch. Infraorbital foramen.

All the boy sees is a heavy jawbone that detached would be a weapon in itself. Flat molars for grinding grass that no longer seem benign. Empty holes where eyes should be that see him all the same.

Mari Lwyd's festivities are associated in his childish memory with Christmas. The Winter Solstice's wassailing from house to house is blurred with the press of bodies in living rooms decorated with baubled trees, tinsel, and mince pies.

Now the boy is old enough to understand it as a separate entity. To register its weight and solemnity. Mari Lwyd is a ritual from time out of mind, origins lost but still deep rooted. It's a reminder that despite the darkness, light will come again. The dead will be kept at bay.

Winter Solstice. The day's chores chafe but animals still need feeding and bedding down, dishes need washing, seasoned wood needs bringing in. Then they can begin in earnest.

Mother is ostler this year. Her top hat has pheasant feathers in the band, her frockcoat covered in coloured tatters. The children wear homemade waistcoats, the boy shorn-off antlers.

The horse skull is mounted on a broom handle, garlanded with holly, ivy and mistletoe, beribboned in red, green and white. Its eye sockets are stuffed with a pair of Christmas baubles shining like mercury, the gaping nasal cavity syphilitic.

Father holds it. He's draped in sackcloth. Transformed into an underworld hobby horse, its mouth opens and closes in awful guffaws. It chases them around the kitchen at a gallop and the boy screams with laughter, feeling terrified joy. Or joyous terror.

The family always start the proceedings. Their boots crunch as they walk, the torchlight sweeping the glittering lane and frosted hedges. The cold pinches the boy's cheeks and shapes his breath.

They knock at the first house they come to. The Christmas wreath looks jolly on the red door which opens in a rectangle of brightness. Then comes the stand-off. A contest of rhymes and song. Failing occupants stand aside to let the victors in to be fed and watered but this ritual has evolved. The household follows them out with their own Mari Lywd in tow.

On they go, separating to bang on doors with ribald calls. Their numbers swell exponentially until the whole village is out, a herd of Mari Lwyds with them.

They're an arresting sight. Bejewelled, eyes full of fairy lights, bridled, rosetted, hung with bells that tinkle as they canter.

The parade ends at the village boundary, the weathered marker a gravestone. There's a bonfire and dancing. An old woman plays an accordion with twisted fingers. It wheezes along with her. A drummer beats the time on stretched hide. A man fiddles on an instrument of his own making.

Candles glow in the skulls that line the border. This darkest, frost bitten day is when the divisions are weakest. Worlds abut one another. Darkness must be satisfied or it will devour the light.

The final Mari Lwyd is brought out, bridle tied with enough ropes to keep it from bolting. It tosses its head, gives a jolt, but the fight it had when they took it has gone out of it.

When it smells the fire, hears its crackle, it grunts and bucks. An ostler puts her foot into the back of its knee to fell it. They all crowd around. Divested of its decoration it's just a man. Young, blonde topknot, heavy beard. He says something in a guttural, foreign tongue, then, "Please."

He looks directly at the boy who looks back at him impassive, taking his cue from the faces around him, the steady weight of his mother's hand on his shoulder.

Death is a swift knife to the throat. Blood caught in a cup to be sprinkled on the borderline. It anoints the skulls in splashes.

The rest of the young man will be steeped in lime and his skull retrieved to join the others in the farm's earth, ready for retrieval the following year.

The boy goes over, holding his mother's hand. They touch the handsome face by way of thanks. Next year he'll bear the candle in the empty space that now holds his brain. He'll join the other emissaries, for the dead only listen to the dead and he can go where the living have no place.

FOOTNOTES TO THE TRAVEL GUIDE

Location: To access Pinel Island from the Saint-Martin mainland, drive through the sleepy area known as Cul-de-Sac ("cul-de-sac" translates from French to "bottom of the bag"; however, most English speakers use "cul-de-sac" to mean "dead end") on the French side of this Caribbean island and park in the lot near the dock marked "Pinel". Pay the ferryman a fee of $12 USD; you will be dropped at Pinel Island, and the fee includes a return trip. Note that the last return ferry of the day leaves Pinel Island at 4:30 PM.

Description: Formerly used to house lunatics from the mainland right around the time that slavery was abolished on Saint-Martin, Pinel Island ("pinel" is Portuguese for "crazy") has become a day-tripper's snorkeling paradise. The main beach, directly to the left of the ferry dock on the north side of the island, offers white sand and clear shallow waters that are protected from the trade winds. An ideal spot for snorkeling or sunbathing, and the two beach-side open restaurants rent chairs and umbrellas; they offer drink service as well.

To access the wilder and uninhabited south side of Pinel Island, turn right off the ferry – away from the palm and grapefruit trees that will be gently swaying in the breeze – and follow the narrow footpath for Pinel Island Marine Trail through a lush, tropical green rush of vegetation that swallows one whole until it

NICOLE M WOLVERTON

opens onto a short-scrubbed expanse of rocky land. Do not tarry off the trail. In addition to the north side of the island being a protected green sanctuary, there have been dozens of reports of missing persons (see conclusionary note at the end of this report).

Supernatural Manifestations: "It was just me and my boyfriend Mike," says Olive Satterwaite, who lives in Blue Ridge, Georgia. "I told him not to go, but he wanted to see the mysterious wagon everyone was telling us about. He climbed up over the little hill just before the Marine Trail descends to the beach, and that was it. I yelled his name for an hour, but the only thing that answered me back were birds. It sounded like thousands of them."

The wagon has been a legend on Pinel Island for well over a century. Satterwaite did not see the wagon on the day that Michael Blanke disappeared; however, for those who have caught a glimpse from the trail, it is described as dark green, with a curved roof stretched over with dirty white fabric. While no horse has ever been sighted, a hitch has been visible, along with a shallow grass green porch built off the entryway to the wagon.

Extensive drone footage of Pinel Island has never revealed the location of a wagon of any type, nor the bodies of the missing trail hikers. Saint-Martin authorities call claims of missing persons and sightings of the wagon "unsubstantiated".

However, local Cul-de-Sac resident Jérôme Ledee says that authorities are afraid to launch an investigation because of what they may find. "You live here long enough, you see things after dark. Lights moving around on Pinel Island, long after no one is supposed to be out there. That's why the last ferry comes back so early – you won't find anyone with sense in their head anywhere near that island when the sun goes down. Evil things live there."

When asked why the legendary wagon might be part of that evil, Ledee points to Pinel Island's dark past as a haven for the mentally ill. "No one wants to say it, but the people that were forced over there suffered, even after the cruel suffering of slavery – and many of them weren't crazy at all. Legend has it that a doctor – a white man from the States – was charged with looking after the people over there, at least for a time. He brought with him a small green wagon. You could see folks hauling it for him, up over the dunes. People say he did things on that island. To those that lived there."

Charmaine Choisy, who also lives in Cul-de-Sac, has a more sinister explanation. She says, "The wagon was no good. An ancestor escaped Pinel Island and documented it quite well. When the people who were kept on that island heard the squeak of the wheels, they'd hide – they knew that doctor was coming for them. He'd snap one of them up, and for hours all anyone would hear were screams."

Investigation: Paranormal investigators Barry Ash and Nylah Ziegler-Ash, a married couple from Philadelphia, Pennsylvania with many years of experience, were sent to Pinel Island in July 2020 with the intention of purposefully missing the final ferry back to Cul-de-Sac and exacting a thorough search of the island for any signs of the mysterious wagon or the missing hikers. A portion of the following emails, notes, recordings, and videos were received periodically over the course of that night; the remainder were recovered the next day:

[17:30 NZA *email*] – Barry and I watched the final ferry of the day leave the dock from our hiding spot in a grove of grapefruit trees and overgrown shrubs not far from the beach restaurants. We thought the restaurant employees might see us at one point;

however, the second the ferry pulled away from the dock, the employees were frantic about cleaning up and closing the restaurant for the night. A bunch of them came within feet of us, but no matter what sound came from our direction, they studiously refused to even look toward the interior of the island. We even tested it out – we threw a couple of small rocks against the side of the restaurant, whispered loudly. Nothing. No reaction at all, except for the employees moving faster. By 17:15, they were all huddled together on the dock, and a speedboat picked them up, leaving me and Barry alone on Pinel Island. The sky's starting to go pink already – a pretty sunset, but that means it should be dark within the hour. It remains humid and sweaty, even with the breeze off the water.

[18:30 BA *email*] – Completed a thorough exploration of the restaurants and other out-buildings near the beach. Aside from evidence of the hasty effort to get off the island, Nylah and I found nothing out of the ordinary. Night has come, and the island feels as though it is breathing, like a hot huff of air down my neck. I know this to be nothing more than imagination, and Nylah would probably poke fun if I told her, but I admit that my heart races with each exhale. We will now take the Pinel Island Marine Trail for our first true test of the night. Nylah plans to leave the trail – however, I insist that she attach a rope to her belt. Whether or not there is, indeed, something evil on the island, I will feel better if I have some method of finding her should anything truly happen.

[19:30 BA *voice report*] – Nylah has disappeared into the scrub, and I cannot find her. I cannot raise her by cell phone nor walkie. The breathing I feel – the island breathing – grows louder, but the birds that had been chattering away are now silent. It has been forty-five minutes since Nylah left the trail, and I have not moved. The rope tied around her waist is slack, and I am afraid to continue on, lest she stumbles back to me in need of help.

[19:44 NZA *voice report*] – I found a second path! It's definitely not on any of the Pinel Island maps we looked at. I had to untie the rope that Barry insisted on, but I know he'll understand once I get back to him. I know he's probably worrying like crazy, though, and I feel a little bad about it. My cell phone service is shot, so you'll probably get all these reports in a big chunk once I get into a coverage area. Anyway, there's another path about twenty yards off the trail. What's weird, though, is I feel like I should have reached the flat part of the island already – I feel like I've been walking at least twenty minutes. The birds are putting up a real racket. Unless this path goes in circles, I should drop off into the ocean any second now. The island just isn't that big. I've stopped at a large flat rock at the base of a palm tree – at least I think it's a palm tree. I tried to get Barry on the walkie, but I think maybe the trees are causing too much interference.

[20:15 BA *voice report; ed,* Ash's voice is tense and low] – I urge you to call the Saint-Martin authorities when you receive this. Nylah is still missing, and I decided to return to the ferry dock. I must have gotten turned around, though, because I found myself back in the spot where she disappeared after ten minutes. I tried again and achieved the same result. The moon is risen but appears stuck in the sky – I do not understand, and I mostly assume it is an optical illusion. I'm trying to stay calm, but I'm worried. Very worried indeed. Instead of attempting the ferry dock, I decided to continue along the Marine Trail. I thought perhaps when I reached the south side of the shoreline that I might find other pathways through the protected area of the island, but there is nothing but the sea. I just set up emergency flares on the rocky beach on the off-chance a passing boat will notice and offer a rescue. Right now I am sitting on the beach, facing the ocean. The sound and the feel of breathing continues, and I wonder if perhaps it is the waves crashing and being sucked out again. If Nylah doesn't return soon, I may conduct the paranormal investigation without her – maybe it'll help me find her. I feel I can't wait, and perhaps I will discover a clue in the process. Maybe she's hurt.

Oh! I just heard a squeaking noise behind me, almost like metal rubbing against metal. I'll investigate and get back to you. I am hoping it's Nylah. Do let me know if you're receiving these transmissions and if you contacted the authorities.

[20:22 NZA – *voice report; ed*, Ziegler-Ash whispers during the whole of the following transcript] – I can't believe it! I found the wagon. Barry is going to flip! I followed the hidden path I'd been on and wandered into a thicket of tall trees. The wagon is half obscured by the foliage and a tangle of thick, brown roots. [*the sound of rustling and ocean waves*] I almost walked right past it – it's so dark, and this part of the trail is so overgrown. I'm not surprised that people have only caught a glimpse of this thing, even in the daylight when it would be more visible. The air here smells strongly of salt and hibiscus, and something else. Something... dirty. I don't mean dirty as in sex-dirty, I mean like dirt. Old dirt. A light just turned on in the wagon – it's shining through the fabric top, and I swear I just saw a shadow move inside. [*clunking noises, the sound of Nylah's breath*]. Okay, I've decided to hang back in case there really is a vagrant living in the wagon. I remember you briefing us on the island, saying that it used to be home to Saint-Martin's mentally ill. I think you said it was over a hundred or two hundred years ago – so I suppose it's possible that some hermit ancestor of someone who lived here could still be living on the island. While I'm more inclined to believe just that – a human who prefers the isolation of the island – I am going to do a cursory walk-through of the site. Let Barry know I'm being careful, okay? [*a grunt and more quiet clunks*] As I said, the landscape is overgrown and hidden from view – certainly from the main Marine Trail at least, but I can't imagine it'd be easily seen from anywhere, on the island or off. The moonlight only shines through the overgrowth a little, and the wagon itself is green – almost the same green as the brush. On a dark night this whole area would be invisible. Standing next to the wagon, you can't see any lights from Saint-Martin at all. With my flashlight turned off, it's very dim – but I can still see because of the light inside the wagon. I would have expected it to be louder here – the sound of the ocean waves is somewhat muted, maybe by all the trees and bushes? I don't know, but there aren't even any birds. Every now and then I hear the faint sounds of what I assume are small animals – maybe those little lizards skittering around, or mice. The air feels very still, though, and very thick and humid. Like I said, it smells like flowers and the smell of the ocean is very strong, too. I think what I meant when I said that it smells dirty is that it smells earthy, if that makes sense.

Okay, I'm going to take some baseline images. Hold on, I'm going to switch off my recorder and move to video.

[20:51 NZA – *video report*] – This is Nylah Ziegler-Ash on Pinel Island at the site of the hidden wagon on July 8, 2020 at 8:51 PM. Going quiet now. [*ed.*, video footage indicates that Ziegler-Ash crept around the scene in silence; her footsteps are audible but very quiet, and the sound of waves is similar to a dim hiss in the background. The camera does not pick up a great deal, other than thick underbrush and several trees. While Ziegler-Ash refers to the wagon being present, it does not appear in this section of footage at all. At 21:01 the footage indicates that Ziegler-Ash found a spot in which to settle in and observe her surroundings, as the camera becomes stationary. At 21:17, the camera jolts and the image swings wildly.] A curtain across the back of the wagon just swung aside, and light from inside is giving me slightly better visibility. What looks like a human ribcage is resting on the tiny porch. [*loudly*] Hello? My name is Nylah Ziegler-Ash. I'm sorry to disturb you – I'm conducting an investigation of Pinel Island… I'm terribly sorry, sir. I didn't realize anyone was living on the island. Do you mind if I ask you a few questions?… [*ed.*, footage does not pick up the sound of a second voice, nor an image of to whom Ziegler-Ash is speaking] No, I'm not here alone – my husband is on the Marine Trail, probably waiting for me on the beach… have you lived here long?… oh, yes, I'd love to come in for a cup of tea. [*ed.*, footage indicates that Ziegler-Ash walks into a shadowed space, and her footsteps can be heard on what sound like wooden stairs. A few seconds later, hinges squeak, and bright light floods the camera. The view is of a dented wood-planked floor with dark stains – there is speculation that perhaps Ziegler-Ash did not want the subject to know they were being filmed] Thank you, Mr.… oh, Dr. Holmes. Thank you – this is so nice of you. Your little house is so hidden – you must have lived here a very long time… wow, that *is* a long time… how have you managed to evade detection? There are rumors about the island, but… and you live here alone? Oh… you know, maybe I should go – you seem busy. That's quite a collection of tools you have. I don't want to keep you from – uh, no, I wasn't aware. That's – I'll pass, thank you. It's not something I'd like to see. Did you... is there something in this tea? I feel [*Ziegler-Ash's shoes come into view – brown hiking boots with blue laces – and she appears to be staggering. Seconds later, falls to her knees, then collapses to the floor. The camera points at her chin, picking up Ziegler-Ash's mouth.*] Let me... no... I... please let... [*a force pulls Ziegler-Ash quickly away from the camera, and her body is flung backward and up at an angle. She lands heavily on the floor seconds later with a high-pitched groan. The camara struggles to focus on a small white object that bounces toward it until finally the focus crystallizes on a single molar. Ziegler-Ash's breathing is wet – and she is yanked backward again and lands off camera with a hard thud. What looks like blood splashes across the floor. Ziegler-Ash screams for the next twenty minutes, then falls silent. The lights go out, and the screen is dark once more. Several sounds are picked up in the next 33 minutes, but nothing definitive. We assume the battery power failed at 22:00, as there is nothing more recorded on the camera beyond that point.*[1]]

[22:07 BA *voice report; ed.*, Ash's voice is ragged, his words rushed – as if he is running] – It won't stop. It's been hours – it follows, and a woman... been hearing screams, horrible screams. It sounds like my Nylah, but I can't... whenever I turn toward, it gets in front of me and seems to come straight for... the squeak of the wheels, whatever is... not sure if you're getting these... I'm in trouble. Have to find Nylah. Can't shake it. The island... the whole island... breathing, breathing, like I'm in the lungs of some awful thing. God, help me!

---

1   Audio recordings from Ziegler-Ash's phone and camera were analyzed for electronic voice phenomenon (EVP). Several anomalies were picked up, particularly when Ziegler-Ash was inside the wagon. At 21:19, a low voice is heard to growl, "come in," and at 20:24 we hear several voices laughing, which continues for well over a fifteen minute period. Outside the wagon, a voice can be heard whispering "Holmes comes," "please go," and "no" at various points.

[22:32 BA *voice report*; *ed.*, the VM opens with Ash screeching. When he speaks, his voice is high-pitched and panicked] – Oh, god. Oh god! I found a body, and so help me I think it's Nylah. It's her pack on the ground. The body is – oh my god. [*Ash screams and gibbers*] Oh god, Nylah, hang on, baby. You have to send help right now – she's alive. Nylah, sweetie, what… is that… is that the wagon? [*Ash screams again, and the phone goes dead*]

Conclusion: Barry Ash was discovered at approximately 08:00 the following morning by employees of the restaurants on Pinel Island. He was found, lying face-down, at the entrance to the Marine Trail. His equipment, as well as Nylah Ziegler-Ash's bag and equipment, were found with him. Ash suffered several injuries too gruesome to describe. Those that found him report that he could do nothing but whimper, although he did scream the words "wagon" and "Holmes", as well as Nylah's name, until he succumbed of his injuries at approximately 08:57. Nylah Ziegler-Ash's body has never been recovered. Since her disappearance, at least two other hikers have gone missing. We cannot rule out a murderous person living in a wagon on Pinel Island; however, given the EVP work done inside and outside the alleged wagon, as well as the disturbing footage from inside the wagon, we feel comfortable labeling the island haunted, and dangerously so. Do not risk staying on Pinel Island after the last ferry leaves for the day – and do not, under any circumstances, go in search of the wagon (which we assume to be the source of the haunting) at any time of day.

VIOLET GREEN

The wing case reflects the sun in furious emerald, as Erika twists and angles the beetle towards and against the light. For every beam that strikes the shell, it lashes another back at the sun in a blaze of jet black and electric green. 'It's beautiful,' I say.

Erika's icy bemusement hits as sharply as the light. I might as well have said *it's dead*, which is equally self-evident. 'It's perfect,' she replies. Barely smothered victory sparkles behind her tight purple lips, contoured cheeks and hard, kohl eyes.

'For what?' But I know, feel the answer tipping in my chest on the balance point between excitement and dread. My throat is so tense I don't know if I want to smile or throw up.

'For you, Vi.' Erika tilts the beetle again, playing it off against the sun. It's barely as long as an index fingernail but Erika, a year into her apprenticeship as a taxidermist, is already practiced in finding exactly the level of pressure to bend her subject into position with just enough force to keep it from breaking. She's nearly a foot shorter than me but has only ever seemed to look down on any other person, just as I can only ever imagine looking up at her. 'I'll set it in resin. Easily be dry by tonight.'

'I thought we weren't going tonight,' I say.

She stiffens, only a little, the cat who senses the prey but doesn't even let its ears twitch. Just before the shimmer on the pavement stopped us dead, we'd admitted to each other how, for our own opposite reasons, neither was ready: to accept Luke's invitation, to face the Gatekeepers, to see The House again. Returning might show everyone else how little we cared, how far we'd moved on; all it would show us would be the extent of our addiction. 'Look, it's dead,' Erika says. 'I really don't see the problem.'

I look down at the empty pavement, a duller grey than it ever seemed before the beetle. No, Erika doesn't see the problem. Problems melt obediently as Erika steps through them, unharmed and unaffected as a ghost through what to me would be a solid wall.

'It'll draw the right attention. On you, anyway.' She glares her practiced beam of kind, encouraging jealousy at my chest.

I smile acceptance of the compliment, but cannot make it reach my eyes. Yes, I have boobs, and height. But Erika has everything else. Instinct. Courage. History. And Erika left by choice.

Yet all it would take is my agreement, to melt reality to a future of Erika's chosen shape. And that thought is more hypnotic than the sparks of light from the shell, drawing my eyes back to the way she's still turning the beetle towards and against the sun.

The House grabs you by the corner of your eye as soon as you step through the mess of willows into Luke's thin, entirely missable private road. Just five minutes from the university they all left two summers ago and I, a year to go without them, feel I've barely entered. I never even noticed this road before they brought me here, as if their world existed by invitation only.

At first The House is just a red-grey slanted roof, peering over the cherry blossoms that line the path. It hides there, deliberately badly, watching and following, skipping beside you above the hedges all the way to the corner of the pond, where the path joins the tarmac and veers left. That's where The House leaps out at you from behind the bushes, blazing its brilliant white-brick welcome and filling my throat with knots because every time I've ever seen it I've known this should – must – be the last. Known as surely as the Gatekeepers let me know I was never meant to be here in the first place, did not fit, could not belong. That the best I can hope for is permission to disappear under Erika's folded wings. And with this wretched, vibrant beetle glowing around my neck on her orders, I can't even hope to do that.

I grip the resin pendant, feeling only the hard, smooth surface, none of the power and colour beneath. I turn to Erika, just a little, the better to hear her ash-grey stilettos stab at the tarmac over the apologetic swishes of my cork wedge sandals. 'I fucking hated living here,' she says as we turn the corner.

I look at her without breaking stride; if I stop walking I will never find the courage to start again. 'Really?'

'You kidding?' She comes into focus with every tree that blocks the sun, her precise steps so smooth it's like the row of trees are passing behind her, rather than her passing in front them. 'Grandiose bollocks.'

When I met Erika and Luke they were still very much together with every appearance of forever, eternity seeming to stretch as far behind as ahead of them. The reason I barely noticed my fascination for Luke back then was it didn't seem any greater than my fascination for Erika, this black queen and red king of the hard, solid chess set of our college – which if I'm honest I still think of as theirs. Each piece proud and certain, knowing its place. Watching them dancing at the centre of a nightclub, talking to them in cigarette breaks that stretched over lectures, vivid and real to me in a way I hadn't known I wasn't to myself, before that became all I knew.

'Here it comes,' Erika hisses from the corner of a smile already set for the audience that will be gathered on the terrace, though we're still too blinded by the dazzle of the sun to see them yet. Multiples of invisible eyes prickle my skin until the dazzle fades enough to see them looking, not at Violet and Erika but at Erika and her strange, oversized shadow that won't seem to fall away. 'Don't know what possessed me, Vi,' she hisses through that practiced, perfect smile. She isn't talking about The House. It's not The House's fault Luke's parents left it to him. All he did was stay, and open it in indiscriminate welcome to their set. I think she left because that was all he was ever likely to do. I don't blame her – even I do not look at The House and see a home – but for a moment I let myself hate her, though I don't quite know what for: having what I want, or not wanting it. I should never have let her bring me back here, in this pathetic attempt to climb back over the gates of paradise.

As we close in on the terrace, The House blocks out the sun. The air is full of honeysuckle, wine and cigarettes, toxic and reassuring, familiar and natural. I never want to be anywhere but here, even if right now I would pay in my own blood to be anywhere else.

The dazzle fades, leaving floating ghosts of green and purple swimming over my vision. As I blink my own imagined colours away, they are upstaged from the corner of my eye by a flash of red. Not the quiet off-red of Luke's hair above the heads of the others – not yet. This red is a stranger. And I know exactly who she is.

'Luke's latest fucking flamingo,' Erika whisper-hisses from the corner of the smile she's aiming at the Gatekeepers. 'There's always a new one. No offence. You were different.' I feel the nickname tightening around my mind, sticking to the image like a label to a bottle, as I follow her in.

The Gatekeepers stand either side of the stranger. I

never remember which is Karl and which is Kyle, but their identical smiles freeze in position as we close in: the one with jet-black gelled hair and white skin so thin it looks like it should hurt; the other confidently obese with bleach-white hair, an exaggerated smile and narrow, angry eyes.

Luke's new flamingo leans back from them, on the edge of the terrace. Like me, and like him, she's taller than everyone else. Unlike me, she barely listens to the Gatekeepers, looks less at them than at the steak tartare finger-food she grips between long silver nails, at a distance from the mesh and glitter of her strapless scarlet dress. I see before we move into earshot, with certainty that wraps itself around my throat, the difference between her response and mine to the stories I know they're telling. She isn't offering – fighting back with – her own, desperately proving her existence under the onslaught of theirs as I did. She's listening comfortably, from the distance of our natural height. It could have been that easy.

'Darlings!'

The Gatekeepers' twin pairs of eyes turn, and they greet Erika with the embraces her aura of entitlement demands. The thin one – Karl? – wraps his arms around her for a moment, like a puzzle that doesn't quite fit. He leans back to nod a greeting, not so much to me as over my shoulder and beyond as if hoping someone better is behind. It's unbearable how recently I saw them as Luke's cheerleaders; that I was banished before I realised they were his generals.

As Erika joins in and the recitation of previous parties flows beneath us, I watch Luke's new flamingo watching them. There's real blood on her blood-red lipstick from the steak, a dark drip becoming a stain at the corner. I'd never known the difference between blood-red and the red of blood till now. Her lips part around the words, 'Is that a mouse skull?'

'Thanks for noticing.' Erika strokes the silver chain looping through its gold-leaf eye sockets. 'I found it here, actually. When we were doing up the front room.' Her smile belies the powerplay, but her use of a more distant past than theirs flickers in Karl and Kyle's eyes, deliberate and significant as a drawn sword. 'All my pieces are found.'

'Ahh, you're *that* Erika.' The flamingo's blood-red smile is lazily confident, only watching the show because it happens to be on. 'The, err...'

'Vegan taxidermist?' As she indicates the front room window where she found the mouse, I let myself look when the others do. Beyond the glass, the fireplace is almost visible between the mahogany shelves and green velvet curtains where previous versions of Luke and me sit, stand, lie together. The pictures of us are so vivid in my mind I wonder how no one else can see them. 'I only use what's died naturally.'

'The word I think Luke used was...'

'Witch?' Erika's smile has a rich, invisible layer of challenge.

The flamingo returns it. I can't tell blood from lipstick now, the shades have smeared into one. 'Is your company really called "Dead of Islington"? Or is that just Luke's joke?'

'Not Luke's, my grandfather's. This is my latest piece, this morning's work.' She puts a hand on my shoulder, encourages me to give the beetle a demonstrative twist. 'Karl, Kyle, you remember Violet?'

'Ahh, the fresher in the library. How are you, Violet,' says one without a question mark, the other obediently looking at my chest without passing my eyes. I always forget which of them it was I threw out for smoking, but not the hatred in both their eyes when Luke stayed talking to me at the till.

'This morning?' The flamingo frowns. 'How could it set that quickly?'

'Magic,' Erika says. The challenge is solid as iron, hard and delicate as ice. She leaves a pause long enough to show everyone no one dares challenge her, before she laughs and pats the flamingo's arm, looking down despite being a foot below. 'The colour's turned out well, hasn't it?'

It's almost comforting, that the ghosts I see walking that room must be so much shallower than the years of ghosts Erika must see. Mine only cover and eclipse my fresher year, weeknights when I "might as well stay", "no point in extra journeys", until I "might as well" stay at weekends too. Then, that Friday night just as the cold spell broke, when we'd had the whole weekend ahead of us, he hadn't mentioned the Gatekeepers or the outside world once, then Karl or Kyle texted they were on their way. I took my silent orders from Luke as unquestioningly as he took his from them; had minutes to leave by what Luke calls the back door but was built to be the servants' entrance.

'Taxidermy's a steady job,' Erika is telling the flamingo. 'Someone's always going to want a moment in time stuffed.'

'They should stuff us here, in this one, shouldn't they?' The fatter, white-blond Gatekeeper nudges the thin, darker one. 'I don't remember much about last year's party! Never do after Luke's parties do we?'

I haven't dared look up at Luke's bedroom window since we arrived, especially now we're right below it. I know I'll see her if I do: the ghost of the self I so briefly, standing where I left her. I dare not meet my own eyes, staring down at the terrace and know that behind her, invisible from down here, will be Luke's chin resting briefly on her bare shoulder. "Nice, isn't it, this?" was all he'd said in that eternal moment, my smile returning his flicker of a smile reflected in the glass, before he walked off to shower and I stayed at the window, looking down at the white terrace, both it and the future a clean, blank page. I cannot bear the peace I will see in my – her – face if I look up there now: my own ghost, the part of me that will always be standing at that window. I cannot look up, cannot meet her eyes, cannot tell her why I gave in so easily, why I let her become a ghost.

The flamingo is looking at me.

I feel it before I raise my eyes. Sympathy flashes between us, the first real smile of the night. We look away again, silent allies, sharing the joke that is everyone else. Then the flamingo looks back at the others, smiles much as Erika does, brightly and safely encased in her own resin. Exactly what I hadn't done. Where I only ever saw tragedy, she's already seen the joke. It's ludicrous. This game they play. This whole ridiculous chess set, each piece so carefully shaped and positioned there may as well be nothing left beneath, hollow and empty and pouring whatever's left of its soul into the shape of its armour until all that's left is the outside. Yet I let them win, took myself at their evaluation, disappeared from the board.

I grab Erika's hand, emulating with all my strength the casual confidence of disappearing for something socially acceptable like drugs, not socially unacceptable like tears. When the bathroom door is locked behind us I stop moving completely, caught and frozen by my own eyes in the mirror. My face could be anyone's. The beetle is bright around my neck, but my face is blank but for tears, white against the purple walls and gold framed mirror. I do not see myself in that mirror. My only self is the ghost at Luke's window, that only I can see.

Out of my eyeline, in the corner of the mirror, Erika sits down on the lid of the toilet. Sometime in the silence there's a knock and a yell, and Erika's voice yelling back at the yeller to fuck off, claiming some detailed and elaborate rite of blood or make-up or both. It must work, because all goes quiet beyond the door except for one of the albums I bought Luke at Christmas playing through the speaker system all over The House.

'Vi? Violet?'

'It's so bright. So itself.' The tears running down my face miss the rock of resin. I press my fingers over it. 'Why the hell would you give it to me?'

'Because I knew you wanted it.' My face in the mirror is replaced by Erika's dark, perfumed shoulder. 'Flock of fucking flamingos.' Her voice is muffled, stretched by the possibility of tears. 'The Gatekeepers. Those smiles. The same smiles they were at seventeen. Every party, every year, trying harder and harder to capture the first. To crawl back. This terrified, hypnotised little world, climbing into its own dream, dancing in front of its own mirrors. Afraid to look away from its own reflection in case it realises it doesn't fucking exist.'

'This beetle...' I say.

'As if growing up and moving on was more frightening than being trapped in a fucking photograph. As if holding on to a moment in time like a hostage was fucking immortality.'

'I thought...'

'You thought it was an example?' She pulls away, reaches for the beetle around my neck. It shimmers lightly, glittering green and gold under the electric light. 'It's not an example, Vi. It's a warning. Find the right conditions and light will go right on shining without anything left inside. Call it desperation, or call it magic...' She shrugs, sits back down on the lid of the toilet. 'You dodged a bullet. You dodged the bullet I took. I'm still bleeding, Vi. Why would you come back for this?'

'Because I want it.' I sit on the edge of the bath, look from the beetle to her eyes.

'Are you sure, Vi?' she says. Because I know what

I'm seeing is impossible, I ignore her eyes changing colour as she looks at me. 'Because I don't. I don't want you sealed in resin. Something of you will die.'

'Yes.' I look into her eyes, as hard as she ever looked at me. Something of me needs to die. Something of me should have cared less, fought more. 'I want my shell, Erika.' It doesn't matter that what I'm seeing makes no sense. It must be just that I've never looked up long enough, that's why I thought her eyes were brown not blue. Or I'm so drunk I'm just imagining that their strange centres look like balls of flickering blue fire. 'I have as much right to be here as anyone else.'

'I know that, Vi.'

'But I didn't!' I look down at the beetle. As impossible as I know it to be, her eyes seem to be mirrored, looking back at me from inside the pendant: bright blue fire, burning electric as the green did under the sun, flowing like water inside what I thought was solid resin. 'So neither did the world.'

'Violet…'

I shake my head, gripping the beetle in one hand, reach for hers with the other.

She looks at me like she's seeing me for the first time.

For what could be minutes or hours, I watch myself appearing in the mirror, beside the reflection of Erika's face considering my own. Her kohl eyes, brown again, glimmer with a mixture of pride and sadness. With every streak of the brush, the beetle and I look more and more like we belong. There are moments I want to tell Erika to stop, to take the make-up off and leave me as I was; that the absolute safety of disappearing under her wings is too great a loss for the gain of being myself, of standing alone. But then I blink and watch my eyelids shimmering the exact electric green as the beetle around my neck, the colour she'd spotted on the grey pavement and recognised as perfect. The edges are sharper, the colours precise and vivid, and I recognise the beginnings of the face she saw in me. This face is not mine, not yet. But I feel myself rising to meet it, filling my armour. I am ready to look the world eye to eye, safe behind the mask of my own face.

In the glass, Erika smiles. Beside her, as the same person I've always been smiles beneath it, I watch the face that is becoming mine smile back.

There's rain in the air when we return to the terrace. It hasn't quite begun but it's hanging there, a heavy, present absence. The Gatekeepers home in, curious and intent as drawn swords. 'Violet, you look great,' one of them says, and both wait for me to provide an explanation.

'Thanks,' I say, looking over their heads to wave at Luke's new flamingo, not that I think she has any intention of being that after tonight. Erika imperceptibly leans into my shoulder, a nudge that might be drawing in the reins as much as it might be support or congratulation. She needn't worry. There will be no apology for myself, no more permission sought.

'I've just realised I don't know your name,' I say when she's close enough.

'Bridget.' Her smile is uncomplicated, real, making me realise how very little else is. 'I love your dress.'

'Thanks.' It's the one thing about me that predates The House. 'Yours too.'

'Thanks, but it's not really me.' Beside us, the Gatekeepers have started telling Erika and each other as loudly as they can about how drunk they are, and previous parties where they'd been drunker still. 'Doesn't this place…' Luke's hair blazes in the corner of my eye, from one of the gaggles around the buffet tables. She sees it too and turns her back, lowering her voice in spite of the noise. 'Does it make you feel like you're… you know, playing yourself?'

'Not the place,' I say. Strange to look at someone cast as my enemy and find a genuine friend, and know she wouldn't even be standing here if I hadn't broken the rules, refused to play the game. All this strategizing in the ranks, yet the king only moves one inch at a time, barely registering the wider game being played around him. 'It's just some of the people.'

'Violet and Luke met in the *library* of all things…' Kyle or Karl shouts over their conversation – or recitation – with Erika. His voice is too fast, too urgently casual. 'Can you believe it Bridget, Luke and a librarian?' He pauses for the laughter. 'Of course, anywhere but university Luke and Violet would never have looked at each other—'

Yeah,' I interrupt, 'because no two people ever just met in a bar.'

It's a new kind of silence, and lasts only a moment before Erika and Bridget laugh with me, a louder, truer sound. Karl and Kyle try laughing too, their desperate looks to each other for cues perfect reflections of each other, too far off script to find their way back without giving away that there is a script; that the double-act is a performance. My eyes drift higher, to the bedroom window where I know my ghost still stands.

She hasn't faded at all. Why was I so afraid to look at her when she was me all the time? Now I look at her, can smile back at that moment, I wonder if perhaps that's the feeling of belonging I've had since I first walked in here: not pulled by the ghost of a past I didn't rise to meet, but a ghost of the future? What if that's what the Gatekeepers' fear: that my presence haunts them not from a badly fitting moment of the past, but from a future they do not rule? A pawn that reaches the opposite side of the board, becomes a queen on her own terms?

'Did the mouse really die here?' Bridget asks as we edge from the Gatekeepers towards the buffet table at the end of the terrace.

'Luke and Erika tell the dead mouse story in different ways.' I let myself smile, let it be my joke to share. After all, I've reached the other side of the board. The endgame has begun. 'What does overlap is Erika sold all the jewellery he'd ever given her when she left, but kept the skull.' Karl and Kyle look over and glare or smile from time to time, and we smile back until they look away. 'She only kept what she'd found or created, what was truly hers.'

Bridget looks at the Gatekeepers, then at the climbing ivy hanging down the wall by the French windows, as if trying to tell the difference. 'Make sure you do too. Whether you stay or go. Be yourself. It scares them.'

'I kind of felt like I didn't have one.'

'You kidding?' She looks at me, not the make-up. 'You're the only real person here.'

'Don't believe everything you hear about me,' Luke grins as the taxi pulls up. The silence between the first words we've spoken to each other all night is packed with apology and hope. Knowing the language now, I pretend not to notice either. 'She's an accomplished witch.'

'Not a witch. A vegan taxidermist.' Erika's air-kisses just miss his cheeks, as if she can't quite be bothered to reach any higher. Then she steps down to the driveway.

'It's alright, I'm protected.' I kiss his cheek for only slightly too long before I turn away and feel his eyes following.

'So,' Luke says.

I turn back. The same shy, open smile as always, its polite, chivalrous expectation that someone else will make the choices, pick their cues. I'm not going to. Not this time. I just wait, listening, and don't look away.

'See you soon then?' he says at last.

'I'd like that,' I say. Beneath where we stand on the steps to the hallway, somewhere in the garden Karl and Kyle's matching, desperate laughter rises in the dark. Bridget is long gone, with my phone number and a second-year librarian she'd asked me to introduce. The bushes of the driveway are full of crickets and the scent of wine and cigarettes is fading behind lilac and jasmine. I can feel the private world Luke and I knew here underneath this public one, no longer ghost images but finding each other, returning to each other, settling into one reality.

I smile back at Luke as I close the door, then the silhouettes of the cherry trees along the driveway are flying by us. I had no idea it had got so dark; every star is visible now I look up. As we turn out of the drive, I don't need to look back. For the first time, I can see every detail rush past, can watch the stars and lampposts shooting by beyond the glass and know I'll see it again.

'Tighten the cord.'

I'd almost forgotten her. Beside me, on the backseat by the other window, Erika is smiling, more quietly than I've ever seen. Her eyes flash blue briefly, and then it's like looking at black glass. Somehow I know I won't ever see those colours again. As the drive rolls away behind us I see her bending to the pavement this morning, picking up the electric green beetle from the hot ground; recognizing it, not for what it was but for what it was waiting for permission to be. 'Erika…'

'Tighten the cord,' she says again. 'It's yours now. Own it.'

I sit beside her in the dark as the ever-changing world flashes past us, turning the beetle so all the passing streetlamps and headlights bounce fluorescent beams off the wing-case, enough colour that some of the sparks will find her as hers found mine, and keep on reflecting back.

TO PRAY AT YOUR TEMPLE

She danced like no one was watching. The lights slick as they bathed her body in violet and blue, a settling bruise that twisted and spun in time to the music, or at least to the music that played in her head. An adipocere of sweat gathered in the hollows of her neck, clavicles imprisoning the neon lights, a penumbral necklace that cojoined and snaked its way down between her meagre breasts. Saying a prayer to Saint Vitus, she shook off the shackles they tied her down with. Raising skeletal arms she devoted herself to the litany. Stigmata encircling her at the wrist and ankle, a memento, a remembrance of those left behind, of those held in beds, and chairs, and arms. Of those not allowed this dance.

~×~

In the beginning they called us vain, as we averted our eyes from the very image of ourselves.

Then they called us wanton, as we swathed ourselves in habit and mantle.

They called us histrionic, as we kept our heads down at our father's table.

Before finally they called us ill.

~×~

There was to be no supplication to our gods here, no devotions made to our saints, to Jerome, to Catherine de Siena, or Rosa de Lima. Instead we're told to put our faith in Aesculapius, in

P
E
N
N
Y

J
O
N
E
S

Aceso and Aegle. That our enlightenment is only possible, if we turn our backs on our old beliefs and give ourselves completely to their new faith. Though I do not know why they would covet our conversion, we are unsuitable as acolytes; unwilling to take communion, unable to find meaning in their words. They say we are blind to the truth, our perceptions as warped as our bodies, as we sit, heads bowed, waiting for them to leave so we can find meaning in their silence, truth in their echoes, solace in the quiet they leave in their wake.

There were many of us there in those hallowed halls, those unbelievers hollowed in stomach and spirit. For most of us, we had taken up our vows, our tears hushed, our prayers whispered to deities that we dared not address, except in secret. Though occasionally those gods of Paean would trip up, and the heretic that stumbled through those doors would not be broken, would not have retreated fearfully inside the withered husk of their body. But instead would call upon us to worship at their temple, to gaze upon their sharp angles, to lay our hands upon their fragile skin, to understand the message that they brought to us within that desiccated parchment. They did not come quietly, with muted liturgies hidden behind cracked lips and parched tongues. They came shouting and screaming, speaking in tongues that no one understood, a glossology of threats and curses and promises.

It was due to the sacrifice of one of these martyrs that I finally managed to escape those sainted halls. As they lay upon the ground that their feet had worn twisted paths along, crucified by attendants who held them still as their skin was pinched and prepped, pierced by angels who swoop down, waiting for them to quiet, to lay in peace, to sleep. So they could bind their feet, calloused and blistered from the miles they walked within their miniscule cell, their penance. An attrition which even when they removed those martyrs shoes they couldn't stop.

When all the eyes were upon the fallen, I slipped away, a shadow, staying close to those who had come to visit, the mothers, the fathers, the lovers, the enemies. Hiding my bare feet and unorthodox clothes amongst those who had dressed for outside, for normality, for the world. I escaped amongst the fug of smoke that masked the doorway, ash and embers my shoes, holding my head aloft – my only disguise – I looked ahead.

I returned to where it first began. To that time when I stood erect and elegant, poised and pointed as my body melted to the music. Where my limbs were twisted. Where my feet and torso were bound in silk and bone until I shone above the polished ground. I thought I was beautiful then as I waited in repose, as their hands grasped and their fingers gripped, as they lifted and turned me, an awkward pirouette, as I straightened and folded, as their voices cut me deep: *Too limp, too round, too soft…* Their words hardened me, made me slice away at the layers that held me back.

Now I have returned again to dance for them. The music plays, a jarring of notes, of hard accents, sharp and precise. I turn to face them, their judgement masked by the discordance of the notes. I dance for them. I dance for me. I dance for those who I left behind. I dance until my feet are shod in sanguine slippers, until my skin is swathed in sweat and my peardrop-sweet breath is cut short. I dance my dance, and my dance is sublime.

THE FALL OF PAN

It was always in the hazel grove I heard him, whimpering softly like a new born lamb. I walked this way often, taking in the view that carved across the land, changing and morphing from hill to crag, dale to wood and patchwork fields to finally the cold bleak sea where the power station coughed its foul breath. A smattering of rooftops rose up the valley like an invasion to meet the farms that dotted the lower hills.

It was early spring and the trees were budding, returning to life after winter's death. Dark green moss furred the trunks and hung from the limbs as lichen sprouted, pale and frosted silver, over the branches. The scent of earth filled my lungs as, breathing deeply, my boots disturbed the leafy mulch, and soft black pressed through the crisp rusted woodland floor.

It came again, a whimper, and a small movement flitted behind the mossy trunks. I called out, following my line of sight to where the movement occurred. As I stared I noticed tiny fingertips gripping either side of a narrow trunk. Bony and twig-like they unfurled and pulled sharply away. Approaching slowly, I begun to hum a tune, an old folk song of mist and mountain tops. Turning softly my gaze reached behind the tree and stared down into tangled bramble and bracken.

A small flash of fur, brown and tattered, scrabbled with little hands clutching and burrowing into the moss. A head turned away cowering and shook as the whimpers increased. I

JULIE ANN REES

smoothed the hunched and shuddering shoulders, cold and scabby to the touch. My hand recoiled and I flushed with embarrassment. The shaggy body contorted into misshapen legs, twisted and swollen, where little hooves, cloven and cracked, kicked at the dirt.

He was smaller and weaker than last time. His head looked up from a spine of neck, wobbling, the once-mighty horns broken and shrunken. I sat and pulled off my rucksack, handing him an apple, a cox's from the tree in my garden. Crooked fingers reached and took whilst chipped yellow teeth struggled to break the skin. He chewed slowly, glancing at me. I could feel his shame.

I opened my flask and poured some chamomile tea, sweetened with honey. His nostrils widened and after a sip I offered the cup. He drank, flinching from the heat, his lips twisting a growl, his eyes flashing with a glimpse of old power. I smiled and shrugged. "It's hot, be careful." He offered it to me, his face a grimace. I blew on the liquid and gave it back. He continued to drink and soon his expression relaxed.

"Why do you come?" His voice was like the whispering of leaves, the rumble of thunder, the burble of brooks and the pattering of rain on the forest floor. Again I shrugged, then looking around me at the wonder of nature and at a loss for words, I indicated the little wood and the view saying, "Because it's beautiful and helps me feel alive."

"Then why am I dying?" His voice cracked as he handed me the cup. I didn't know what to say. How could I apologise for the human race, when I knew they would not stop until everything was dead. Sighing, I replaced the cup and flask into my rucksack and watched the boughs of the hazel sway and dance in the breeze. A squirrel screeched from above and I noticed a black-nosed prickly rustling under a pile of leaves, uncurling from hibernation.

"Walk with me?" I asked, and he nodded. At first he struggled to stand, his crumpled limbs buckled under a body so frail that he fell to the mud. I thought he'd disappeared but a gnarled hand reached out and I helped him, taking his weight whilst he slipped and tottered on shaky bent legs, to stand on crumbling hooves, quivering.

We moved slowly to the edge of the grove and listened to the tapping drum of a woodpecker shaping a nest deep in the bowels of a tree. Honeysuckle had begun to tangle itself through the shrubs, twisting and turning, the small clusters of green not yet ready for blooming the heady sweet fragrance that would engulf this side of the wood in summer. As I breathed the sharp fresh scent of spring he did too. His aged nut brown nostrils cracked and flared, his eyes opened wider to absorb the scene of green and life emerging, the cold earth birthing once more.

My eyes closed and I heard his breath snort forth, and my mind's eye saw the proud king strut and cajole with the woodland creatures leaping over the mountains, a haunting tune in his wake. He was tall and muscled, toned and handsome, his skin smooth to the touch, covered with downy hair that smelt of animal musk, both raw and primal. My vision joined his and I gasped at the wild and vigorous land stretching before me through eyelids held shut.

That ancient view was not divided into patchwork farms; rather the swaying heads of trees swarmed up the sides of mountains giving way only to the golden gorse or purple heather shrubs that crowned the crags. Even the sea shone with crystal intensity, the power station just a future nightmare, unformed. I gripped his hand and opened my eyes when, weakly, he sagged against me. Taking the brittle body into my arms I carried him back to the hazel grove and placed his twisted form safely in the hollow of a tree.

Tears were flowing down my cheeks and I wiped them away, not wanting him to feel my pity. What worth is the pity of a silly weeping woman to his kind? He began to whimper once more and his breath slowed. I kissed his scared and scabbed cheeks, my lips catching against the coarseness of his skin. His little hoof slipped out of the hollow and I repositioned him, tucking him in safely and womb-like out of sight.

"They are coming," he said. "Even now I can feel the Earth tremble beneath the huge machines that tear and murder." I lowered my eyes, not wanting to know, but I knew he was right.

"I can still see you, and have done for years," I stated, attempting to sound positive, like a mother consoling a child with lies. A low wheezy rumble escaped his lips and I thought he was choking so I helped him sit up, then realised it was a chuckle. He held my face in his small twiggy hands, sharp and bark-like on my cheeks. His eyes bored into mine, beady like a blackbird's.

"That's because you believe," he said simply, and his chapped lips, edged with sap-like spittle, brushed my forehead in a woody kiss. Tears blurred my sight causing me to blink and I inhaled the scent of decaying wood. My eyes refocused and where a knotted brown hand had gripped my own, a hazel branch, green with buds, pressed into my palm. I traced my fingers over the rough-shaped knoll of the tree where his outline remained carved in bark.

I planted the branch in my garden and watched it take root and thrive, becoming a sapling and then a small tree. I celebrated when the first male catkins sprouted in autumn and relished in gathering the abundance of hazelnuts for Yule. The old hazel wood and most of the fields are long gone these days. A housing estate has grown in their place and litter decorates the land like cancerous moles.

I never saw the sad beast again but every midsummer I hear an uncanny fluting and imagine I see him curve his body forth from the young hazel in my garden and spring leaping and cavorting through the land. He is followed by an array of forgotten creatures streaming forth on hoof, wing and claw.

I lean out of my bedroom window into the cool evening air and relish the sensation of goosebumps pricking my skin through the thin silk of my blouse. "I believe I believe I believe," I cry out, watching June's rose-blushed moon rise over the rooftops. The scent of musk hangs heavy in the night and the soft brush of beasty breath dances along my spine to tremble through my hair, and my heart flutters to the beat of a cloven hoof.

SKY EYES

Stories are spells.

They can enchant, beguile, destroy or transform. The correct words, arranged in a particular way, can raise and dash hopes, make the reader laugh, cry, fall in love. It is essential, then, to tell a story – an event, after all, that has occurred somewhere, in a time past, present or yet to come – in the best way possible. This story is about events that will be unable to occur until you, the reader, has read every word.

～≻≺～

The Beast-Boy sat on his chair and gazed around the room. It was sparsely furnished, perhaps too sparsely, he thought, although he liked to live frugally – in material terms, anyway. The building was ruined in places but it was home, the only real indulgence being the lush rugs that had been bought rather than rescued from a skip. He got up and walked through the long room, glancing at the shaft of sunlight that suddenly intruded through the hole in the roof, lighting a circle of floor. He left the building and stood in the yard. The bushes there were overgrown but he liked them that way for the privacy they provided. The oak tree was heavy with acorns. He picked one and looked it over, then took out the bone he'd been carrying in his pocket. If he swallowed the acorn he could be fairly sure of the outcome, but he didn't know what type of animal the bone came from.

J
U
L
I
E

T
R
A
V
I
S

217

Swallowing it would be a step into the unknown. He studied it — it was long and thin and jointed in several places. The Beast-Boy raised his face to the sky, opened his mouth and slipped the bone down his throat. He took a gulp of water from a nearby bucket and returned inside.

When he'd last swallowed an acorn, the effect had been profound. His skin had toughened, its texture rough and dry, and leaves had sprouted from some of his fingers, but it was his mind that had suffered the biggest change. He had begun to *think* like an oak tree; of great expanses of time, of the seasons — two thousand of them — that he would experience, the lives that would come and go, from the birds in his highest branches to the worms and fungus among his roots to the animals that would die under the shade of his canopy. Humans, too, would die within his radius, by murder and suicide. But these would be infinitesimal events, just part of the endless cycle of life and death. When the effect had worn off — when the acorn had passed through him — it had taken days to adjust to being himself again. He would have been quite happy to remain in his altered state for longer or even to have transformed permanently into an oak tree. It had been an illuminating experience. This new experience — whatever it turned out to be — would also enrich his life. And if it ended it, then that, too, would be fascinating.

One day the Beast-Boy hoped to become a Beast-God. It would take a long time, pushing himself to his limits, before there was any chance of becoming so, but he would not wish the time away. There was no hurry; on the contrary, the journey was vital. And it involved, as far as the Beast-Boy was concerned, nothing he considered a sacrifice — just intense indulgence in all the extremes life could offer.

The bone belonged to a creature that didn't exist.

The Beast-Boy was sure of this, but knew he would nevertheless become it. He was happy with the contradiction and wondered whether his imagination would influence the creature he became. The first effects were subtle. He found himself outside again, gathering twigs then dropping them into the most hidden corner of his living room. The untidy twig-nest grew and when it was finished he sat on it and let himself be overwhelmed with the changes to his body.

～✦～

Nikola P____ had never seen the building before, and this gave her hope; if it could remain hidden from her for so long, then it was surely a safe place. Judging by the plants that had forced their way through the concrete around the rear, it had been derelict for years. She stopped and closed her eyes.

Bird song from the nearby bushes. Wings fluttering inside the building. Water dripping onto metal.

If there's a water supply, there's probably been squatters here, she thought. *There may still be.*

Such a hidey-hole, in these days of hyper-gentrification, was rare. She entered silently through the back door. It was possible that here was a place she could remain hidden. And if the building turned out to be full of squatters, she could creep away just as quickly.

She found herself in a kitchen – complete with a tap dripping into the steel sink and a small table with mismatched chairs around it. The building was an industrial unit; part office, part workshop. And so quiet it was surely uninhabited after all. But Nikola P____ crept through the building, ever cautious. Her life depended on it. And she once again blessed her caution, for lying in a corner was an animal sleeping on a bed of twigs.

Marow examined the Emptiness Machine, as she had so many times before. It was still so full. She ran a finger over the tiny, mother-of-pearl dials and around the wooden frame. Inside the small glass case fog swirled malevolently.

A case full of emptiness.

Marow delighted at the poetry of it. But there was work to be done and when the fog had all gone there would be another kind of poetry to it. The machine was so small, but inside it held so much emptiness. She returned it to her mouth for safekeeping and continued her slow pursuit of Nikola P____.

What kind of animal are you? she wondered. It was unlike anything she'd ever seen. A bit like a long, thin cat that had been crossed with…what? Although deeply asleep its features showed great expression. What would such a creature dream about? Nikola P____ spied a mattress on the other side of the room. It was stained and cold to the touch, but comfortable, and she lay down and slept. When she awoke, the creature had become almost human. Tufts of fur remained on the tops of his ears, but they only enhanced his looks.

He was sitting on an uncomfortable looking chair, looking at her with interest rather than suspicion, and she noticed that his army shorts revealed two wooden legs. Not prosthetics, but actual trees – one was distinctively a silver birch. How had he acquired them? They seemed to be part of him.

"You were an animal before I went to sleep," she said, and immediately felt impolite to have mentioned it. But the man smiled and visibly relaxed.

"I was indeed. And a fierce one at that, although I still don't what I was." He paused. "Would you like some coffee?"

He knew she was keeping things from him, but he understood why — she was clearly running away from something and caution was a method of self-protection. And, judging from her reaction to his transformation, she was escaping something quite out of the ordinary. He was happy to have her stay, but he needed to know what the danger was. All he had drawn from her so far was her name and that she needed help. She spoke good English but he couldn't place her accent. When he'd asked where she came from, she'd muttered *from the inside of a Black Hole*. She'd clearly been through a dreadful time. He mentioned, as casually as he could, how calm she'd been at his appearance.

"I cannot think of many people who would have said what you did when you first saw me. How is it that you're so familiar with the extraordinary?"

He was giving her a tour of the building. Nikola P____ slowed down.

"Unfortunately, I have been unable to avoid it," was her terse response.

Ordinary was a land she used to inhabit. She missed it, but she felt this building to be a place of safety, and the strange young man to be an ally.

"Exactly how much trouble are you in?" he asked gently.

And Nikola P____ had to admit that she really didn't know.

Marow felt as old as the hills and the rock beneath them but she continued nonetheless. It was more than worth it; the Emptiness Machine was all that mattered.

But there was pain, too, the aches and troubles of age. Mere twinges of arthritis in her joints – so long ago! – had become great pain, had become agony. She had built up her muscles and ligaments to cushion the joints, to the extent of deforming her body. An observer would notice movement underneath the skin, bones pushing outwards as Marow moved, at times threatening to tear through flesh but never quite breaking skin. An elongated neck and limbs were a price worth paying for an easing of the pain and more freedom of movement.

She was often alone but never lonely. She spoke to everything – birds, the air, the stars, the souls of dead trees. She spoke to people, too, when the mood took her. Then she would pick the spike from its clever hiding place within the Emptiness Machine's case and drive it into their hearts.

There would be little conversation of worth afterwards.

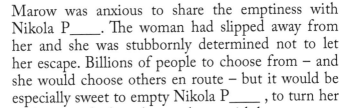

Marow was anxious to share the emptiness with Nikola P____. The woman had slipped away from her and she was stubbornly determined not to let her escape. Billions of people to choose from – and she would choose others en route – but it would be especially sweet to empty Nikola P____ , to turn her soul to a void when she caught up with her.

Marow laughed suddenly. The sound made the birds flee from a nearby tree. A man passing by smiled condescendingly at her. She wheeled around silently behind him, opened her mouth and reached under her tongue with thumb and forefinger. Another short delay wouldn't do any harm.

～∽⊱

Their previous encounter had opened Nikola P____'s eyes to possibilities she had never wanted to consider.

On a rare foray to her local pub, she'd slipped out to the·beer garden for a cigarette and was lighting up when she noticed a man staring at her. He stood, stock still, while a woman next to him attempted to tattoo his chest.

At least, that's what it looked like.

Then she saw the little glass case in the woman's hand, the mist swirling around inside it, the needle penetrating the man's chest. The woman heard the *click* of her lighter and turned her head. Her manner was so ghastly that Nikola P____ dropped her cigarette and ran back into the pub. She was at the front door before she decided that she'd be safer among the drinkers. Eventually the woman appeared and looked slowly around the room. Nikola P____ guessed the woman was older than herself, although it was difficult to tell. In any normal situation she would have wanted the woman to notice her; she had an attractive intensity. But this was not a normal situation. Their eyes met. In contrast to the man's blank stare, the woman's gaze promised so many things. At that moment Nikola P____ knew she should have run from the building, and keep running.

Marow crossed the room. Nikola P____'s expression was one she'd seen before but was no less enjoyable for it; a combination of dread and *want*. Then she was by Nikola P____'s side and whispering in her ear, suggesting the delightful things that would happen if Nikola P____ would follow her to the pub's toilets.

And Nikola P____ was tempted.

Then she remembered the man in the yard. The things this woman promised were lies. She slipped out of Marow's reach and weaved around the drinkers. Fuelled by adrenalin, she was out of the door within moments. Marow ordered a whisky before following.

And so began the hunt.

Nikola P____ had described the encounter as best she could but she couldn't do it justice. How could she describe the air of menace that night? But it was clearly enough for the Beast-Boy. He was suddenly very serious. It was not reassuring.

"Do you know who she is?" she asked him. "Perhaps *you* can tell me how much trouble I'm in?"

The Beast-Boy shook his head as he replied. "I have no idea who she is or what she was doing to that man. If it was a drug it isn't any I've heard of."

Or partaken in.

That meeting had been nine dreadful months ago. Nine months of being on the run – at first going home when she was desperate, sneaking in like an errant teenager to shower, change her clothes and, if she felt safe enough, sleep a little. She had toured her friends' sofas, giving them unconvincing reasons why she couldn't be at home. She worked for as long as she could. For a while she felt safe there and began to think the woman wasn't trying to find her after all. Then came the phone call, the whispering voice promising obscene pleasures, but there was a chill in the tone that froze Nikola P____'s blood and she screamed her own obscenity into the phone and threw her headpiece to the floor. After that it was only a matter of time before she didn't return.

Her life fell apart quickly. The normality and

structure that had often bored her was soon just a memory. All that mattered was survival, fleeing an enemy she knew nothing about – who knew nothing about her – and imagining a dreadful fate if she did not run fast enough. Time went on and her savings were disappearing, so she gave up her flat. No longer wanting to involve her friends she took to staying in cheap b&bs, with increasing paranoia. Most nights she had different neighbours. Many were noisy and argumentative, shattered by illness, redundancy, relationship breakdown. Others were silent. Those were the worse. She imagined them plotting, noting her movements. In one drab hotel she'd seen monsters; outlandish shadows with strange voices. She fled from it after a terrifying, sleepless night. She trusted no one.

By the time she reached the abandoned industrial building and the Beast-Boy she was beginning to think there was only one option left: to let the mysterious woman catch up with her. Facing her might be the only way to stop her life spiralling forever downwards.

All there is is emptiness.

In his sixty seven years on the planet, Karl thought he'd seen everything.

But not this. This was different.

He was floating in Space now. Not in an exhilarating, exploratory way, but in darkness and isolation. Going nowhere, from nowhere.

Karl had obtained his thrills anywhere he could find them, in every country he had hitched and blagged his way around. He'd found pleasure with both women and men, and when a woman had approached him in The Lamb Inn suggesting a unique experience, he had readily agreed. And now here he was. He wasn't dead, he was sure of that. The woman had injected him with something. He felt full and yet empty, his bones and blood and muscles dissolved to nothing. All that was left was his mind. And he dearly wished that it would dissolve, too.

Nikola P____ was a fugitive, then, thought the Beast-Boy. They were sitting in the most habitable room in the building. It was decorated with what looked like ancient cave paintings, the grey, industrial walls almost hidden beneath colourful handprints and outlines of fabulous animals. He observed Nikola P____ as she sat quietly, taking it all in. A smile briefly crossed her face and she closed her eyes.

While she slept, the Beast-Boy pondered the situation they were both now in. Nikola P____ was probably as safe here as she would be anywhere, but her pursuer was an unknown entity. He needed to know what they were up against. Nikola P____ claimed to know nothing about the woman, but having evaded her for this amount of time meant she probably knew more than she was aware of. He walked quietly around the room, found a space on the wall, a good space opposite the window that faced the rising sun, and began to paint. He began with some basic shapes to represent Nikola P____ and himself. He placed them within a protective circle and depicted the building with Marow unable to enter, the trees and bushes acting as spies and defenders. The room had other spells on its walls, most of them lust or luck spells but there were others: a solar eclipse, powerful storms, the Beast-Boy dancing in the garden. The building was in a powerful location – two leys crossed at its centre, which was undoubtedly the reason why the place had been abandoned. The energy rumbled around, creating cracks in the walls and forcing dirty water from the drains. It could have been harnessed for the benefit of whoever was occupying the building, but the Beast-Boy guessed that successive tenants thought the place haunted or just troublesome and didn't stay for long. It would also be the reason the place was impossible to sell. The owner had given up, the 'For Sale' board rotting on the ground near the building's entrance.

The Beast-Boy, of course, was able to use the energy to his advantage – hence the painted spells and the attraction of some strange waifs and strays over the years. Was it this energy that had brought Nikola P____ to his home? She claimed to have been in the area before and had returned to try to give her pursuer the slip, but hadn't felt any pull towards this particular destination. But the Beast-Boy was sure she'd been attracted subconsciously to what she felt was a safe space. It was possible that her pursuer would be confused by the energy of the building and pass by, but it was too risky to hope for and the spell was essential.

When the painting was finished the Beast-Boy crossed to the window. It was quiet outside. He sat by the heater to warm his tree stump legs. He'd been born with them, and they'd grown as he'd grown. In warmer weather he would sit in the sunshine, watching beetles burrowing their way in and out of them. Once he'd fallen asleep and had been woken by a woodpecker drilling into his shin. It had hurt but he was happy to have been so close to such a beautiful bird. The bark on his legs felt dry and sore so he massaged them with a little oil. It was enough to make them feel better without killing the insects that lived inside.

The Beast-Boy looked out at the city. He saw it as a forest, the buildings towering like giant redwoods, the intermittent smog acting as a canopy. And the city, of course, had its predators, the hierarchy of the urban food chain; from domestic cats to foxes to the

Peregrine falcons that lived on the roof of the church. There was also, of course, the human kind of predator. Nikola P____ was certainly being hunted, but for what reason neither of them knew. As far as he could tell she hadn't crossed or offended anyone, living or dead. It seemed this woman had picked Nikola P____ at random and was determined to find her for whatever purpose. He needed to know more if they were to be safe. He picked up his phone and began texting his most reliable contacts.

Karl was aware that he was walking. He could see that he was moving but he felt uninvolved, like a pilot forced to relinquish control of his plane. Everything was happening from a distance – the light rain on his face, the kerb that scuffed his shoe, the piss trickling down his leg. Normally, of course, he would have been mortified to do such a thing, but he was too far away from it to care. It could have been a day or a decade since that fateful meeting at The Lamb Inn. *A suitable place to have been slaughtered,* he thought. Since then he had drifted – quite literally – through life. There was no pleasure to be found in anything, just yawning nothingness. Until now. He'd stood up from the chair he'd been sitting on for so long and had left his house. To go where? He didn't know. His body, now weak and unfamiliar with itself, made its way to wherever it was going. It boarded a bus and stumbled along pavements. Finally it stopped and leant, face forward, onto a chain link fence that surrounded a derelict industrial site.

How does one acquire an Emptiness Machine? Is it something that can be bought or sold? Or does it need to be made specifically for whoever requires it? Marow couldn't answer these questions. She only knew that her own, unique Emptiness Machine had been given to her by her grandmother. Quietly. Secretly. Marow had lived in the same street as her, and the family were frequent visitors. On one occasion, when she had been left alone with her grandmother for a few minutes, the old woman gathered her hair up and took something from behind her ear. *"There are many of us, but this is the only Emptiness Machine,"* she had said mysteriously as she handed the object over. Over the next few weeks – with Marow old enough to visit on her own – they investigated the peculiar device. Her grandmother claimed not to have used it for many years and needed a magnifying glass to view it in detail. For Marow it was an adventure, a continuation of the magic in the fairy tales she loved. The more she learned, the more exciting it became. It was real, it was dark and, she knew, it had to remain secret. Her parents were unaware, her grandmother not wanting to pass it on to a son who believed only in the power of money. Marow asked her many times how she'd come across the machine but her grandmother, becoming more forgetful as time progressed, gave a different answer on each occasion – her mother had passed it down to her, she'd been given it in a Satanic rite, she'd made it herself from the wood of an African witch's coffin, with ice sheets for glass, the dials and other electronic parts designed and made by a medieval peasant woman in Spain.

Marow believed these explanations and at the same time knew they couldn't all be true. This paradox faded into insignificance compared to the beauty of the Emptiness Machine. Everything about it fascinated her – her grandmother, a woman she'd thought of as ancient and loving but not capable of very much – had done amazing things that her family knew nothing about. And keeping it secret from her parents was exciting.

What could such a device be used for? Marow didn't ask for some while, so fascinating was the device itself, as well as its former keeper. She would brush her grandmother's hair and look for the device's hiding place. At first there was a large indentation in the old woman's skull, just behind her left ear, but now the machine had been passed on the hiding place was no longer required and the indentation gradually grew out.

As to the device's purpose – when she finally gathered the courage to ask – it was nothing less than delightful.

"Look inside the case," instructed her grandmother. "What do you see?"

"Clouds," said Marow. "Grey clouds, like a storm's on its way."

Her grandmother nodded. "It's full of clouds, but the clouds are full of emptiness. There is nothing and everything in this machine."

As Marow sat, transfixed by the movement in the case, the old woman continued. "When it was handed down to me, it was different. The clouds were every colour you could think of. They were full of contentment. My mother would find people who were sad and used the needle here," she held it up for Marow to see, "to pass some happiness to them. She made no charge for this. It was enough for her to see them smile."

Marow frowned. "So where did all the colours go? Your mum must have been very nice."

"She was a fool!" snapped her grandmother. "After she died I took the machine apart. I changed how it worked."

Her smile became wider and wider and she broke into laughter. Marow was almost frightened.

"I find people who are too full of happiness. I swap it for clouds," she said.

The conversation ended as Marow's father arrived to take her home. The next time they were alone together Marow was desperate to ask why she'd changed the device's purpose but she was too nervous. She was worried that it might be taken away if she asked too many questions. Her grandmother had given her an extraordinary thing which excited and daunted her. The old woman could see this, and after instructing Marow on how to use the machine added, "Perhaps one day the clouds will all be gone and you can stop." It was not long after this that the old woman died. Marow was ten years old, and all she could think was that there couldn't be enough emptiness in the machine to take away her sadness.

⇜⇝

Nikola P____ woke to find the Beast-Boy looking out of the window. He heard her stir.

"I'm used to having all kinds of visitors," he said, "but I can't tell if the man out there wants to come in. He looks ill. Or even dying, actually."

Nikola P____ looked and shuddered. What a lost soul! There was something about his bearing, the way he leant against the fence, that was both resigned and desperate. And then, in the pit of her stomach, was the realisation that she'd seen the man before.

"It's him," she spluttered. "The man in the pub. Why is he here?"

He was evidently not going to leave so they went outside and approached him.

"Are you alright?" asked the Beast-Boy.

Karl tried to raise his head but it no longer belonged to him. With a great effort he managed to whisper, "Is she here?"

The Beast-Boy looked at Nikola P____. "Has he been following you, do you think?"

Nikola P____ shook her head. "I haven't seen him since that time at the pub. Why would he, anyway? I can't help him."

"Perhaps it's not you he's looking for," said the Beast-Boy. Perhaps, he thought, for whatever reason, the man needed to see the woman who'd done this to him.

The man spoke again and they just caught his words.

"She emptied my heart."

He was a ruin of a man. The Beast-Boy's initial thought – that he intended to do Nikola P____ harm – was clearly groundless. He was almost non-functioning.

"She's not here," said Nikola P____. "Why do you want to see her?"

Karl took the deepest breath he could muster.

"I want her to see what she's done."

For the first time in years, the Beast-Boy was afraid.

Fear, excitement, pain, joy; the Beast-Boy had lived his life surrounded by them. This was a new kind of danger. This woman had the ability – and the intent – to destroy people. And he had no idea how she was doing it. Nikola P____ had seen it happen but nobody – including the victim – knew what it was. And the Beast-Boy's most reliable contact had come back to him with unsettling stories of others in a similar condition to their guest.

She would find them now, of that he had no doubt. And, despite the danger, it might be better that she did; Nikola P____'s life as a fugitive was no life at all and Karl wanted closure of some kind, perhaps so he could let go and die in peace. The three of them sat, then, in the Beast-Boy's living room. Nikola P____ on the edge of her seat. He'd had to talk her into staying. She had mostly given in, he thought, because she was too tired to keep running.

Marow held the woman close and laid her gently on the sofa. The swirl of cloud in the machine was noticeably reduced. While most of her victims fought before they became glassy-eyed, this one had been disappointingly passive. She'd offered no resistance when Marow had drawn the needle from the Emptiness Machine. Even when she'd realised that this was no foreplay, she'd watched Marow insert the needle and her body had practically gorged on the clouds. This was most unusual. And deeply unsatisfying. After returning the device to her mouth Marow set off once again. Her quarry was nearby. It was time to close in.

Nikola P____ was smoking nervously by the back door when the Beast-Boy approached her.

"I don't think I can stay," she said. "I don't want to end up like *him*. And it's dangerous for you."

The Beast-Boy took a puff of her joint and handed it back to her.

"He's in a bad way," he said. "But do you have the energy to keep running?"

"Can you stop her?" she said, a flicker of hope appearing in her tired eyes.

The Beast-Boy sighed. "I don't know. I know nothing about this woman or what she's doing."

"And that's why you need *me!*" said a triumphant voice.

Nikola P____'s stomach lurched. She was ready to run, but the Beast-Boy was smiling.

"Imp! Great to see you!"

A teenage boy slipped across the yard and into the kitchen. He hugged the Beast-Boy and they returned to the living room. Imp sat down and took a deep, dramatic breath before speaking.

"It's been almost impossible to find out anything about this woman," he said. "But I'm certain that what information I do have is accurate. Sort of, anyway." When he paused again, the Beast-Boy took a small package from his pocket and threw it over.

"This is amazing and a bit confusing," he continued. "But here goes. This woman is one of a handful who own a device that cures severe depression by injecting sufferers with something. It's weird – it's not a medical device and no Class As are involved. It's a contraption that's hundreds of years old. It's called a Euphoria Machine."

Imp looked around the room at the puzzled faces. Well, two puzzled faces – the old man looked as if he might be past such things.

Nikola P____ nodded at Karl. "He's not full of joy, is he?" she snapped.

The Beast-Boy sat up. "So this woman has reversed the function of the machine?"

"I would say so," said Imp wryly. "How many people has she done this to? There are definitely more, but I can't say a number. It's all a bit mad, even for you."

The Beast-Boy smiled. "It's certainly keeping life interesting. It's likely this woman will turn up here…"

Imp rose to his feet. "In which case I'll leave you to it. I'll see you soon." He waved the foil package at the Beast-Boy. "Thanks for this."

With a final glance at Karl he was off.

"Your friend's got the right idea," said Nikola P____. "And I'm no martyr, but it's selfish of me to stay. I'm grateful for your hospitality but now I need to go."

She'd clearly made up her mind. The Beast-Boy was disappointed – this peculiar adversary with her equally peculiar machine would be as fascinating as she was frightening. Nikola P____ collected her few belongings and he reluctantly walked her to the back door. It was dark now and raining, which would at least provide some cover. She donned her hat and was about to say goodbye when she froze.

"We're being watched," she whispered.

It was so quiet out there. The Beast-Boy closed his eyes and heard three people breathing; it was unlikely that Karl was one of them.

"Yes. There's someone out there," he whispered back.

The spell wasn't strong enough, he thought, as a piece of the darkness moved into the light.

It began in a civilised manner. Marow removed her coat and sat at the kitchen table. It was then that Nikola P____ saw her properly for the first time. She looked almost ordinary, but moved awkwardly when shedding her wet coat. Now Nikola P____ could see the woman's overly long limbs and how her neck jerked as if it was continually clicking out of place. Over the course of the last nine months Nikola P____'s fear had reshaped the woman to become monstrous. Now, in the flesh, she was less frightening and clearly suffering. The Beast-Boy, too, had imagined a demonic figure. The woman had great presence, it was true, but looked dowdy.

Marow found the Beast-Boy interesting. This man with tree stumps for legs and tufts of fur on his ears was a type of hybrid she hadn't seen before. Nikola

P____, her prey for so long, looked haggard. Their meeting was long overdue. Marow sniffed the air.

"I smell emptiness," she said. "Who else is here?"

"The man you hurt in The Lamb Inn came here. He wants answers," said Nikola P____. "So do we."

"Hurt," said Marow. "Such a quaint way to put it." And she opened her mouth and took the Emptiness Machine from the cavity beneath her tongue. She set it down on the table with love and care. And caution; she knew her audience were weighing up the possibility of snatching it from her.

"We have a thousand questions," began the Beast-Boy.

"A thousand lights in the darkness," said Marow. "I've no interest in them."

She gazed at Nikola P____.

"She's ready, isn't she?" she said. "Stopped running at last. Does it matter why?"

Nikola P____ didn't want to take her eyes off Marow but couldn't help looking at the device. It was exquisite; assembling the thing would have taken great skill. The little wood and glass case had something swirling inside, just as it had been when she saw it before.

"This was a Euphoria Machine," she said. "Why did you change its use?"

"Why not?" said Marow with a shrug. She wasn't prepared to tell them the device's history.

The Beast-Boy moved then, making a grab for the device but Marow was faster, much faster. In his frustration he turned away. And then he saw it – a single hair on Marow's damp coat. He plucked it away and swallowed it. Marow seemed not to have noticed. He sat back, his breathing slowed, and he felt himself becoming a subtle reflection of her. He didn't want to become her – it would be far too dangerous – but a snapshot of her being might reveal what she was doing and why. Marow gripped the device and held it up so they could view it.

"It's beautiful, isn't it?" she crowed. "Now, my dear, the chase has been fun but it's over. Time to experience the delights of —"

"The Emptiness Machine," said the Beast-Boy. He even sounded like her now. He had glimpses of her life from the inside looking out, a vague understanding of the device as she altered the dials and took out the needle. And the clouds, the blanket greyness, just waiting to fill Nikola P____ with nothingness. He felt for Karl, that poor, empty man who was slowly making his way into the kitchen.

"Why isn't it a Joy Machine?" asked Nikola P____. "Why did you change it? And why me?"

Marow ignored her. She'd been wrong-footed by the unexpected existence of the Beast-Boy but she was in still control of the situation. She was glad that Nikola P____ hadn't given up. She didn't recognise the man shuffling into the room, but he had clearly experienced the device. Why he was dragging himself around here was beyond her.

"You've spent most of your life doing this," said the Beast-Boy. "That device sucks the life out of people."

He was thankful that he'd only swallowed one strand of hair. He wanted to be himself again soon; Marow was not a soul he wanted to inhabit for long. He hadn't learned much about her, but didn't dare try to go further.

Marow turned on him. "There's more than enough emptiness in here for the pair of you."

The Beast-Boy felt her flash of anger like a drug rush and the hair he'd swallowed was full of power again. He experienced more moments from Marow's life, of what it was to be her. The Emptiness Machine – so small! – still had so much to give. And then he was laughing, his voice merging with Marow's as they screeched at Karl's pathetic attempt to confront her. Marow took Karl by the shoulders and dropped him onto the chair where she'd been sitting. This would be an intriguing opportunity to use the device twice on the same person. She plucked the needle out and rammed it into his chest. The Beast-Boy looked on, his own emotions battling with Marow's. Nikola P____ was transfixed by the swirling motion inside the case. The clouds were frantic, whipping around like a tiny tornado. The needle was connected to the case by a wire; Nikola P____ imagined it pulsing as the cloud passed through it into Karl's heart. He didn't struggle and his head slowly dropped as what life had remained in him was snuffed out. It was a little disappointing, Marow thought, to see him die, but the experiment had nevertheless been worthwhile. As she withdrew the needle Nikola P____ gave a cry. And Marow was on her in a second.

The Beast-Boy was at a crossroads. Flesh gave way to bark and fur, fingernails to polished stone. His veins carried traces of dust from a shooting star. And now his vision merged with Marow's. She held Nikola P____ against the wall with one hand and played with the dials on the Emptiness Machine with the other. They were so tiny, but he could see them clearly, how they set the frequency and strength of the output. There were different degrees of nothingness, it seemed. The needle swung underneath the case like a pendulum. Nikola P____ pushed her away.

"What about you?" she said. "Why don't you use that thing on yourself?"

Marow laughed. "Are you trying to appeal to my better nature? My sense of fair play?" She threw her head back and laughed again. Her long neck clicked loudly and the Beast-Boy felt a dagger of pain shoot up and down her spine. He clutched his neck in sympathy and rose to his feet. Marrow whirled around and ordered him to sit down.

"I'll set fire to those kindling legs of yours if you get in my way," she declared, her eyes flickering flames of their own. He could feel how she felt then, how she was equally joking and serious. The Emptiness Machine was a far more sophisticated torture device than her threat but he knew she was capable of anything. He sank down, missing his chair, and as he sprawled on the floor, the neat line of tins he'd knocked off the table clattered around him. He grabbed at one of them and flicked it open. The contents scattered and he threw a small piece into his mouth.

Marow turned her attention back to Nikola P____.

"The longer this has gone on," she said, "the more you need this."

"Why?" Nikola P____ shouted. "I've done nothing to you. You've made my life Hell for no reason."

"No!" said Marow. "Your life is joyous, your desire to live has kept you going all this time. You've never loved life as you've done these last few months. You're perfect."

Nikola P____ struck out at Marow, hard enough to send the Emptiness Machine flying. Marow gave an anguished cry and went to pick it up, and Nikola P____ fled.

~∾≈~

Her first thought was to run again, to use the energy she'd gained from resting at the Beast-Boy's home, but the rain was harder now and she found a bush that was dense enough to hide within and so she sat at its base. It was dry here and the sound of the rain was soothing. The bush had pushed its way up through the concrete. Nikola P____ admired its determination to survive, but as she sat there she wondered whether she was hiding from Marow or waiting for her.

The device was intact. Marow ran a finger over the case to make sure there were no cracks. The clouds were agitated but would soon settle. What *would* it be like to use the Emptiness Machine on herself? She was amused at the thought of joining the empty souls she'd created, then started as the Beast-Boy got to his feet.

"You're a strange one," she said. "What do you care about any of this?"

"She came to me for help," said the Beast-Boy.

"That doesn't mean you had to give it," said Marow.

The Beast-Boy stood his ground. He wanted to give Nikola P____ as much time as possible to get away.

"You do know that I'll catch up with her, don't you? It doesn't matter if it's today or in a year's time. It's inevitable. And she's grateful to me."

"How on Earth would you think that?" asked the Beast-Boy. "You must be a very particular kind of twisted."

Marow was offended. "She's become far more than she was when I first saw her. If I let her go she'll have no reason to carry on."

"If you do catch up with her she'll be incapable of carrying on! You could change the machine back. Reverse the reversal. Do some good."

Pain gripped his stomach, like a hand squeezing his intestines. What had he swallowed? He glanced at the floor. Pieces of iron pyrite glittered up at him.

"You're wasting my time," said Marow. "I may return for you. Think about that tonight. And every night."

The pain was worse and the Beast-Boy was doubled up as she strode out. Forcing himself upright, he staggered after her into the rainy night. The nearby streetlight reflected in the puddles, giving him a better view of the yard and he saw a reflection of Marow crouched next to a bush.

Nikola P____ was inside it, cornered. Already cold, she shook violently as Marow picked open the top buttons of her shirt. She held Marow's gaze as the needle pierced the skin and forced its way to her heart.

The Beast-Boy's stomach was on fire. The tin that he'd opened had been a fortuitous and perfect choice. The iron pyrite had driven the last traces of Marow from him and he lurched towards the bush.

She was transfixed by Marow's gaze. It was almost paralysing, but she found she could move her fingers, and if she could do that she might be able to move her hand to the needle and pull it out. And then the Beast-Boy was there, dropping to his knees next to Marow and spitting at her. His saliva splattered over the Emptiness Machine and the hand that held it.

The Beast-Boy hadn't swallowed iron pyrite before but the effect was even more dramatic than he'd hoped for. His saliva had become sulphuric acid. As it landed it bubbled into life. Marow shrieked as the acid ate into her hand and – worse – began to dissolve the Emptiness Machine's case. She wiped at it with her only intact finger and dropped it.

Nikola P____ crawled out from the bush. The Beast-Boy was vomiting the rest of the acid onto the concrete.

"I hope it's enough," he said, gasping for breath.

Marow screamed for her hand. She thought she'd wiped the device clean and she screamed again when she heard the acid fizzing through it.

"You've done it! You've destroyed it!" said Nikola P____. The needle was still in her chest but she barely noticed.

There was a *chink* of fracturing glass. The Beast-Boy hadn't destroyed the machine, he'd only damaged it. And the fog was escaping. Such a small amount – tiny – in the case, but as it forced its way out it expanded to form a thick cloud. Nikola P____ grabbed the Beast-Boy and they lay on the ground, the cloud hanging just above them.

Marow was horrified that her beloved device had been damaged, but she couldn't deny her fascination; the possible consequences of the cloud escaping were almost unimaginable. She, too, kept low, her damaged hand held close to her.

All three looked up into the cloud. What was inside it? It broke apart for a moment and they saw desolation; dark canyons, cliffs rising on every side, poisoned trees and dry river beds. And Space – endless, claustrophobic Space. It was all only inches away. If they reached up they could touch it. And they would be lost. Marow, too, had a momentary urge to reach into the cloud. But the sights that had made Nikola P____ and the Beast-Boy cower made the hairs on the back of her neck rise in excitement.

They watched as the cloud was gathered up by the wind and taken away, its edges glowing as it passed a streetlight. And as it disappeared the Beast-Boy's anguished howl was matched only by Marow's whoops of joy.

❧

This is where this story ends – or at least this is where we part ways with it. Now that you've read it, the events described can begin. The Beast-Boy, Nikola P____ and Marow now exist, as does poor Karl and the likelihood of disaster. Do not feel guilt for this – you have been reading in good faith. We cannot only do the things that we are sure of the consequences of. Good and bad – even evil – exist and cannot be banished at our convenience. This is a story that needed to be told. And if you still have some misgivings over having read this far, consider this – it's quite possible that your own life, too, is just a story that a reader at some point in time has set in motion.

THE DREAMERS

CATHERINE ADAMS

is an aspiring amateur writer from London. She has been shortlisted for the Exeter Story Prize and for the London Independent Story Prize twice.

EMILY CASTLES

studied at the University of Manchester and Durham University, graduating with an MA in English Literature. Born in Birmingham, she now lives in London and enjoys the theatre and going to metal gigs. She is an upcoming writer with a small scattering of published pieces, all irrevocably cemented in the delicious macabre.

SAM HICKS

lives in Deptford, south east London. Her fiction has appeared in various anthologies, including *The Fiends in the Furrows*, *Nightscript*, *Dark Lane*, *Vastarien*, and *The Best Horror of the Year* volumes 11,12 and 13.

PENNY JONES

knew she was a writer when she started to talk about herself in the third person. Her debut collection *Suffer Little Children* was shortlisted for the 2020 British Fantasy Award for Best Newcomer, and her short story "Dendrochronology" was also shortlisted for Best Short Story. She loves reading and will read pretty much anything you put in front of her, but her favourite authors are Stephen King, Shirley Jackson and John Wyndham. In fact Penny only got into writing to buy books, when she realised that there wasn't that much money in writing she stayed for the cake.

EYGLÓ KARLSDÓTTIR

was born and raised in Iceland but has spent the last twenty years living in the South of Sweden where she lives with her daughter and her dog. She is most at home in the short story format and has a collection available called *Things the Devil Wouldn't Dream Of and Other Stories*. She has also published two novellas, *All the Dark Places* and *In His Mind, Her Shadow*. Apart from that she publishes a short story zine called *The Chestnut* regularly on Patreon.

eyglo.info

RACHEL KNIGHTLEY

has been published in *Great British Horror 5* (Black Shuck Books), *Uncertainties vol. 3* (Swan River Press), *Writer's Forum* (First Prize for Fiction) and by Hull University where she gained her PhD in 2020. Her debut short story collection *Beyond Glass* was published in May 2021 by Black Shuck Books. Rachel is currently writing and presenting *The E.I. of Sci-fi* for Starburst Magazine's YouTube channel. Her non-fiction titles include *Your Creative Writing Toolkit* (Green Ink Writers' Gym) and *Illuminate's Drama Study and Revision Guide*. Rachel founded Green Ink Writers' Gym and coaches writing, speaking and performance.

rachelknightley.com

GISELLE LEEB

has appeared in *Best British Short Stories 2017* (Salt), *Lady Churchill's Rosebud Wristlet*, *Black Static*, *The Shadow Booth*, *Supernatural Tales*, *Unsung Stories*, and other places. She is a 2019 Word Factory Apprentice Award winner and an assistant editor at Reckoning Journal.

giselleleeb.com

SELINA LOCK

is a mild-mannered librarian from Leicester. She is known for editing *The Girly Comic*, and has written strips for various comic strip anthologies, including the double-Eisner nominated *To End All Wars*. She has had several short stories published and her novella *Green Eyed and Grim* is available from Obverse Books. She has M.E./CFS, is a member of The Speculators writing group and one half of Factor Fiction alongside her partner Jay Eales.

factorfictionpress.co.uk

KIRSTY LOGAN

is the author of three short story collections, including her latest book, *Things We Say in the Dark*, two novels (and two more scheduled for publication), two flash fiction chapbooks, a short memoir, and several collaborative works with musicians and visual artists. Her writing has been optioned for TV, adapted for stage, recorded for radio and podcasts, exhibited in galleries and distributed from a vintage Wurlitzer cigarette machine. Her next publication is an original audio novel with a full cast and sound design for Audible, an Arctic-set ghost story, *The Sound at the End*.

ROSALIE PARKER

co-runs independent Tartarus Press with R.B. Russell from the Yorkshire Dales and has been the recipient of four World Fantasy Awards for her editing work. She has written four collections of weird short stories, *The Old Knowledge* (2010), *Damage* (2016), *Sparks from the Fire* (2018) and *Through the Storm* (2020), and her stories have appeared in many anthologies, including *Best New Horror* and *Best British Horror*.

JULIE ANN REES

holds a first class Masters degree in creative writing from the University of Wales Trinity Saint David. Her short stories have been published both online at horla.org and in print with Parthian books and forthcoming anthologies with Sliced Up Press and Improbable Press. Her first book, a memoir entitled *Paper Horses*, will be released by Black Bee Books in October 2021. She is a single mother and works at a busy rural library in Wales, when not riding her horse over the wild Welsh hills.

facebook.com/julieannrees

P J RICHARDS

is a writer and artist living in Somerset surrounded by the nature, myth and history that inspires her work. She's had several short stories published in anthologies and online literary magazines, and is currently writing the sequel to her debut novel *Deeper Older Darker*, published by Snowbooks.

twitter.com/p_j_richards

PRIYA SHARMA

has appeared in such venues as *Interzone*, *Black Static, Nightmare, The Dark* and *Tor*. "Fabulous Beasts" won a British Fantasy Award for Short Fiction. *All the Fabulous Beasts* (Undertow Publications) won a Shirley Jackson Award and British Fantasy Award for Best Collection. *Ormeshadow*, her first novella (available from Tor), won a Shirley Jackson Award and a British Fantasy Award.

priyasharmafiction.wordpress.com

TEIKA MARIJA SMITS

is a Nottinghamshire-based editor and mother-of-two. She writes poetry, fiction and non-fiction, and her speculative fiction has been published in *Reckoning, Best of British Science Fiction* (2018 and 2020), *Enchanted Conversation* and *Great British Horror 6*. Her debut poetry pamphlet, *Russian Doll*, was published by Indigo Dreams in March 2021. A fan of all things fae, she is delighted by the fact that Teika means fairy tale in Latvian.

teikamarijasmits.com

TAYLOR SYKES

is the author of the novella *Many Small Disasters*, forthcoming from Los Galesburg Press. Her fiction has appeared on NPR as part of their Three-Minute Fiction contest, as well as in *The Horror Is Us* (Mason Jar Press). She is the recipient of the 2017 James Hurst Prize for fiction and a 35 in 35 Fellowship from the Vermont Studio Center. Originally from northwest Indiana, she holds an M.F.A. from North Carolina State University and currently teaches writing at UNC Asheville.

JO M THOMAS

is a tech druid by day, genre writer in the evening, and dog-parent all the time. She's pretty sure she used to have other interests, but she's mislaid them in a combination of lockdown and anxiety.

JULIE TRAVIS

is a writer of Surrealist horror fiction. Co-founder of Queeruption international festival and west Cornwall's Dead Unicorn Ventures. Occasional album cover photographer for avant-garde band UNIT. Fan of stone circles, burial chambers and fogous.

NICOLE M WOLVERTON

was raised in the rural hinterlands of Pennsylvania and now lives just outside Philadelphia city limits in a 100-year-old house full of mysteries. Her short fiction and creative nonfiction have appeared in a variety of magazines and anthologies, most recently in the *Saturday Evening Post* and the *Hungry Ghost Project*, and anthologies from Dark Ink Books and Ghost Orchid Press. She is also the author of *The Trajectory of Dreams* (Bitingduck Press) and editor of *Bodies Full of Burning* (Sliced Up Press). Nicole is a speechwriter, gin aficionado, and travel enthusiast.

C A YATES

is a writer, narrator, editor, and genderpunk warrior. She is an advocate for the open discussion and exploration of mental illness, in both life and fiction.

chloeyates.com

blackshuckbooks.co.uk